My
Mother's
Gift

BOOKS BY STEFFANIE EDWARD

This Other Island

My Mother's Gift

STEFFANIE EDWARD

bookouture

Published by Bookouture in 2022

An imprint of Storyfire Ltd.
Carmelite House
50 Victoria Embankment
London EC4Y 0DZ
United Kingdom

www.bookouture.com

ISBN: 978-1-80019-649-0
eBook ISBN: 978-1-80019-648-3

To everyone who has experienced the journey of caring for a loved one living with dementia.

CHAPTER ONE

The warmth and dazzle from the sun hit me. Eyes half-closed, I looked down, thoughts leaping to the shades in my bag as I navigated the narrow metal steps of the plane.

'My waist troubling me,' Auntie Barbara had said, forewarning that she might not be there, but expectation and hope stayed with me all the way through the formalities phase of arrival, until I was outside again and Cousin Headley – with, sadly, no Auntie Barbara nor Mum beside him – shouted, 'Erica!' and waved me over.

'You cut off all your nice hair?' he said, when I got closer.

'Oh, yeah.' I touched my head. 'How are you, cousin?' I gave him a light hug.

'Fine. Fine,' he said, taking my suitcase, though he didn't have to. My four-wheeled case had been gliding over surfaces like grease on a marble floor. Lifting was the problem. Especially this case, packed as it was with mosquito repellents, a four-pack of Heinz baked beans, special M&S tea, butter mintoes, shortbread biscuits, the ginger snaps that Mum loved, and other stuff including shoes for Cousin Headley, Mum and

Auntie, and countless other family requests I'd daren't say no to – even though the list represented three-quarters of the contents of my suitcase.

I followed him, away from the hustle and crowd, towards the car park.

'Leave dat an' go inside,' he said, as he lifted my case into the back of his minibus. I did as he asked, leaving my hand luggage next to him and made for the front seat, where I took a deep inhale, mentally preparing for what lay ahead.

That aside, it was good to be in St Lucia, the place Mum always referred to as 'back home'. Today wasn't the hottest of days. It was rainy season, but as gratifying as a glorious summer's day in England.

Cousin Headley was my second cousin, though no one identified cousins in levels here. First, second or third, you were simply a cousin. Blood. He was around ten years younger than Auntie. They'd grown up together in the same house with my grandmother, grandfather, Mum's other siblings, plus nieces and nephews. Their closeness meant he was always at hand to help Mum and Auntie out, especially with transport.

Although his level of formal education hadn't gone beyond fourteen and he'd never lived abroad, thanks to the acres of farming land his father had left for him and his two brothers, who were settled in America and didn't care for farming or coming back home, Cousin Headley was wealthy. He employed people to work on what he, Auntie, Mum and others referred to as his 'estate'. His main role was coordinating everything, then shipping his tons of green bananas, plantains and other fresh foodstuff like turmeric and ginger, and ground provisions – cassava, yams and sweet potatoes – to the local supermarkets and to the women who ran market stalls in and outside of St Lucia. Driving his old minibus, wearing jeans, slightly worn-out shirts and sandals – gave nothing away about his financial status.

Once seated, we did the 'good flight?' thing, and talked about the weather because outside was still puddley from the on-off rain. 'But better dat dan storm or hurricane. An' de plants need it,' he said, as we began leaving Vieux Fort behind.

I sat back, taking in the views of surrounding mountains and hills in the distance; trees, lush greenery, houses and eating places set back from the road. Hiding in amongst all of that were some less presentable, wooden houses with rusty galvanised roofs and fencing – if they had any. These were houses belonging to poorer families, some living on what they grew and sold in small quantities. If they were lucky, relatives here or abroad could slip a little something their way. It was all part of surviving in the Caribbean. I'd left too young to remember ever living here, but the visits I'd made since my twenties – even more since Mum had come back to live – sometimes made me feel more emotionally anchored here than in England, the country I've lived in practically all of my life.

I sighed. 'Mmm.'

Memories of holidays, times spent on the beach, visits to warm spring baths and simply being in this relaxed atmosphere with all the fresh fruit I could eat, put a glow on things as I took in more of the views: people selling their garden produce by the roadside or roasting corn; sitting on their balconies, watching traffic go by; and music blaring from one of the bars we passed.

Some had a good life here, but the fact was unless you were born into a wealthy family, were a lawyer, doctor, ran a successful business, or were a member, or an active supporter, of the current ruling party, making a living could be rough, requiring one hustle after another to get by.

'So, how long you come for dis time?' Cousin Headley asked, disengaging me from my thoughts.

'Oh, seven weeks,' I said.

'Long.'

'There's a lot to sort out.'

'I know.' His eyes stayed fixed on the road as my mind drifted to Auntie Barbara's call to me in England, a few days ago.

CHAPTER TWO

'Hello?'

'Erica?'

I pushed back the covers. The fact that it was Auntie and not Mum on the line meant at least this conversation would be based on reality.

'Erica. Ione is really too much for me,' Auntie had said.

I sighed. 'Too...? What's happened?' I sat up. 'What's the problem, Auntie? Is she...? Is Mum okay?'

'I cannot manage her any more. When is it you say you coming?'

'In three weeks. What's happened, Auntie? Has something happened?'

Since Mum's diagnosis, four years ago, certain incidences had grown more frequent with her, along with the panicked calls from Auntie.

'Today,' Auntie was saying, 'we go to town, as usual, doing de shopping an' when I turn aroun', Ione not dere.'

'Oh, God. Where was she? Where's she now?' I was fully awake.

'If you know how much time I spend – both me an' Headley

– looking for Ione, an' all de time she in de market saying she buying fish.'

'Oh no,' I said. 'She didn't tell you she was going?'

'Nothing. She don't say nothing, jus' go – leave de shop, jus' like dat.' The line was silent for a couple of seconds. 'She go an' buy fish an' don't tell nobody nothing.'

'Oh, Auntie. She with you now?'

'No. I jus' leave her house an' come home. I really don't know, Erica,' Auntie added after a pause, 'To me? I see Ione getting worse. She believe she seeing Sim, Louis – all... all people dat dead already.'

'I know. I know, Auntie.' They were Mum and Auntie's siblings.

My misgivings over Mum's condition had been rising over the last three years, along with my worry over the limited options open to me for her care. Between each of my visits to her and Auntie in St Lucia, she'd call me at all sorts of hours. More recently, the calls were to accuse me of leaving her on her own, telling me she'd been waiting ages for me to come and take her home. 'What kind of chile you are?' she'd say. 'Leaving me here like dis?'

Her words would bring a lump to my throat. Paralyse me with guilt. There was little I could do from here. Depending on the time, I'd ask to speak to the carer or, if it wasn't too late, call Auntie and ask her to go and check on her.

'How she can do dat without even telling me?'

'Oh, Auntie. I'm so sorry. I... I'll see if I can come a bit earlier. I'll try. I don't know what else we can do.'

'Please try, *ich mwen* my child, because—'

'I... I'll call you back later. I have to speak to my manager. I'll see.'

It frustrated me no end, that I wasn't able to do more of what I knew I should, and *wanted* to, be doing for Mum, but what more could I do when she lived in another country?

'You have to do something,' Auntie said. 'For Ione's sake.'

Damn this. Damn. Why now?

My official end of term wasn't for another two weeks. My flight to St Lucia was booked for a week after that. Could *this* urgency wait until then? Any change in my flight now would mean forking out at least another hundred pounds to the airline. But Auntie shouldn't have to be dealing with this kind of stuff. It was too much. Not at her age. Mum was her baby sister, but *my* responsibility. All I wanted Auntie to do was pay the carer for me and monitor things. But her closeness with Mum meant she saw her every day, anyway. And only last week, she'd called saying Mum had driven away the carer I'd recently put in place. Not a month went by when there wasn't something new to deal with relating to Mum. It was looking more and more like I'd have to get her to come back to England again. Being her only child meant there was no one to fill in for me, share the responsibility or decide on the best thing to do for Mum. My daughter, Millie, was there, of course. At thirty-four she was old enough for me to discuss Mum's condition and situation with, but ultimately the buck stopped with me. I had to make the final decision and deal with the consequences if something I'd put in place didn't work out. I was the legitimate one to get all the calls, the one expected to do something about everything to do with Mum.

Through gritty eyes, I glanced at the clock again and sighed. Mum's sleep pattern wasn't as set as Auntie's. I dialled her number, telling myself I'd hang up if she didn't pick up after four rings, so I wouldn't get her out of bed.

'Mum, it's me,' I said, hearing her voice.

'Erica?'

'Yes, it's me. How are you?'

'What about you?'

'I'm fine. Fine, thanks, Mum.'

'When you coming?'

'Not tonight, but soon. You feeling okay?' It was a potential opening to a can of worms, but I needed to ask.

'When you coming again?'

'Soon. In a few days. Soon. You sure you okay?'

A short silence. Then, 'I miss you,' she said.

'I miss you too, Mum, but I'll be there soon.' Saying less to her was best, especially in situations like this, given what the psychiatrist called her 'cognitive impairment'.

'Oh. All right.'

'I love you, Mum.'

'I love you too, Babes.'

Those words that were supposed to reassure and comfort me, now only added to my guilt. How badly had things progressed since I'd seen her at Easter? Those things couldn't properly be assessed through a telephone conversation. If Auntie was saying she couldn't manage her baby sister any more, it meant that things had escalated, even in the few months since I'd seen her.

'How soon do you need to leave?' my line manager and headteacher, Phillipa, asked after I explained my dilemma.

'As soon as possible,' I replied, torn between commitment to the job I loved as a deputy head, and commitment to Mum – the need to fulfil my daughterly duties.

'Time to bring her back to England and find a decent care home, eh?'

The churn in my stomach intensified as thoughts of what might lie ahead continued to multiply.

'I don't know,' I said, half to myself.

Putting your elderly into a care home wasn't a cultural practice in St Lucia, and in *my* family it would be seen as sacrilege, especially by people like Auntie Barbara. Plus, Mum had made her disapproval of it clear even before

Alzheimer's began to steal bits of her brain. The idea of putting her in a home summoned up a torrent of guilt that hung with me for days. She'd be living in a strange place, with strangers. Strangers doing everything for her. She'd have to eat English meals, which weren't her favourite. She would feel out of place. And I'd feel like I'd abandoned her – left her in a place where she didn't have a say in anything. I just couldn't do it.

She might have felt differently about being in one if it was a viable option in St Lucia. She'd have more in common with the people there: everyone would speak Kwéyòl. She'd be fed her national dish of green bananas and saltfish, and all the other Caribbean meals she was used to, and they'd all be able to reminisce about similar things. She might even meet someone from her past there. *That* situation would be different.

Plus, I'd heard a few horror stories about the poor care and abuse some old people suffered in those places. I couldn't risk that happening to Mum.

St Lucia wasn't like England. There, most old people died at home, which felt nice to me. Dying in a familiar place, with someone or people you knew, love and who loved you, had to be the nicest way to leave the world. *No.* A care home wasn't an option.

When she had last lived with me here, I'd arranged for her to go to a day centre: something to occupy her, give her a chance to socialise more during the day, instead of just going to the shops and back, or visiting her friend, Mrs Gooding. She'd come home with sheets of the songs they'd been singing. 'You Are my Sunshine', 'How Much is That Doggie in the Window?' Nice, fun, sing-along songs, but all foreign to her. And it had saddened me that there wasn't somewhere else she could go to where the goings-on reflected more of her own culture. Where the songs might be a Harry Belafonte: 'Day-o', 'Island in the Sun', 'Come Back Liza', 'Brown Skin Girl', or even one of

Mighty Sparrow's calypsos from her younger days. She was sure to get more fulfilment from that.

Last year, with Auntie's help, I'd put two carers in place for Mum so she could stay in St Lucia – where she'd insisted she wanted to end her days – but that was becoming a rocky road. She was constantly accusing them of stealing her things, and chasing them away.

'I'll most likely have to bring her back to live with me, unless I can sort out a good alternative,' I told Phillipa.

'And how would you manage then?'

I shrugged. 'I'd just have to, somehow.' I couldn't allow my mind to stray to that place. Not right now. Though I knew I'd have to bring her back.

Phillipa agreed to give me an extra four days as dependence leave and said I could leave three days before the official end of term. That gave me two days to pack and wrap things up at work, before heading to St Lucia.

Phillipa was due for retirement next year and was well aware of my intention to apply for her post. Retiring on a head-ship's salary would mean a better pension. And as Phillipa herself had pointed out, I was more than capable of doing the job. I planned to ask her to help me with the application. We worked well together, and went for the odd after-work drink or Saturday pub lunch, and spoke quite a bit outside of work. I kind of saw her as a work friend. But there was always that cultural difference you couldn't get rid of and had to sidestep.

Since I had been brought up in her culture as well as mine, I understood hers more than she got mine.

After work that day, I called Millie.

'Two weeks' time?' she said.

'Yeah. Auntie sounded like it was urgent,' I said.

'She should have stayed here in the first place, instead of

you having to do all of that running up and down every few months. Must cost a bomb, as well.'

'I know, but we couldn't force her, could we? And at least I get regular breaks in the sun.' I chuckled, trying to make light of it.

'There are other places you can get a break in the sun in, Mum.'

'I know, but—'

'Okay,' Millie said, like I'd worn her down.

'I hope, this time, I'll be able to convince her to come back with me.'

'She doesn't have a choice now.'

'You know Nannie. How stubborn she can be. But I'll drag her on that plane kicking and screaming, if I have to,' I said, dreading the idea.

CHAPTER THREE

Cherry Orchard sat between Dennery and Micoud, in the south-east of the island – no more than forty-five minutes from the airport. It was no hot spot and a good distance from the most happening part of the island, up north, but it was well designed, peaceful and pretty. People who lived there were mainly returnees – Caribbean people who'd come back home after spending most of their lives in western countries like Canada, England or America. It represented a suburbia those who'd left the Caribbean for a better life had returned and gifted to themselves.

Every road on the development was named after a tropical plant or fruit and conjured up an image of something pleasing, succulent or sweetly scented, gifted from nature. Mum lived on Sweet Lime Grove; Auntie – Ginger Lily Close which was further downhill, near the main road. Hers was one of the first houses there seventeen years ago. Mum and Mr Frank's came five years later. Unlike Auntie, who had glimpses of the road between the tall trees, and the noise that went with it, Mum and Mr Frank had chosen an elevated plot with a sea view.

After passing Micoud village, Cousin Headley swung the minibus left into Cherry Orchard, up Heliconia Avenue passing fancy houses edged with bougainvillea, rose of Sharon, frangipani, ginger lilies and other eye-catching flowers and plants I couldn't name. The sound of his engine brought dogs racing up to fences and gates. Barks and snarls warning their owners of strangers approaching, and visitors to be aware.

Further downhill we went, then up again, pulling up outside Mum's gate. I got out and pushed at it – green paint giving way to rust – but it was locked. I'd told Mum a number of times that I was coming, and so would have Auntie. Unless she was asleep, she would have heard the minibus doors opening and slamming. Where was she?

'Mum?' I shouted, rattling the gate some more. I should have been better prepared, with my keys handy, and considered retrieving them from my hand luggage.

'Cousin Ione?' Cousin Headley was around six inches above my five feet six, but stood on tiptoe, stretching his neck to lengthen his voice so it would catch Mum's ears, wherever she was beyond the gate.

After the fourth call, she appeared at the kitchen door, her head wrapped in a Creole print cloth, no different to a Scottish tartan. 'Eh-eh,' she said, surprise in her voice. 'Good evening. Who's dere?'

'It's me, Mum. Erica,' I said, trying to keep my voice down.

'Who?'

'Mum, come and open the gate.' Half the neighbourhood must have known I'd arrived by now.

'You don't see is your daughter dat's dere, Cousin Ione?' Cousin Headley said, as Mum tottered towards us.

'Eh-eh, it's you?'

'Hi, Mum,' I said, eager to get beyond the gate.

She was wearing a brown skirt with wide-open flowers

printed on it, and a striped blouse. The clash reminded me of her condition. 'Jus' now,' she said, trying to fit a key into the lock on the gate.

I scrutinised what I could see of her face, her movements, as I pushed through the half-opened gate. 'Mum,' I said, getting a closer look at her.

Dark shadows around her eyes, tell-tale signs of late nights or broken sleep. The scars from the last fall Auntie had told me about, were still visible over her nose and forehead. So were the pale patches, left by fallen scabs, waiting for pigmentation to return. Auntie had had to take her to the clinic then. It tugged at my heart that I'd been nowhere near to tend to her.

Once again, as with my previous visits, a multitude of emotions descended on me: joy to see Mum again, sadness surrounding the reasons for these regular visits and regret and the guilt that's plagued me since her diagnosis.

I wrapped my arms around her and tried to dismiss the faint scent of body odour that came with it. 'See, I'm here! How're you doing, Mum?'

There was a time, when we'd have regular Skype calls, where we could talk and see each other on screen, but she'd forgotten how to use it a while back.

'Why you din tell me you was coming, Erica? You-all trying to surprise me?' She smiled and tapped my arm, as we came apart.

Cousin Headley appeared with my cases and went on ahead while Mum and I took our time making our way to the side veranda. The path closest to my room.

'I'm not stopping, eh?' he said, stepping back out.

I thanked him, and offered him something for his petrol, which sometimes he'd take. Today, he insisted it was okay and left, saying he'd see us soon.

Mum followed me to my room. The second largest bedroom

in the house. She'd thrown a mustard-coloured candlewick spread over the bed. *Where on earth had she got that from?*

The heat in there was unbearable. I lifted the latch on the windows and pushed them open.

'How are you?' I said again, hugging her.

'You look good,' she said. 'How is everybody? Millie?'

'Millie's fine, Mum.' I stood in front of her, with a hand on each of her shoulders, my eyes trying to read hers. 'You okay?'

'Of course,' she said, turning away. 'You hungry?'

I was. My meal on that eight-hour flight had turned out to be the tuna sandwich and nuts I'd brought with me, not the sprinkling of overcooked veg, handful of rice and two pieces of meat in a yellow sauce claiming to be a curry that they'd handed me for dinner.

'I need to use the loo,' I said, pushing open the door to my en-suite. 'Ooo!' I let out a quiet scream which forced the stench of stale pee in the air further into my nostrils, smack into the back of my throat. I gagged, reached for the handle on the small window above the cistern, opened it, then flushed the toilet before lifting the lid. Who'd been using my bathroom?

When I came out, Mum was gone. I paused to look out of my bedroom window; taking in the view of the bay where the rage of the Atlantic eased as it met the mangroves. There wasn't a decent beach for miles from here, but a sea view was a sea view. In London, I'd be looking at my little patio garden and houses beyond that, or the street at the front. *No competition.* I went to find Mum.

'Why's it so dark in here?' I opened the blinds and was reaching for the window when Mum said: 'People passing an' looking inside here.'

'Mum, they can't see in here all the way from the road,' I said. 'Not through the net curtains and the hedge. And it's just your kitchen. Not your bed or bathroom.'

'How is everybody? Millie. She all right? How's de boyfriend?'

'Millie's fine. Everyone's fine, Mum,' I said, rubbing my nose. There was a funny smell around. 'Actually, I'd better call her – let her know I got here safely.' I kissed her cheek. 'She sent that for you.' I smiled.

A small green lizard scurried past Mum's foot and headed for cover under the washing machine. 'Did you see that?' I said.

'What?' She glanced at me.

'A lizard just ran under the washing machine.'

'Dey does come in sometimes.' She shrugged. The zest she once had for the war against little creatures trying to make her house their home was becoming history too. Until recently, lizards, spiders – especially flies, had to have had a death wish to venture in.

I peered through the sweaty glass lid of the pot she had on the stove.

'A *bouyon*,' she said. The sweat on the outside of the pot told me it had been in the fridge, for a while too. Had she really forgotten I was coming today?

I looked around the kitchen. 'Don't worry about me, Mum. I'll sort myself out in a minute.'

It would be around nine o'clock in the UK now. There was no answer from Millie's phone. I left a message, then quickly called Delia. We'd been friends since primary school. She came from Mauritius, and could hardly speak English then. Our first common ground was that I understood what we used to call the 'broken' French or patois she spoke because it was close to the Kwéyòl that Mum, and the rest of the big people in my family spoke. Delia looked black like me, but with eyes you'd associate with someone who was Chinese. She wore her long wavy hair parted in the middle and pulled into in a bun in the middle of her head. Our friendship has lasted until today.

'I'm here. All in one piece,' I said.

'You've arrived? Oh, good,' she said. 'How is it?'

Mum didn't have internet anymore, so my calls needed to be short. 'Okay, I think. I'll call again when I'm a bit more sorted. We're about to eat.'

'Okay. Glad things are okay. Enjoy,' she said. 'Love to your mum.'

'Okay.' I disconnected the call and let out a breath. Then heard footsteps on the path outside, followed by a voice.

'Ione?' Auntie Barbara was here. 'Erica reach yet?'

'I'm here, Auntie,' I said, following Mum to the kitchen door.

Before we could get there, Auntie was inside, holding a cloth bag. 'Look, I bring some food for you,' she said, giving me her one-dimple smile.

'Thanks, Auntie.' I hugged her and took the bag. 'But Mum's cooked.'

She turned to Mum with a sad, sorry face. 'But, Ione, I din tell you I was going to cook for Erica?'

Mum shrugged, stepped back and sat at the table.

'Jus' put dat back in de fridge,' Auntie told me. 'You-all can eat dat tomorrow.'

'So, how are you, Auntie?' I asked.

'I'm dere. You know. But you get fat,' she said, giving me a playful tap on the bum.

I hadn't got fat, or fatter, in the three months since she'd last seen me. Thankfully, I still fitted into the size fourteen menopause had drawn me into since hitting my fifties. This was just Auntie Barbara's usual greeting whenever she saw me. Even when I was a size twelve. I was past being offended by it.

Besides, Auntie and Mum's generation didn't think being slim was the thing. Having some flesh on the body was a sign of good health and happiness to them. It also helped if ever you got sick and couldn't eat, because then you wouldn't look too skinny after losing the weight the illness had caused you to. So, in a way, telling me I was getting fat was a kind of a compliment from her.

'What did you cook?' I asked her.

'Saltfish an' hard food.'

'Dumplings?'

'With green *fig,* bananas, an' dashine. Look at you. I know dat's what you like.' She smiled again. 'It still hot.'

That did sound tastier than the *bouyon*.

'Come on. Let's sit outside,' she continued. 'You don't find it hot in here? Your mudder don't like to open window. Don't like to use de fan. Come. Let's go outside.' She waved her hands like she was drawing me and Mum into her arms.

'Okay. Come on, Mum. Shall we eat the *bouyon* tomorrow?'

'All right,' Mum said.

'Or I can have some later,' I said, not wanting her to feel her effort wasn't appreciated.

I put the pot of soup back in the fridge, grabbed a fork and followed Auntie and Mum out, with Auntie still complaining about Mum not keeping windows and doors opened. I ate, half listening to Auntie's updates on the neighbours' affairs: who'd died, were being neglected by their children, whose husbands were letting young girls 'eat' their money – one of Auntie's favourites, but touchy for Mum – and how much the cost of living was rising in St Lucia.

'Mum?' I tapped her knee.

'Uh?' She gave me one of her half-dazed looks.

'You okay?' I asked.

'She all right,' Auntie said. 'An' if she not all right now, she will be all right now you reach. You know how she like it when you come.'

'Mum? Are you all right?' I asked again, ignoring Auntie's blasé attitude towards Mum's feelings.

'Mmm,' Mum replied, looking half interested.

With Auntie gone, and Mum in her room, the house fell into a hush. I stepped out from the shower I'd been craving since getting here, smiling inwardly, contented with my plans for wrapping things up and taking Mum back to England with me.

'Who is there?'

'Mum?' Her voice had an odd tone. I glanced at the doorway.

'What you doing in dere?' she shouted.

'Just had a shower,' I shouted back, pulling the towel right to left, across my back.

She appeared.

'You okay?' I continued drying my skin. Her seeing me naked wasn't a big deal. We'd been seeing each other naked forever.

'Get out!'

I slowed down my movements. The aggression, menace in her voice, threw me back to childhood; to when I'd badly displeased her. But this I hadn't seen for so many years.

'Wha—?' My shoulders tightened. I pulled the ends of the towel closer as she came towards me, her pace steady, expression calculating, but unsure. 'Mum, what's—? What you doing with that knife?'

She had reached the foot of the bed. I stepped backwards, closer to the window, my gaze fixed on the knife in her hand. *What was happening here?*

'I said get out of my house, or I will kill you,' she said. The wildness in her eyes sent fear buckling up my spine, impinging my attempt to focus.

'What the hell?' The words shot out of my mouth. *Is this my mother? The woman who's taken care of me...? Coming at me with a—?*

'Mum!' I shouted. How was I going to get out of this? My eyes switched back to the knife. 'Mum, I'm Erica. It's me. *Erica.*'

But my words flew past her, with no effect. Whatever was going on in her head, I was close to being trapped between that knife in her hand and the window, which was secured with burglar bars and too high off the ground for me to leap or scramble out of.

'You hear me?' Her scream mustered up another layer of fear. Heat rose under my skin as her eyebrows drew closer together, creating rows of swollen flesh over her forehead. As she passed the foot of the bed, the hand holding the knife rose a touch higher above her head.

'Mum! Mum, don't!' I shouted again, waving a hand I hoped would snap the craziness out of her. 'Mum, it's me. Your daughter. It's Erica.' I couldn't shout any louder.

'Erica?' She stilled herself and glanced over her shoulder. 'Where you?'

Heart racing, I took what was likely to be my only chance: throwing myself onto the bed, scrambling across it and out through the doorway behind her.

At the end of the corridor, I stopped to catch my breath.

'Here I am,' I said, facing her coming out of the bedroom.

The towel I'd been wrapped in had fallen off en route, leaving me standing naked, sweat dripping from my face. Was I safe enough standing here, close to the kitchen and living room? The doors leading to the outside could all be locked. I pressed the light on, surprised at how suddenly darkness had filled the house.

'Who...? Who's there?' Mum shouted.

'Me. Erica. Mum, I'm out here,' I answered, scanning the area for something bigger than a tea towel to cover myself. Feeling weird and awkward, I watched Mum pad down the corridor towards me. 'I'm here, Mum.'

'Erica? What you doing dere?'

I wipe a dribble of sweat from my nose, before it hit the floor. Mum's face was crumpled, shoulders dropped, hands hanging. The knife's blade flashed at the end of her right hand. *I had to get it from her.*

'You all right, Mum?' I said, in my best befriending, getting-on-side voice that hardly ever failed with children. Though being naked had never been part of the scenario.

'Erica?' she said, in a searching, curious tone. 'I was... Eh-eh. Why you don't put on some clothes?' The anger had gone. Her voice childlike.

'They're in my room,' I said. *Could I pull this off?* I placed myself at Rushmede Primary, talking down a hysterical six-year-old intent on destroying the class room, harming anyone in their path, and re-summoned my best gentle and pleasing tone. 'Shall I take that?' I braved a few soft steps in her direction.

Her expression suggested it was okay.

I stooped and wrapped my hand gently, but firmly, around the hand holding the knife. She flinched. 'It's okay, Mum. Everything's okay.' I slipped the knife from her hand, straightened up and backed away, eyes still on her.

'I don't feel well in myself,' she said, softly.

'I know, Mum,' I responded, discreetly dropping the knife behind the microwave.

What had I walked into? This whole incident could have gone horribly wrong.

'Come.' I took her hand and led her, gentle steps, to my bedroom. Sat her at the foot of the bed, next to the dress I'd planned to wear after the shower, then slipped it on.

'Look at your big backside,' she teased, tapping my bottom before I sat next to her.

'You gave it to me.' It was a banter we shared.

Nerves still settling, I chuckled, hoping things really were back to normal. That the mother I'd known had returned. I put my arm around her shoulders, the whiff of her body odour no longer such a bother compared to what had just happened. 'Mum? What's going on with you?' I asked.

'What you mean?'

'Oh, Mum.' I sighed. 'It'll be all right.' I hugged her.

'You think so?'

'Yeah. I'm here now. We'll sort it out.'

'Mmm.'

'You must be tired.' She shook her head. 'Why don't you have a nice shower and get ready for bed?'

'But I am not sleepy.'

'Well, take a shower while I make you a nice warm drink, then.' We both stood up. 'I'll bring the drink in for you.'

I saw her to her room. Whilst waiting to hear the shower running, I found her a nightdress.

Mum was drying herself, looking drawn and drained, when I brought the drink in for her. I sniffed the air. 'You smell nice.'

'Mmm.' She put the nightdress on, sat down and took the drink from me. 'Milk?' she said, after the first sip.

'Yeah.' I'd put a teaspoon of honey in, a trick that worked with getting Millie to sleep when she was little.

Leaving her to finish her drink, I popped back to the kitchen to get rid of the other knives in there.

Mum's new docility made it easy to settle her into bed.

'Good night,' I said, before closing her door.

'Good night, *ich mwen*, my child.'

I'd won her back.

I wanted to call Auntie Barbara – someone I could offload on – but Auntie's bedtime – like the chickens, and most people around here – was close to dusk. It would be after midnight in England. Everyone asleep.

The key to my bedroom door wasn't in its usual place – in the keyhole. It wasn't in the dresser drawers, either. Mum was likely to sleep well after that drink but, just in case, I wedged a chair between the floor and door handle. She'd never push that away without waking me.

CHAPTER FOUR

The first indication that something wasn't right with Mum had come four years ago, a couple of years after my stepfather, Mr Frank, died. On one of what had become her annual three-month-long visits to England, I'd noticed a new distance in her. She'd kept locking her keys in her suitcase, and taking ages to shower and get dressed when she was usually the one waiting anxiously for me if we were going anywhere.

I mentioned what I'd observed about her to Auntie Barbara, who had brushed it off. 'Dat's how Ione is. We all getting ole, you know,' she was quick to remind me.

But seventy-four didn't feel that old, not when you're hitting fifty, and I'd never known Mum to be scatty.

That year, I'd managed to talk Mum into going to the doctor, who gave her a memory test, but she'd bottled out of the second stage, which required a brain scan, so the diagnosis was inconclusive. I didn't want to make a big deal of it at the time because I could see how scared Mum was about going into the machine for the scan. Maybe she was okay. Maybe Auntie was right. Heads in the sand, we'd left it.

The following year when I'd gone to St Lucia to see her,

as usual, more observations had been thrown into the mix. She was retelling the same stories again and again, asking the same questions, forgetting more, reporting back on incidents I'd been privy to – but her report had discrepancies. Then she started forgetting her PIN for withdrawing money from the cashpoint. I told Auntie again that things weren't right.

With her help, I encouraged Mum to come back up to England with me, partly so I could observe her more closely, but hoping that this time I could convince her to go all the way with the tests.

That year, I'd given her a basic mobile phone to keep with her. Showed her how to make calls and how to answer them. As with all of her other visits, if I could, I'd drop her off to wherever she wanted to go, and pick her up. Often, she'd insist on making her own way. I worked with that. She wasn't usually on a tight schedule.

One day she was coming back to my house after visiting her friend, Mrs Gooding, a journey she'd made a trillion times. Half an hour after the time I'd expected her to get home, I called her three times before she picked up.

'Where are you?' I asked and was stunned when she hesitated and said she wasn't sure.

'What... what can you see?' The description she'd given me wasn't clear. I told her to walk to the nearest bus stop. 'And when the bus comes, ask the driver the name of the road you're on.' It was something she could have read on the bus stop herself, but I thought asking would be easier.

'Don't move,' I'd said, my coat and keys in hand even before she'd told me.

'My mind was far away an' I missed de stop,' she said, after I found her outside one of the nail shops on the high street.

'But, Mum, you know you have to get off the stop after the pound shop.'

'I jus' wasn't looking,' she said.

Bluffing. I could tell. She'd gotten off a stop too soon and not recognised where she was.

Days later, I got in from work to find her sitting in the front room staring at the window. I asked why she wasn't watching her regular dose of *CSI*.

'De telly not working,' she'd said.

I got the remote and switched on the television. 'Course it is. Here.' I pointed out the on-off button and handed the remote to her.

Later that night, I was sitting in bed going through the assembly plan for the next day at school when she came to my bedroom, like a child dragging themselves towards a pending unpleasant experience – a telling-off or punishment. 'Erica?' she'd said, sitting on the bed by my feet. 'What is wrong with me?'

I'd put my pen down. 'I'm not sure, Mum. That's why I think you need to take the rest of the tests.'

I'd reassured her that whatever it was, I'd be there to help her.

'Well, okay,' she'd said.

The next day, when I told her I'd made the appointment for her to see the doctor, she asked: 'For what?'

'The tests you agreed you'd go for to see why you're forgetting so many things.'

'Everybody does forget things,' she said.

The night before the doctor's appointment, I called Auntie Barbara so she could encourage Mum to go. Whatever Auntie

Barbara had said worked, and I got her to the doctor's appointment.

Thankfully, Mum had great respect for doctors, so I used the fact that the doctor had said it was very important she went to the hospital for the other tests, and got her to have the scan.

'If something is wrong, de doctor will be able to give me med'cine?' she asked.

'Yeah. They should be able to,' I'd said, though I knew if she had what I thought she had, all they could do was give her something to slow down the progression.

Flutters in my chest became intense whenever I thought about it too hard. I was anxious, as I knew she had to be, and prayed I'd end up being wrong. But if I was, what else could be going on with Mum? Something *worse* than dementia?

Every test, starting with the basic memory one at the GP, filled me with dread. Before Mum could give a response to the questions put to her, I was assessing the likelihood of her giving the correct answer. Some were unfair. For example, being someone who didn't watch the news, Mum couldn't recall a recent news event.

She failed – and not because of that particular item.

The two weeks waiting for the final, conclusive result were worse. And I couldn't let her know how worried I was: my fears might feed hers and that wouldn't be good for either of us.

On the morning of her appointment, we'd sat in the room they'd put us in, me, Millie and Mum, the muscles in my throat growing more rigid, pushing down into my chest as one professional after another filed in to break the news. Until now, we'd been using chit-chat, jokes and trivial comments to keep the tension at bay. It was time to face the truth.

Everyone was introduced: psychiatrist, specialist support worker, nurse and us. I'd become lost for words when they confirmed it: Mum had Alzheimer's.

I had looked at her, my insides tightening, but for her sake, determined not to cry. Someone had handed Millie a tissue from a box on the table.

The psychiatrist explained the dementia umbrella that Alzheimer's sat under, told us it was the most common type and suggested putting Mum on a tablet which might help to slow down the progression of the disease.

There was a deafening pause after she'd finished speaking, which she broke by talking about the support and advise that would be available to us through the memory clinic.

I wasn't sure what Mum had made of everything that was being said and hoped she wouldn't want to talk about it until we got home, when – I hoped –logic, clarity and acceptance would have replaced the panic and fear. Brought some answers to the questions racing around in my head.

In the five-minute walk to the bus stop, I put my arm through Mum's, for the need to get close to her. 'Cold, isn't it?' I said.

Millie followed my lead and linked Mum's other arm. 'Your pockets feel cosy,' she told Mum.

'What is dis thing dey say I have?' Mum asked.

'It's called Alzheimer's, Mum,' I said, squinting, clenching my jaw in submission to the harsh wind on my face.

'Alsymuss?' Mum said.

'Our bus is here,' Millie interrupted, hurrying us along.

'We'll talk about it when we get home,' I said. 'All right?'

She looked perplexed. We unlinked arms and stepped into the bus. I welcomed the forced silence and took her hand.

The Rivastigmine tablet they'd put her on ended up making her nauseous, so they changed it to a patch, which for a long time she managed herself, changing it religiously every morning, like her life depended on it. Poor Mum had made herself believe this patch was her saviour – a cure for the condition she knew was changing her world for the worse. She hoped it would give her back the confidence she was losing; the ability to manage her life.

But, soon she started asking me where the toilet was in the house. I continued pointing it out – next to her bedroom and imagined her checking behind all the doors, when I was at work and she was at home on her own, until she'd located it.

In between all of this, were the regular appointments at the memory clinic and I followed up on the advice from the support worker there to get a power of attorney, which Mum cooperated with, though her comment: 'I have one daughter. When I die everything is for her,' made me – and I'm sure the doctor who witnessed her signing it – wonder if she believed she was signing her will.

Four years on, it was daunting, thinking of Mum being this far along the road into dementia; so far, in fact, that she'd forget who I was to the extent of wanting to harm – even kill me.

I lay across my bed drained, worried, fear spreading as the ceiling fan spun above me. How far had Mum's condition progressed? What if she'd had this kind of episode with one of the carers I'd put in place, or even Auntie? The thought wouldn't leave my mind. I wasn't safe alone with her.

CHAPTER FIVE

Marrying Mr Frank had been a financial blessing, but an emotional horror, for Mum.

He'd come into my life when I was nine years old. Back then, I'd hoped he'd be the man I'd spent the last few years wishing and hoping Mum would meet: the one who would be nice, kind, help her manage things, love her – maybe even marry her and become something like a father to me. They might have a baby and make me a big sister.

She was thirty-three at the time. Of course, I didn't have a clue about her age then. So young, when I worked it out, years later.

Before that, it was just me and her in the one bedroom she rented in an old Victorian house in Haringey.

Isn't he old? was what had entered my head when she'd first introduced him to me as her 'friend'. Later, I learnt he wasn't much older than her. Just looked it. He was a builder and owned three houses, not including the one we moved into with him. A quietly smug and shrewd man, he figured himself clever because he'd discovered how lucrative it was to buy a rundown or derelict house, fix it up, rent it out, raise enough money to buy another one to fix up, and then rent that out too.

We moved in with him soon after Mum had introduced him to me. At first, sharing the three-bedroom house with a basement kitchen double the size of the room Mum and I had vacated, with his tenants. Then they left and we had the whole three-bedroom to ourselves. It felt like Mum and I had won the pools – which she used to play sometimes, and talk about her dream to move out of that one-room place, get a house of her own and have enough money to buy a piece of land and build a house back home before she got too old.

The rise in our standard of living had started before we moved in with Mr Frank. Mum had bought me new shoes earlier than normal, before I had to – unknown to her – fit a piece of cardboard in my old pair to keep pebbles from pricking me through the hole at the ball of my foot, and also sop up the water getting in when it rained. After we moved in with him, Mum didn't have to carry heavy shopping bags any more. And if we missed the paraffin truck, she didn't have to drag the empty five-gallon paraffin container in her shopping trolley half an hour up to the hardware shop and back again, after filling it up to feed our heater for the week. We didn't eat the same meal almost every day any more, either. Mr Frank liked change. So Mum had dropped her old habit of cooking the 'one-pot' rice and chicken with frozen vegetables, herbs and spices thrown in – a pot that would last for at least four days. And I started getting pocket money, though that ended after I turned sixteen and got a part-time job at the local library.

But little things remained: I still added up all the change she had in her purse when she came home from work. She still brought me a buttered bun from the canteen and I still enjoyed it. Her habit of challenging the white man selling the yam and green bananas on the market stall, or arguing with the Indian butchers about the prices they charged, and getting a few pence knocked off continued. As did washing our smalls by hand in a basin at the kitchen sink even though they could have been thrown in with the other clothes we now took to the launderette.

The changes brought a more relaxed way of being to her. She laughed and smiled more. Her display of happiness was genuine for a long time, until later on, when it became a façade.

Maybe it all started on the Saturday when she was out shopping and that woman came to the house. I'd usually go with Mum, but that day I had the horrible periods, a new and unwelcomed addition to my bodily changes, so she said I could stay home.

I was downstairs at the kitchen table doing homework, Mr Frank upstairs somewhere, when a banging on the front door, and a finger pressing on the bell for longer than usual, startled me.

I rushed up the stairs to hear a woman's voice shouting: 'Frank! Frank!' through the letter box. 'Frank Simpson, find yourself here now. I warning you.'

My first thought was that this woman was mad. Made a mistake and was knocking on the wrong door, but she was calling for Mr Frank. So I dashed upstairs to find him. 'Mr Frank? Mr Frank?' Catching my breath, I knocked at his and Mum's bedroom door.

He came out, adjusting the belt on his trousers. 'What happen?'

'There's a woman outside – at the front door.' I pointed behind me. 'Can't you hear? She's calling you,' I said.

'Woman? Calling me? What woman?' He gave me an agitated look. 'What you talking about?'

The banging started again.

'It's a woman. At the front door for you,' I repeated. 'She sounds angry.'

'Angry?' He buckled the belt and started making his way downstairs.

'Frank?' the woman was shouting.

Mr Frank didn't answer, but took firm, determined steps towards the door. I stepped back and watched as he opened it.

'What the fu—? What the hell you doing here, woman?'

The woman, who had lighter skin than Mum, me or Mr Frank, was wearing a black coat with fur around the collar. A brown handbag hung on her left shoulder. She took a couple of steps away from the front door, her eyes never moving from Mr Frank.

'What you doing here?' Mr Frank asked, then, turning from the woman to me, said: 'Go about your business.' He pulled the door closer to him, reducing my view of outside.

I hesitated. Couldn't just leave. Who was she? Why was she here behaving like this?

'Where is what you owe me?' she said.

Mr Frank turned and glared at me. I moved slowly downstairs, but only far away enough to be out of his sight, then took another step up, straining my ears so as not to miss a syllable. There was shuffling, then the door slammed. I stepped as softly as a kitten back to the table. His own heavy steps told me he was on his way down. Back at the table, I picked up my pen and fixed my eyes on the book in front of me. What was going on? What did he owe her? What for? Had he given it to her to make her go away? And did Mum know about this?

'Erica?' He was standing above me.

'Yes, Mr Frank?' I looked up, faking surprise.

'Listen to me good,' he'd said, in a new Mr Frank voice I hadn't been exposed to in the three years we'd been living with him – his disciplining of me had always come across as advice: the real stuff was left to Mum. I wasn't his child and though at times, in the past, I'd wished he would, he'd never tried to make me feel otherwise.

I lifted my head a little higher, forced my eyes to settle on his, but couldn't do anything about the wobbling going on inside me. My brain was still adjusting to this other side of Mr Frank.

'You... you never see or hear what jus' happen there, eh? You understan' me?' he said. 'Dat lady there was a frien'. Your mother don't have to know nothing about. You hear?'

I nodded.

'What de eyes don't see de heart don't grieve,' he said, raising his eyebrows.

I pulled my eyes away from his and he made his way back up the stairs. Minutes later, when I was still trying to refocus and finish my homework, I heard the front door slam. He'd gone to pick Mum up.

Days after that Saturday came sneaky warning looks from him, a raise in my pocket money and him always defending me anytime Mum got on my case about something. I stayed up nights, rolling the whole thing over in my mind. I had to tell Mum. Wanted to, but couldn't.

Every time I saw her and him together, interacting: her preparing or dishing out his meals; washing and ironing his clothes; or heard her talk about him in a fond and caring way, the temptation to tell niggled at me. But I fought hard against it. My biggest fear, the pain and disruptions it would cause.

I didn't want things going bad between Mum and Mr Frank. The house we lived in belonged to him and Mum's job as a kitchen assistant at the sweet factory wasn't going to be enough to give us anything near to what we had with him. I imagined we'd manage, like we'd done before him, but visions of that hardship flashed across my mind. I couldn't do that to Mum, to us – take Mum's happiness and our comforts away.

Days, weeks passed, as my desperation to tell Mum grew to bursting point. The whole thing gnawed at me, put me on edge.

'What is wrong with you?' Mum finally asked me one morning, when the pot of milk I had on the stove boiled over. Mr Frank had already left for work.

'Nothing.' I avoided meeting her eyes.

'I find you to be very absent-minded dese days. You letting de milk boil over, burning de toast, forgetting dis, forgetting dat... What is going on with you?'

My thirteen-year-old brain couldn't take any more. I told her, and watched the expression on her face turn sour, moisture settle in her eyes.

'I'm sorry, Mum,' I said. 'I'm so sorry,' when she turned away.

The tears I half expected to see didn't come. 'Why you never tell me before?' she said.

'I was scared. Please don't tell him I told you, Mum. Please.'

'Don't worry,' she said. 'It's okay. Don't worry.'

'Okay.' But I did worry. Every time I saw him, I half expected him to say something. Lash out at me. Do something to punish me in some way. I wasn't often alone with him, but actively avoided it now; convinced I'd done the wrong thing by telling Mum. I'd let go of one fear to replace it with another.

But, weeks later, I came home from school and Mum told me she and Mr Frank were going to get married.

'When? When?' I said, excited for her.

'Next month.'

'I can be a bridesmaid?'

'Of course,' she said.

'And Auntie Barbara and everyone will be coming?'

'Yes... yes, of course.' She nodded, her face lit up, matching my anticipation and joy.

The pending marriage meant everything was okay. Whatever discussions they'd had, everything was okay. I could put the whole thing about Mr Frank and that woman behind me. More importantly, so could Mum. Mr Frank was going to marry her.

That proved he loved her and that there was nothing funny going on with him and that woman.

We started to prepare. Saturday after Saturday, we shopped until we found the right bridesmaid dress for me. Mum shopped for her wedding gown with Auntie Barbara and showed it to me when she brought it home.

I begged her to put it on so I could see what she'd look like, like I'd done with mine. 'And the shoes too. Put them on,' I said.

'All right. All right,' she said, 'but quick before Frank come.'

'You look beautiful,' I said. 'Like a princess.'

She twirled, smiled. It was a moment of happiness for both of us. My wishes for her were coming true.

But the month came and went. Her mood changed. Worry came back. I watched. Watched and listened for signs of what was to come between her and Mr Frank. More months followed, with no new date for the wedding. And the bridesmaid dressed stayed pressed up against the end of the rail in my wardrobe, keeping the possibility of the marriage alive, until I'd outgrown it.

CHAPTER SIX

I woke up groggy, my body clock still on UK time. The fan had been spinning above my head all night, but I'd kicked the sheets off in my sleep.

Knocking off the five hours we were behind the UK made it six thirty. The phone was ringing, then Mum was talking. I could have drifted back to sleep but the sight of the chair wedged behind my door stirred up memories of last night's episode with Mum. I sat up. Sniffed. Scents of cinnamon, nutmeg, seeping in through the gaps in the door suggested she was making porridge. My stomach began to grumble.

I scratched my arm. Counted five itchy, raised bumps. Mosquitoes. Damn pests had made a three-course meal out of my blood during the night. With all the drama, I'd forgotten to use my repellent or take my antihistamine.

I got out of bed, opened the curtains and looked out towards the bay, where a man stood in the water holding a fishing line. He'd be trying to catch snappers, jacks and other fish swimming up from the Atlantic to lay eggs in the mangroves.

A gentle hum of 'I Can't Stop Loving You' made me turn towards my bedroom door. She was humming that old favourite of hers, bringing up memories of the days when it was just me and her in our one-bedroom. I sat on the edge of the bed.

Back then, she'd often start with a hum, then say something like: 'Come on, take a little dance with me,' and take my hand. She'd sing, that song I'd learnt to love, and lead us in a waltz around the narrow space in our bedroom.

I focused on that memory for a while, allowing the sense of wholeness, safety and contentment to pour over me. In those days, I'd imagine she was singing to me. And she wouldn't ever stop loving me, as I wouldn't her.

The humming faded.

'Mum?'

Only her footsteps. I opened the door and the aroma of spices flooded in.

She was in the kitchen.

'Morning, Mum,' I said. 'Ooo, that looks nice.' As expected, it was cornmeal porridge and she was about to start eating.

'Good morning,' she replied, looking up at me. 'I leave some for you. An' tea on de stove.'

'Thanks. You okay? Sleep well?' She wasn't likely to remember what had happened last night, but part of me hoped she would. Wished we could talk about it: she could apologise and we could acknowledge the problem, together.

'Uh-huh,' she replied. 'How you sleep?'

'Got lots of bites,' I said. 'Mosquitoes love my blood.'

'How is Millie?'

'Millie? Millie's fine, Mum. She sends her love.'

'She doesn't phone me – forget all about me.'

She'd spoken to Millie a few days before I arrived, and had obviously forgotten our exchange yesterday, about how Millie was.

I sat opposite her with my bowl of porridge, though there hadn't been much for me to get because half of what was left in the pan had burnt.

She took a small white pill from one of the small transparent plastic bags on the table and popped one in her mouth.

'What's that?' I said.

'My med'cine.'

She'd left the early stage of Alzheimer's years ago, so had stopped taking the medication for that.

I checked the label on the bags. One was 'Aspirin 75mg', and the other was 'Paracetamol'. 'What you taking these for?'

'De doctor say, one every day,' she said. She was always cooperative when it came to taking medicine, conventional or herbal.

'What, both? Paracetamol is for pain. Are you getting pain?'

'Sometimes.'

'Where?'

'I does get headaches at times.'

'Everyday?'

'I don't know. Sometimes.'

'You don't need to be taking these, Mum,' I said.

'I have to go to town today.'

'I think we need to go and see your doctor.'

Those paracetamols would definitely be disappearing, once her back was turned. Did she need the aspirin for blood thinning? Did she have other health issues I didn't know about? How had I missed this?

'I'll see you later,' Mum said, standing up with her tea cup and spoon on her plate.

'Where you going?'

'Town, I tell you.' She headed for the sink.

'Castries?'

'Yes. We going shopping. Me an' Barbara.'

'Oh. Nice. I'll come too.' I perked up with the prospect of a trip to town. A chance for distraction. 'I could change some money. I'll need to have a shower first.' I rushed off.

Last night's events skimmed through my mind again. I

lodged the chair behind the door before going into the shower. Questions around other aspects of Mum's health kept coming.

'I'm ready,' I shouted, making my way to her room. I knocked and went in. 'Mum?' She wasn't there.

The sound of a car engine outside sent me darting towards the kitchen door.

'Hey?' I shouted, waving after Cousin Headley's minibus as it drove away from the gate. I tried chasing after it, still shouting, but he couldn't have heard nor seen me because he kept going. I rushed back inside and called Auntie Barbara. No answer.

Great. No Mum and no Auntie Barbara.

Had Mum knowingly left without me, or had the conversation we'd had under half an hour ago already fizzled out of her mind?

Disappointed and idle, I unpacked the rest of my clothes and started putting the food stuff I'd brought from England away. The sweets needed to be somewhere cool to stop them melting. As I opened the fridge door, a magnet fell, followed by an old telephone bill and other bits of paper. One reminded Mum to 'call gas people'. Another, 'outside pipe', and another: 'Erica Sunday'. A memory method we'd started in England. What I could see confirmed my own deduction that it wasn't working any more: she hadn't remembered I was arriving yesterday.

I put the 'Erica' note in the bin. Poured out a cup of bay-leaf tea and sipped it while strolling around Mum's garden. The gardener clearly hadn't been for a while. The grass needed cutting and wild flowers were growing all around the shed in the far corner of the garden.

Scattered around the grassy areas were different fruit trees: sweet orange, lime, mangoes, soursop, sugar apple and coconut; towards the back: bananas, plantain and a moringa tree with its delicate leaves, white flowers and hanging pods filled with seeds claiming to be a cure-for-all.

The sun was rising higher in the sky, dishing out heat the intermittent breeze alleviated. Ripe and green mangoes hung off both mango trees and the ground was littered with rotting ones, some half-eaten by birds or fruit bats before falling. I prodded, with my feet, at a couple but didn't pick them up. The rule was never to eat a mango you hadn't seen fall. They could be filled with worms. The sickly-sweet scent of rot and the sight of the flies feasting on them brought on a queasiness that made me shift my direction, back into the sunlight that fell onto the side of my face. I headed for another shaded area to inspect the two orchid plants Mum had sitting on her unused raised bed, partially sheltered by overhanging branches from the huge breadfruit tree in the garden backing onto hers. Healthy, but, sadly, not flowering. 'Does anyone remember you're here?' I asked them, lifting one of the pots. I left them alone.

The sun had found the back of my neck now. Stirring up the itch to get out. Go somewhere. I could take the bus into town, couldn't I?

I'd always left the loose change I hadn't spent after each visit in a jar that I kept in the far corner of a cupboard in my room. I headed off to find it, but it was gone. I looked around me. Surely there was some kind of loose change hanging around somewhere in the house? I didn't need more than five dollars for a fare. Mum's room would be the best place to find it.

I pulled the top drawer out of her dressing table and was met by a large jar of coffee, a box of tea bags and one side of a pair of pink flip-flops amongst her knickers and bras.

I sighed. 'Oh, Mum,' and began taking out the things that didn't belong in there. This ritual, though a losing battle, ruffled me. It was a revolving door. I'd take stuff out that didn't belong where Mum had put it, then Alzheimer's would instruct her to reverse it again.

Pairs of shoes were amongst her clothes in the two other drawers below, with loose photographs of Mr Frank, herself, me,

Millie. Evoking memories of occasions I didn't want to be drawn into. There were trinkets, the old mobile phone I'd given her when she came to England, candles, pens, loose buttons, but no coins.

I sat on her bed, exasperated, worries over Mum's condition and the way forward niggling at me, the money needed for the bus now secondary in my concerns. Taking a deep breath, I glanced around. Being in there was beginning to stifle me. I approached the wardrobe and my eyes fell on two bags hanging on the door handle. Turning them upside down over the bed, I scraped up three dollars' worth of loose coins, then a five-dollar note tucked into a zipped-up compartment inside one of them and a bunch of keys with a wooden carving of an 'F' hanging on the key ring. *His* keys. I detached the carving, dropped it in the bin, got myself ready again and left the house.

Cherry Orchard had one designated entry and a separate exit for vehicles. On foot, you could take either one. I aimed for the entry road, perspiration building up on my face and underarms. As I lifted my shades to dab some of the moisture off, I spotted a woman coming towards me, carrying a bag in one hand, a walking stick in the other. Her wide-rim hat conjured up an image of Little Bo Peep.

'Mrs Andrews?' I said.

'Good morning, my dear,' Mrs Andrews shouted, when we got closer.

'Good morning.'

'You arrived?'

'I have.'

My school-breaks visits had become a routine, and anyone close enough to Mum knew when to expect me. Three times a year, all roads led to St Lucia so I could make sure things were okay with Mum and put right what wasn't.

'A mind told me the person was you,' Mrs Andrews said.

'It is. How are you?'

'Not too bad, darling. Not too bad, by the grace of God. You taking a stroll?'

'Yeah.' Her accent quickly reminded me she was originally from Barbados. Her husband, Mr Andrews, was the St Lucian one, but they'd spent most of their lives in Canada. 'Here. Let me help.'

She sighed and began to unravel the bags from her hand. 'Thank you, darling. It's very nice of you.'

The five or ten-minute walk to her house wouldn't eat too much into my time. Besides, what was my hurry?

'How is your mudder – Ione, doing?' she asked.

'She's gone to town with Auntie Barbara.'

'An' leave you to thaw?' She laughed.

I dabbed more sweat from my forehead. 'I was thinking of joining them, but I'm not sure now.'

'The heat will have you melting in town. Castries is hot.'

It had taken me a while to get my head around the phenomena: valleys trapping the heat and the mountains and hills above benefitting from the wind and breezes.

We turned the corner into Anthurium Mews, where Mrs Andrews lived. I flinched at the sight of the three Alsatian dogs bouncing towards us, barking, from behind a nearby fence.

'Don't worry yourself 'bout dem dogs. They just doing their jobs. Keeping their master's house safe.' Mrs Andrews continued talking, telling me how much she missed her husband, who'd died seven years ago. 'As you know, he was the driver. I never did take to the driving thing,' she said. 'So I can only buy a little shopping at a time an' try to stay out of the hot sun.'

I stood back to let her open her gate, and followed her up the four steps to her front door.

'Here you are,' I said, handing her the bags. Her veranda

was similar to Mum's, with four chairs around a glass and bamboo table.

'Thank you very much, darling. God bless you.'

'I'll see you again soon,' I said, wiping the perspiration trapped inside the rim of my shades.

'Oh, no. You mus' take a cold drink to see you up the road. Come on. Coca cola? Juice? Take a seat. You not in no hurry, are you? I tell you Castries too hot.'

'Well...' I hesitated. 'A glass of water would be nice. Thank you.'

She disappeared inside, and I looked out at the nearby houses, all prettied with shrubs and flowers. Behind them grew mango, soursop, citrus and other tropical trees, like at Mum's place.

Mrs Andrews was soon back with two glasses of water, which she placed on the table and sat down. 'Phew.' She sighed.

'Thank you. I'll have to pay you a proper visit another time,' I said, sitting on the chair next to her. 'I need to get to the bank.' I reached for my glass.

'The bank?' she said. 'At dis time?' She gave me a puzzled look, which suggested I ought to know better. 'The line will be out the door.'

The bank wasn't a dire emergency, but on such a lovely day, it would be nice to go somewhere apart from Mrs Andrews' house.

'That cake you gave me to take back with me at Easter was delicious,' I said, trying to change the subject.

'Cake? Oh, not cake,' she said. 'Coconut sweet bread.'

'Well, it was lovely. You must give me the recipe.'

'Of course. I don't do much baking any more. You know. It's me alone here in the house and now they tell me I have the sugar.'

'Diabetes?'

'Yes. Fifty-five years – almost fifty-six, we was together. Me and Mr Andrews.'

'Mmm. Long time,' I said, her words triggering thoughts about their ups and downs. Had he been faithful? Had she, in all of that time?

Mum had been with Mr Frank for thirty-nine years and she, and anyone else who cared to work it out, knew that he'd stayed with her, but not faithfully.

People go on and on about the length of time they or other couples have been together, but the litmus test shouldn't be the length of time together. It should be about the quality. How happy they'd been, and are, together. Not the fact that they'd stayed and endured, in spite of everything. And what was 'marriage' anyway, but a piece of paper? Though there was a time, for me, when it was something precious to aim for in life.

I listened some more to Mrs Andrews singing the praises of her dead husband. It was like that with her sometimes. Other times it would be about her children. Then: 'Ione is lucky to have you,' she said.

The mention of Mum's name drew me back into the conversation. 'When my turn comes – when I am too old or too sick to manage – I will no doubt check myself into St Patrick's.'

'St Patrick's?' I said.

'Dat nice ole people's home down in town.'

'They have a care home here? I didn't realise they had such a thing.'

'Lucky for people like me, they do.'

'But what about your children in Canada?'

'Yes, and dat's where they say they intend to stay.' Her face closed and pity swelled in me.

'What about you? Wouldn't you go back there? I mean, if things got too hard to manage here?'

'Oh. No. Do you know how cold Canada can get, chile?' She glared at me.

'I've heard,' I said. 'Anyway, I'm sure one of your children would come and sort things out for you, when you'll need them to.'

She took a deep breath. 'We'll see. When dat time comes.'

'I'm sure they will.' I thanked her for the drink and said I'd better be off. This time, determined to leave.

'Oh.' Mrs Andrews jerked as if startled, then looked at me with dull, sad eyes. 'I hope to see you again,' she said. 'Maybe we can make some sweet bread together.'

'Yes, yes – we must.' The sharpness of her memory, though a wonderful thing for her, brought sadness and disappointment to me. Why couldn't Mum still have hers? She was even younger than Mrs Andrew.

'You planning to take you mudder up with you?'

'Yes,' I said.

'She really want to go back there?'

'We don't have much of a choice.'

'Dat's what happens when you get ole – you run out of choice.'

'I'm still working,' I said.

'Of course.'

I hurried off before she engaged me in any other issues or stories about her dead husband.

CHAPTER SEVEN

The visit to Mrs Andrews had brought up more of the past. Questions of loyalty, choice and love.

Living with Mr Frank had bumped us up from the lower ranks of hardship to a bit more than okay, but it wasn't long before a distance begun to grow between me and Mum. And my excitement, optimism and hope for better things to come, slowly began to dissolve. She was developing an alternative friendship. Every inch closer she grew to Mr Frank pulled her an inch further away from what we had before him.

He was taking my space at the centre of her life.

She'd have his dinner on the table ten minutes after he arrived home. Not on a plate dished straight out of the pots, like we had. He had gravy in one bowl, rice in another and vegetables in a third. His large empty plate sat waiting with cutlery close by. That was something we'd only had at Christmas. But Christmas came every day for Mr Frank.

Soon after he'd eaten, and loosened his belt, he and Mum would sit together, chatting, him sometimes whispering stuff in her ears, her responding with laughter, chuckle or a comment in a voice and tone I didn't know. I took to my room more and

more, gradually learning to accept my assigned space in the trio
– further away from Mum. That in itself didn't kill my love for
her, but that love started to become dented by hurt, disappointment and resentment towards Mr Frank.

After another year of waiting for news of a new wedding
date, I'd noticed a gold band on Mum's married finger.

'You've got a ring?' I said, expecting confirmation.

'Frank give it to me,' she said. 'You like it?' She put her left
hand out to show me, smiling.

'Is... is it a wedding ring?'

'In a way,' she said.

'So you got married? Without me there?'

'No. Not yet,' she said.

'So why have you got a ring?'

'I tell you Frank give it to me. We will get married when de
time is right.' What she meant was when *he* thought the time
was right. And in thirty-nine years, he never did. But she kept
the ring on her 'married' finger.

She'd lost him way before he died, six years ago. Good job
he died before her, or what would her life have been like? What
would he have done, if he had been alive to experience this?
Mum. Ione, with Alzheimer's. How would that have
worked out?

Those thoughts deepened my need for distraction. I
couldn't go back to the house and just sit around waiting for
Mum and Auntie to get back. Any cashpoint would give me
local currency. And since neither Mum nor Auntie had internet, I had to renew and top-up my local telephone chip too, so I
could stay in touch with Millie, Delia and Phillipa.

Vieux Fort was sleepy for St Lucia's second town, but this was a
small island, smaller even than London.

I got some money out then strolled along the market strip

where vendors displayed their produce of ground provisions, green bananas, mangoes galore, plums, watermelons, pumpkins and all sorts. They were all placed in carts, wooden trays or empty flour bags on the pavement. Behind the stalls were shops selling what you weren't likely to know until you walked in, since window displays were a rarity: a practice that did away with the concept of window shopping.

I asked a young man with a shopping trolley packed with ackees and plums for a small bag of each. 'Hope they're sweet,' I said. It was meant to be a joke, but he offered me one of each to try. The juice inside the skin of the little green fruit, with texture similar to a lychee, trickled first, then burst into my mouth as my tongue and teeth manoeuvred the flesh off the seed. 'Mmm. Okay,' I said, not bothering to try the plum.

'Dey both sweet,' he said.

I put them in my handbag, paid and kept walking through the intensifying heat, which pointed me in one direction alone: the air-conditioned mall, even though I had no intention of buying anything. Everything to do with goods and services was on a mini scale: quality and choice at a level lower than I was used to. And quality didn't accompany the high prices.

One of the things I couldn't complain about, however, was the food and beverages. Also the weather, which was all in all glorious, so long as you took proper precautions, and didn't come out with your head exposed, like I'd done today.

I browsed through the little clothes and souvenir shops, going from floor to floor, checking prices and the quality of things that caught my eye.

The smell of food confirmed I was approaching the food court on the third floor. The ackee had tickled my appetite. It was lunch time. The morning's porridge had been digested and my stomach was rumbling again.

'Erica? It's you?' a voice from behind me said, as I sat

tucking into my plate of stewed fish, ground provisions and salad.

I turned, mouth full of food, to face a woman, maybe in her early forties. Thick eyebrows raised above a questioning smile.

'You forget me?'

She looked familiar, but her name was lost to me.

'Claire,' she said, moving for me to get a better look at her.

I swallowed the food in my mouth. 'Oh, yes. Yes. Are you...?' I hesitated. 'Mum's neighbour. Your house is behind Mum's.'

'You remember now?'

'Mmm.... Yeah.' The most I'd seen of her was when she came over after Mr Frank died. She'd helped out with some of the other neighbours, preparing and serving food and drinks at the wake Mum held at the house for people who'd attended the funeral. And I'd seen her around Cherry Orchard on my visits. 'How are you doing?'

'Good. Good. I'm doing good,' she said, nodding. 'You come back for your dose of sunshine?'

'Yeah.' We both knew I wasn't only here for the sunshine. 'Things are getting... you know? I have to see about my mum.'

'Of course. And how is your daughter?'

'Millie? Oh, she's doing well. Very well, thanks. Do you want to sit down?' I nudged at a chair opposite me with my foot.

'No. No. I ate already.'

I was geared up for some alone time, so was partly relieved.

'But I'll get a drink,' she said, and asked if I wanted one.

'No, thanks.' I pointed at my small plastic bottle of water and carried on eating, hoping to be finished by the time she got back.

'It's nice to see you back again,' Claire said, on her return, and pulled a chair out to sit. 'But I cannot believe you forgot me.' She tilted her head to the side, as if studying me.

'No. It was your name. I just couldn't – and I'm normally

good with names.' I tried to explain. 'And you caught me by surprise. I wasn't expecting to meet anyone who knew me in here.'

'Don't worry. Tease! I teasing you.' She chuckled and glanced at her watch.

'Your twists are nice.'

'Thank you. A friend did them for me.'

'She's good,' I said.

'You cut yours and I'm growing mine.'

'Yeah. Needed a change.'

'I can't stay, anyway. I have five minutes to get back to work. Eat your food. We bound to see each other again.' She pushed her chair back and got up. 'Take care, eh?'

I was about to ask where she worked, but she seemed in a hurry to leave. I finished eating and went to get the bus back to Cherry Orchard.

I opened my eyes. Blinked a few times and looked up at a woman who'd touched my knee.

'Er, sorry,' I said.

She was trying to get off the bus. Just as well she'd woken me because the stop after that was mine. That high carb meal had sent me to sleep as soon as the bus started moving. I took a few sips of my water before getting off and starting the short walk to Mum's.

Cousin Headley's minibus was parked outside the opened gate. Voices coming from the house confirmed they were back, and on the veranda.

'Where you was?' Auntie asked as soon as she saw me.

'Where were *you*? You-all went and left me,' I said, my voice and tone displaying my disappointment.

'What you mean?' Cousin Headley said.

'Yes, I told Mum I'd come with her, went to get dressed and

when I came out she was gone. I called after you when you were driving away, but you just kept going.'

'Eh-eh. I din see you, *on*,' Cousin Headley said.

Auntie Barbara turned to Mum, frowning. 'Dat's true, Ione?'

'I... I call you but you din answer. I believe you was sleeping – you did go back to sleep.'

Could this be true?

'Mum, I told you I was coming. I had to have a shower. I rushed like crazy, came out and no Mum.' We were all staring at Mum. I couldn't see how she would have deliberately left me. She'd forgotten I was coming. Just as she'd forgotten trying to attack me last night. 'Never mind,' I said, trying to ease the pressure off her.

'An' you managed to go to Vieux Fort an' come back already?' Auntie said.

'I needed to get some dollars,' I said.

The conversation drew to a silence.

'Well, let's go, you hear,' Auntie said. 'Take me up de road please, Headley?' She looked at her favourite cousin, who stood up as instructed.

Auntie lived alone in her three-bedroom house, fifteen minutes' walk away. Ten years ago, her husband, Uncle Vic, thinking he was closer to forty-seven than the seventy-four-year-old man he was, had climbed up a ladder to adjust one of their outdoor lights, fallen off, had a heart attack and died. Auntie looked good and was sprightly for eighty, despite her chubbiness, but had shown no interest in replacing Uncle Vic.

'No man not coming to eat me an' Victor money,' she said, when anyone suggested a replacement.

I walked Auntie and Cousin Headley to the gate and told her I wanted to speak to her. I found it uncomfortable discussing Mum and her condition in front of her. In the early days of diagnosis, she'd reprimanded me for telling the dentist she had dementia. I'd been cautious about it ever since. She didn't seem to care much about that any more, but I was aware that she didn't always say what she was feeling and I couldn't be sure how much of a conversation she was grasping.

'Come up later,' Auntie said. 'But not too late, eh?'

When I went back inside, Mum was in her room, lying down.

'You okay?' I asked, quietly.

'Uh-huh,' she responded.

I bagged the gifts I'd brought for Auntie, Cousin Headley and other relatives I hardly knew, then told Mum I was popping up to Auntie's. 'You'll be all right for a bit, won't you?'

'Of course,' she said.

Cousin Headley was gone and Auntie was putting her shopping away. 'Ione all right?' she asked.

I told her Mum was resting. 'Here's the stuff I brought from England.' I normally left them with her for dispersing.

'Rest dem dere,' she said. 'Dat's nice of you, *ich mwen*. Your cousins will appreciate it.'

'This one's for you.' I put her bag on the table and the others on one of the chairs.

'You din have to bring anything for me, you know. I'm ole already, but thank you.'

'It's not a problem, Auntie.' I sat down. 'Mum really did go off and leave me this morning, you know.'

'I suspect she did forget she had dat conversation with you.'

'I know.'

'She even forgetting to take back her change an' pick up de thing she buy in de shop. Sometimes she giving people ten dollars for five.'

'Oh, dear.'

'I'm sorry you come an' find de house in such a state. I—'

'That's okay, Auntie,' I said. 'I'll be clearing things out before we leave.'

'You going to take her with you?'

'I think that's the best thing. Don't you?'

'Yes. I believe so.'

'She won't be able to stay here on her own like this anymore. It would have been good if she still had a carer, but... And she scared the life out of me last night.'

'How?' Auntie sat down and I told her what had happened. '*Bondyé*. I caa believe she mistake you for a stranger. Her head not good at all. I tired of her asking me for de others: Sim, Ellen, Louis – everybody dat die so long already. God rest their soul.'

Auntie looked up at the ceiling and made the sign of the cross, tapping her forehead, the middle of her chest, then each collar bone. 'An' no matter how much you tell her dey dead, she saying nobody never tell her, as if we deliberately keep it from her.'

'Auntie, when she asks, you have to tell her they've gone out. She'll see them later or something like that.' I'd told her this too many times. 'It's better to enter her world.'

'Her world? Pretend my head not good like her?'

'It's upsetting to her every time someone tells her people she remembers are dead. It's best to tell her they're out or something.'

'Huh. Dese days she doesn't even always shower.'

'When did that start?' I asked, recalling the funky odour on Mum when I hugged her yesterday.

Auntie shrugged. 'Erica.' She stared at the table. 'If I tell you...'

Guilt descended on me. 'I'm sorry you've been having to deal with all of that, Auntie. She wasn't forgetting to do that when I was last here.'

'Is me dat should be telling you I sorry. Ione come after you with a knife? She din know it was you in de house? Suppose she did kill you? *Bondyé!*'

'She probably forgot I was there. And didn't recognise me either. She wouldn't have done that otherwise. She wouldn't have tried to kill *me*.'

'Well, at least you get to see how she is for yourself.'

'I'm wondering if she needs some kind of medication, you know? Auntie, I was really scared. Imagine if she had stabbed me or I'd have had to wrestle with her to get the knife away?'

I told her about the tablets Mum was taking and got a worried look from her.

'But it must be Dr Finch dat give dem to her,' she said. 'You can take her to de doctor when you-all get to Englan'.' She looked at me again. 'You want me to come an' sleep with you-all tonight?'

'No. It's okay, Auntie.' Knowing what was possible with Mum, I'd now be better prepared.

'I will miss Ione a lot, when you take her, but I believe Englan' is de bes' place for her.' Auntie looked at her hands.

'I know. You can come with us, if you like and stay for a bit.'

'Me? Uh-uh.' She shook her head.

'Hope she doesn't give me any trouble when I tell her. She's always said she wants to die here.'

'When an' where we die is for God to decide,' Auntie said, firmly. 'You should try to persuade her. She will listen to you.'

I didn't share Auntie's confidence in that.

Daylight was beginning to fade on my way home but the jaunty butterflies hadn't stopped flirting, sipping nectar from any available flowers. The air was cooling to a temperature much like what we'd consider a wonderful summer's day in England. Days we didn't often get there. A tinge of homesickness struck me. I imagined sitting in my little garden, in temperatures similar to this one, chatting with Delia, or reading a book with a glass of wine.

'I'm back,' I announced, to the side of Mum's face.

She was about to open the fridge and turned to look at me. 'Oh, it's you?'

I suspected she might have forgotten I was in the country, but at least she'd recognised me. 'I'm hungry,' I said. 'Shall we eat?'

'Where is Barbara?'

'At home. I just left her.'

That pot of soup she'd made for my arrival yesterday was in the fridge. 'It's lovely outside. We can eat there.'

'All right.' She released the door.

The bottom of the pot was burnt. I salvaged as much as I could, avoiding scraping close to the bottom, then put the pot to soak in the sink.

My favourite seat at the table on the veranda was the one facing the far side of the garden, with my back to the gate. As if knowing that, Mum had left it vacant. We ate in silence, interrupted only by me asking her if the soup was too hot. She said it was fine, but continued blowing the first few spoonfuls before putting it in her mouth.

'Thanks, Mum,' I said, finishing before her. The meat was shredded from overcooking, the flavour a little acrid, but edible.

'Dat's okay.'

Was this the right time to broach returning to England?

'How you feeling about things?' I said.

'I don't know.' She dropped her spoon in her bowl. 'Sometimes I don't feel good at all in myself.' She frowned.

I suspected she was talking about something to do with dementia – feelings, sensations. Not actual pains in her body. 'How...? How do you feel?'

'I don't know. Jus'... I don't know.'

Seconds slipped by. Had Alzheimer's already taken away

her memory of diagnosis? I let my gaze fall on Claire's house over the fence, at the back of the garden. 'I'm not sure if you should be taking those pills you took this morning,' I said. 'I mean, did the doctor say why you should be taking them every day?'

'Dr Finch?'

'Yeah. Usually, aspirin is to thin someone's blood. Did he say you might have blood clots?'

'I... no. Of course not,' she said, her voice shaky.

'Maybe we should go and see another doctor.'

'If you think so.'

'We'll ask for a full check-up. How about that?'

'Mmm.'

'Are you still happy living here, Mum?' I asked, banishing the awkward silence.

'Happy?' she repeated, like she didn't understand the word.

'Yes. You used to be happy being here... in St Lucia. In your house, living close to Auntie Barbara. You know – with all of this.' I opened an arm out towards the garden, beyond the gate.

A few seconds went by again with me looking at her – her eyes near still. 'Mum?'

'Uh?' She shifted her gaze.

'You still like it here?'

'I... of course I still like it. I like everything I have. I... I jus'... jus' find myself feeling funny at times.' Her shoulders rose slightly, then fell. 'I don't know.'

'Oh, Mum.' The urge to make things right for her; to be there as her right hand, a replacement for the abilities she'd lost and was still losing, brimmed inside me. 'Don't worry. We'll sort it out,' I said.

It was insincere not telling her, upfront, about my plan to take her back to England with me for good, but I wanted her on board and didn't want to upset her. This delicate matter had to be broached with care. I'd have to make her understand why it had to happen.

'I brought a few things for you from England,' I said, hoping to lighten the conversation. 'Some little pressies and treats.' I listed them. 'And Mrs Gooding sent you some lovely soaps.'

'Gooding?'

'Your mate, Jean. Remember?'

'Oh. Dat's nice,' she said. 'Jean. Yes.' Her eyes brightened up with a smile.

Silence came again. I picked up our bowls. 'I'll be back in a minute. I'll bring the ginger snaps for dessert, yeah?'

'Okay.'

I came back with a plate of biscuits. She thanked me, and bit into one.

'Mum?' I broke a tiny piece from another.

'Uh?' She looked at me.

'Would you like to come back to England to live?'

'Live where?'

'In England. With me.'

'For what? Eh-eh.' Her gentle tone had given way to a more assertive, defiant one. 'I have my house here. My home.'

'I know you do, Mum, but I was wondering if everything would be better... and if you'd be happier if you lived in England with me.'

'Me? Live in Englan'? With you?'

'Yeah.'

'Eh-eh. Not me. I don't want to live in Englan'. Here I'm staying – in my house,' she said, emphatically.

Then looked away.

CHAPTER EIGHT

Mum couldn't have been happier, thirteen years ago, when she and Mr Frank started building their house here in Cherry Orchard. Full of life she'd been then, experiencing the dream – that many in her generation held onto over the years, saving all the pennies they could working abroad – come to fruition.

Auntie Barbara had made the same move four years before Mum and couldn't wait for her younger sister to join her. I'd tried to keep my personal loss hidden. With her leaving, gone were our trips to the markets, cosy takeaways or visits to the cinema together. There was no more lying on the sofa, watching her favourite *CSI*, my head in her lap. Millie wasn't able to spend all the time she used to with her grandmother. Contact between us was much less and mainly by phone. She was far away. Mr Frank had won her, again.

I'd told her repeatedly how much I'd miss her, and my effort to stay away from Mr Frank meant a whole year passed before my first visit to see her.

I'd cry after each one, turning my face towards the window on the aeroplane hoping no one, especially Millie, would notice. My tears weren't only because I missed Mum or hadn't wanted the holiday to end. It was because I could also see the happiness she'd left England with fading. When I asked if everything was okay, she'd answer: 'Yes. I'm fine. It's fine.' But I suspected different.

Years later, Auntie Barbara confirmed it.

The sky was clouding over, a breeze picking up. The pitch of excitement from the melody of whistling frogs suggested rain was on its way. That didn't matter much. We'd still be warm, as long as we stayed dry.

'You sure you're happy here?' I asked Mum, still angling for a way to persuade her to willingly come back with me.

'Of course.'

'Mmm.'

'Why you think I am not happy here? St Lucia is my home, where I was born.'

'I know, Mum. But... I'm not sure if you'll be able to get the health care or help you need here, in St Lucia.'

'What is dat nonsense you talking about? Health care? Help?'

'You know you've got demen—Alzheimer's, Mum, and I think it's getting worse. Don't you?'

She glared at me. Thoughts were gaining strength, Alzheimer's was stirring something up, behind those eyes. Should I have left this discussion for another time? Would there *be* a better time?

'I'm gonna wash up,' I said, and left her staring at the plate of ginger snaps.

I'd almost finished the dishes when I heard her come in. 'Mum?'

'Yes?' She was heading for her bedroom, but hesitated and paused for a couple of seconds when she heard me.

'I'm sorry,' I said, moving towards her.

'For what?'

'It's okay,' I said. 'You're okay. Right?' I touched her arm.

'I know.'

'Know what?'

'I know you don't want to look after me.'

'Why... why d'you say that?' I asked the question knowing there was an element of truth there. 'I... I do!'

She opened her bedroom door and walked in, closing it behind her. There was a time when the front room was where she'd spent her relaxing time indoors. But since losing interest in the television, her bedroom had become the alternative.

Persuade was what I needed to do. Not pressure her. But what if she was adamant? Refused to come back with me?

I finished up in the kitchen. Was there another way of getting through to her? Of convincing her that my suggestion was the best one? Was there another method or argument I could put to her so she could better understand? If there was, I didn't know it. But now, we both needed a little space to let things settle down between us.

I went to my room. There was a missed call from Millie on my phone and a message saying she'd got mine and was fine. Rain had started to fall. I closed the window and called Millie back.

'You need to be careful, Mum,' she said, after hearing about last night's fiasco.

'I know,' I said. 'I will. How are you doing?'

'Okay. I'm okay,' she said.

'And Adwin?'

'He's fine, too. We're fine. He's doing some work. Hold on, he'll want to say hello.'

Millie and Adwin had been together for over two years and recently bought their own place. Before I could put her off interrupting him, he was on the phone.

He asked how it was all going.

'Not too bad,' I said. 'Millie will fill you in.'

'Give Nannie my regards,' he said, 'Enjoy St Lucia for me. And take care.'

I said I would and he put Millie back on.

'Has he made the appointment for the test, yet?'

Recently, not a day went by without the sad possibility of Adwin testing positive for the sickle cell trait, which Millie was also carrying, coming to my mind.

'Mmm.' That told me she didn't want Adwin to hear and the likely answer was no. 'We'll talk soon,' she said.

Rain was pelting down so loud outside I had to press the phone against my ear to hear her. 'Okay. But—'

'It's okay, Mum.'

'It's only because I want the best for you, you know, Millie.'

'I know,' she said. 'Stop worrying. We'll sort it. And let me know what happens with the doctor. Go get a swim. Try to relax a bit.'

'A swim? Huh. Yeah.'

'Get Cousin wotsisname to take you.'

'Headley. Cousin Headley.' I chuckled.

Millie had put off having children until she was sure she'd met the right person, and had already mentioned thirty-six as being her cut-off point. 'People have children in their forties,' I'd told her, knowing that was late.

'It gets more risky, though, Mum,' she'd replied.

Adwin seemed to be the one she'd decided on. I liked him too, but didn't want to see her go through what I had with her brother, Shane, all those years ago. At the time, we hadn't had any proof of whether Shane was carrying the sickle cell trait or not. The NHS didn't run those tests at birth back then, but from my assessment, there was a strong likelihood that he was.

Millie was twenty when we discovered that she had the trait. And she only found out because she had to have blood tests done before dental treatment. I got myself tested and discovered I was carrying it too, so the likelihood was that she'd got it from me. Now if Adwin, or anyone else Millie had a child with, was also carrying it, there'd be a twenty-five per cent chance of them having a child with full-blown sickle cell anaemia. I couldn't bear the thought of Millie, or any grand-child of mine, having to live with that condition.

Really, she should have checked it out before they even got together. But love, too often, makes us blind to logic and ratio-nale. I'd been nagging her for months to talk him into going for the test. I dreaded to think about the torment an 'accidental' pregnancy could bring to them, and to me.

I missed her. Wished she could have come with me, but her new business needed her there. What I needed was a nice man of my own, but at fifty-four, when days of clubbing, partying and frequenting bars were growing more and more infrequent, the chances of meeting that special person who ticked even near enough to the right boxes, was close to non-existent.

Besides which, in the thirty-one years since, Millie's father, Leo, left us and disappeared, I hadn't felt for any man the way I did for him. Maybe I just hadn't wanted to. But it would have been nice to have had a special someone I could connect with. Have laughs, good times, add a special flavour to each other's lives.

Leo and I had met in the library, where I worked part-time. He came in regularly to renew his books – mainly on history and colonialism. I was eighteen, he was twenty-one.

His sleepy caramel-brown eyes drew me in first.

'What, them big eyes?' Delia had said, when I'd told her that.

But it wasn't just the eyes. I loved the swagger in his walk and would secretly watch as he walked towards the door on his way out of the library. Once he turned, caught me doing it and smiled. I never told Delia that bit. I loved his strong views on slavery and racism. Though I did think it weird, since his mother was white.

'I don't care what anybody says or thinks. I'm black,' he said, when I raised it with him. 'When I walk down the street, I'm black. When I go for a job interview, I'm black. I'm just black. You know how many jobs I went for before I got that one at Sainsbury's? Being mixed only makes my complexion lighter.'

When I asked how his mother and father had got together he said, 'My mother was taking a walk on the wild side, I reckon, when she got with Dad. And here I am.'

Sometimes I felt sorry for him, and that 'sorry' made him more lovable somehow. It was sad that he wasn't close to either his mother or his father.

I ended my call with Millie then went and knocked lightly on Mum's bedroom door. 'Mum?' No answer.

The energy to discuss her future, health worries – anything – with her had been sapped. She had probably forgotten about our earlier conversation and my suggestion to go back to England, but where had the idea that I didn't want to look after her come from? Would she have forgotten that too? I hoped she had.

I found her sitting on her bed, facing the window. She didn't turn or say anything to acknowledge my presence, and flinched when I touched her shoulder.

'Is you,' she said, glancing up at me then reassuming her gaze.

I walked round so that I was in front of her. 'You okay?'

'De woman dat live across dere,' she said quietly, lifting her chin and indicating towards the neighbour to the right, 'was in hospital with cancer.'

'Oh, no. The lady with the fluffy dog? Quite old, isn't she? Who's looking after her?'

'She have her chil'ren.'

'Oh, good. So she has help and company.'

'An' me?' She sighed, heavily. If it wasn't for Barbara, I could die in here an' nobody would know. I wouldn't have one person to bring me a glass of water.'

'Oh, come on, Mum,' I said. 'That would never happen. I'd make sure of that.'

'You?' She turned to me. 'You never here.'

'I'm here as often as I can be.'

She glared at me. 'You? I don't know when las' I see you.'

I swallowed. 'I have to work, Mum.' *Mum's memory is messed up, I know, but is this really her reality? The truth for her?* 'Mum, I... I was here in April – for Easter. Three months ago. And you've had helpers that—'

She slid her eyes over my face. 'You mean de people you putting here to come an' steal my things?'

'You need helpers, Mum. Someone—'

'I don't need no helper,' she snapped. 'No stranger in my house. No *visyéz épi vòlè*, hypocrite an' thief. Every time dey leave I find something is missing... a cup, a glass, even my spoons dey taking.'

I sat on the chair opposite her, by the dresser. Knew that what she was saying about the helpers was untrue, and all in her imagination, but telling her that could bring on another row.

'That's why I want you to come back to England with me. I could look after you properly there.'

'Eh-eh. I have Barbara, Headley. Plenty fam'ly here.'

Alzheimer's had a way of manipulating, switching between logic and fantasy. It all clawed at me.

A slow breath summoned up another layer of resilience, suppressing my urge to cry. 'Well, I'm here now,' I said, partly wishing I was somewhere else. 'And while I'm here, we'll sort things out.'

The reality was that, apart from Auntie Barbara and

Cousin Headley, Mum had no one else to look out for her. The 'relatives' she, or we, had rarely showed up around there and Cousin Headley or Auntie Barbara could only do so much. Mum's care was a role assigned to me by birth, enshrined in my DNA, just as taking care of her own mother was in hers. Throughout my childhood she'd told me countless times about how she had taken care of my grandmother, and hadn't left St Lucia until whatever it had been that was making her mother ill had won. I didn't detect a hint of resentment in her when she relayed that story to me. Only love. A glow and pride. The responsibilities of her other siblings were to contribute towards the means, since they'd escaped to England.

But I'm not *her,* am I? Crush the guilt, banish that engrained expectation. Resign from the role.

Could I? Or was it too late?

My biggest fantasy had been for Mum and Auntie Barbara to move in together. They were both getting old and would have been good company for each other. I could have employed a helper for them, monitored things, come over every few months to check everything was okay. That could have worked for a few years, until I was closer to sixty. But with Mum's illness, I hadn't had the bottle to suggest it to Auntie.

I didn't want her thinking I was trying to palm the responsibility for Mum onto her.

'You're getting old,' I said to Mum. 'You have Alzheimer's. You need to be taken care of. You need someone with you to make sure you're all right.' I'd told her all of this before. 'You've said yourself that you don't feel well.'

'I say dat?' She straightened her spine and threw me a look that called me a liar.

Great. I didn't answer.

'Well, by de grace of God, I will be all right,' she said.

'You gonna get ready for bed now?' It was the most appropriate thing I could think of to say. And a good escape from the issue.

'In a while,' she replied.

I got up. 'Let me know if you need any help with anything.' Fresh air was waiting for me on the veranda. Mental space too.

When Mum pulled this wall up between us, I could do little more than walk away. Her dementia, affected her thinking, her processing, but the feelings her rejection brought took me way back to a time when she didn't have dementia. When she'd rendered me and Millie – the unborn baby I was carrying – practically homeless.

I'd held on to the knowledge of my pregnancy for long enough and was sure she'd soon notice, due to my constant sleepiness and bulging belly.

'Mum,' I'd said. 'I... I don't know how to tell you, really—'

'Tell me what?' she'd said.

'I... I'm pregnant.'

'Pregnant?' she'd repeated, her shudder suggesting the word had disturbed her very core. *Damaged* her. 'You mean to say—'

'I... we didn't mean for it to happen.'

'We? You mean to say, after so much study you say you do to go to university, you go an' let dat boy make you pregnant?' she said.

'It was an accident, Mum.'

'An accident? When dere is so much protection nowadays? Is man you did want so much, Erica?'

'It's not just – we love each other, Mum.' I swallowed. 'We want to get married one day.'

'Married? One day?' she mocked. 'Yes.' She paused. 'Erica, you jus' start university.'

'I know, Mum.' Tears pooled in my eyes.

'You know? An'... so what you going to do?'

'I... I'll finish this year and postpone. Til later – after the baby.'

'An' where you think you going to live?'

'I... I'm not sure.'

'You will see if dat boy stay to see dat baby born.'

'Leo's not like that. He loves me,' I said.

'Loves you? Your father did love me too, but after I have you, if I din have fam'ly to help me, I would have suck salt.'

'I'm not stupid,' I said, dismissing the story I'd heard too many times.

She gave me a cutting stare. 'So, *I* was stupid? I'm stupid? A focking ass? Focking stupid?'

Her words jolted me. She'd never been one to curse and had brought me up to believe that using that kind of language was indecent. Degrading.

'That's not what I meant—!' My words, maybe the whole situation had spun her into a world of let-downs, disappointments and hurt. My father had let her down, then Mr Frank had taken her for a fool with the promise of a marriage that had left her wearing a pretend wedding ring. But it hadn't been my intention to stir all of that up.

She looked at me. The fury in her eyes threatening to obliterate me. 'Stupid I was when your father give me you, an' go?'

'That's not what I meant. I... I meant—' Tears spilt from my eyes.

'Good luck to you,' she said, like she was done with it.

'I... Leo's finishing uni next year. He'll get a job. And I can—'

'Well, he better find a place for you to live too.'

'But—'

'He have to take responsibility for his chile – an' for you.'

I hadn't meant to hurt her in any way. Just wanted her support. Understanding. But her anger, her words – everything said she despised me.

CHAPTER NINE

Sitting on the veranda, I switched my thoughts to the present and went inside for a drink, then searched through the fridge and freezer to see what was possible for lunch tomorrow. Prepping meats were out of the question – they'd need to be defrosted, and seasoned overnight. Saltfish and green bananas it would be. I put the saltfish to soak and squeezed the remnants of the washing-up liquid onto my hands to get the raw, pungent scent off. As I put my head in the cupboard under the sink to retrieve another bottle, a musty odour rushed me. Mum had mice.

They had been everywhere in the house we lived in before we moved in with Mr Frank. Back then, it had been normal for me to step out of our room and see two or three of them scatter to their nearest escape route – under a cupboard door, or under the cooker in the kitchen we shared with other tenants. I'd scream each time.

Mum would come running. 'What happen?' she'd say.

'A mouse.' And I'd point in the direction I'd seen one shoot off in.

Mum would exhale. 'Dey not going to do you nothing.'

Dead or alive, I hated them. And now that I knew how unhygienic they were, the thought of them being in the house made everything everywhere feel yucky and unclean. The germs, droppings, the pee they left in their tracks. I had to get rid of them.

Shuddering, I gave my hands a second wash, poured a rum and Coke and took myself back to the veranda. Mice, dementia and sorting Mum out... I needed to make concrete plans.

Minutes to eleven. I peeked into Mum's room. She was in bed. *Should have gone in earlier to make sure she had a wash.* Too late now. I showered, then lay across my bed in my knickers and a sleeveless T-shirt, Joan Armatrading singing 'Drop The Pilot' through my earbuds.

The handle on my door was turning. I pulled the earbuds out and looked up.

'Mmmm.'

The humming began to fade. Gently, to avoid Mum hearing, I unlocked the door, kicked away the old towel I'd stuffed under it to stop mice from getting in, then edged it open. No sign of anyone. Battling pangs of anxiety and fears of another attack, I tiptoed to her room, knocked and waited guardedly for a response. The knives were still hidden, but she could have found another type of weapon.

It was back – the humming. Behind me. I made a sharp turn towards an approaching shadow. 'Mum?' I said, in a shaky, deeper-than-normal voice.

'Mmmmm.'

The shadow came to light wearing a long, striped night-dress, one sleeve hanging off her shoulder, her head wrapped in her usual night scarf.

'Mum?' I repeated, scanning for weapons. 'What are you doing up?'

'De chile – de baby. Don't let him cry. An' move dat cat,' she said, pointing casually behind her.

A child? Baby? Cat? Where? That couldn't be. 'Show me,' I said, making my way to the front room, with the hope that some of what she'd said might be true, that she wasn't that confused. A cat could have got in through an open window. A door. But a child? A crying baby? I hadn't heard any crying.

There was no one there, of course. Nothing. No baby. No cat. Only furniture: her wall cabinet filled with glasses and porcelain figurines, the floor fan, three-seater couch, two armchairs and a coffee table with the doily and horse-shaped porcelain vase with plastic flowers sticking out of it.

But her mention of the baby... a boy? Had she said a boy? Could memories of Shane still be alive in her head?

I batted back the thoughts and took her arm. 'Come on, Mum.' She shrugged it off and strolled past me. 'It's late. Let's go to bed.'

'I'm not tired.' She passed hers and headed for my room.

An hour and a half later, after a cup of milk and honey, she was in her bed and I in mine, fighting off sleep in case I zonked out before she did.

Auntie should have called me sooner.

CHAPTER TEN

Sounds of activity in the kitchen squashed hopes of Mum still being asleep. I forced myself out of bed.

'Morning, Mum.' She glanced at me. 'You sleep well?'

'Good morning.'

She had breakfast laid out on a tray. Two boiled eggs and a creole loaf, which was like a slim French stick, but softer, with the ends rolled into tiny pointed crusts – my favourite part of the little loaf.

'Yummy,' I said, looking at it.

'You want some?'

'No. It's okay. It's yours.'

'You can have it, *ich mwen*. I don't feel hungry for two eggs today.'

I thanked her. 'You've got mice, you know.'

'Mice?' She looked at me as she lifted her breakfast tray from the counter.

'There're droppings, and their smell's in that cupboard.' I pointed under the sink.

She looked at her feet. 'An' I never see none. I never see one mice inside here,' she mumbled, shuffling to her room with the tray.

This bedroom eating couldn't be helping keep the mice away.

After breakfast, I called Auntie, told her about the mice and my planned trip to the shops for mouse traps. 'She should be all right here on her own, shouldn't she? I won't be long.'

'Of course,' Auntie said. 'I will check on her. If she get fed up, she will call me or come down.'

Before leaving, I called to let Auntie know I was gone. Mum had eaten and was lying in bed again.

I got a Vieux Fort bus straight away, went directly to the supermarket, picked up what I needed and headed back to find Mum dressed, sitting on the veranda wearing a sun hat and looking towards the gate. I thought she was waiting for me to get home before going off somewhere, or for Auntie Barbara to arrive. But the huge bundle on the floor between her legs and her handbag on her shoulder, suggested something else.

'Er, Mum?' I said. 'Why...? What's that?'

'I'm waiting for Frank to come an' take me home,' she said.

'Mr Frank? Home?' There was no point in telling her she was already there.

'He coming jus' now.'

'What?' My eyes went to the bundle – a sheet filled with stuff, all four ends tied together securing whatever she had in there. It resembled a giant model of the one Dick Whittington carried over his shoulder on his travels. But Mum's makeshift luggage was so big she'd probably had to drag it out here. 'Mum?' I said, frustration starting to get the better of me. 'This is your house. You're already at home. Can't you see?' The words left my mouth, with no consideration for Alzheimer's.

She looked up at me, unsure. Anger and fear in her eyes. 'What you talking about?' She kissed her teeth, straightened up and turned her gaze to the gate. Was this where she used to sit waiting for Mr Frank to come home, wondering who he was with and where?

I went inside, dropped my bags of shopping on the table then went back to her. 'Come on, Mum.' I bent to pick up the huge bundle.

'Leave—'

'Mum?' A swift step backwards helped me avoid her raised leg smacking my face. 'Fine,' I shouted, storming off. 'Wait for Mr Frank. Wait all your life for all I care. Cos he'd dead. You understand? Dead. He's dead and he's not coming back. Thank God!'

'Who—?' Her voice startled me. 'Who say Frank dead?' She'd left her bundle and followed me to my room.

'Me. He's been dead for years.'

'If he is dead, is you dat kill him. You...? You see you? You no good. You did never like Frank.'

'What was there to like?' I shouted. 'You put him up there' – I held an opened hand up above my head – 'like he was some-thing... important! Before... before me! And look how he treated you.'

'What? What you talking about? He... if it wasn't for him, where your ass would be?'

'My arse?' I shouted. '*My* arse? He didn't save my arse. You might think he saved yours, but he humiliated you. Cheated on you... treated you like... like...' Rage had me scrambling for words. 'And... and you're even still wearing the fake wedding ring! Pretending to be married to him!' Something broke inside me. 'Oh, leave me alone, Mum.' I turned away.

'All he used to give you.'

'Give *me*?' She was referring to the gifts of expensive jewellery he gave me on each birthday while I was living with them. Gifts I didn't value and kept in a box I never opened except to put the next gift in.

'You think I need you? I don't need you,' she said.

'Good. Well, I'm glad you don't. Cos I've got a life that I want to live.'

'Well go.' She began walking away.

I sat on my bed, jaws clenched, my mind congested with conflicting thoughts. Why was she still so attached to Mr Frank? She'd clearly forgotten how he'd treated her, all what he'd put her through.

His birthday fell soon after he'd given her the ring. In her happy state, she had organised a celebration for him. Had a special cake made and cooked a special meal. It was only for the three of us.

'Jus' a little thing,' she'd said. 'Frank will appreciate dat.'

She'd taken a half-day from work, and I'd rushed home from school to help her prepare what was the equivalent of a Sunday meal: rice, stewed peas, roast chicken and a salad, which we laid out for six-thirty when he'd normally come home. Seven, eight o'clock came, but there was no Mr Frank.

Mum began to get anxious, nervous. 'He will soon come,' she said, after another glance at the clock. Another hour passed. I reached for a second apple to help relieve my hunger. 'I'll give you your food.'

I was fast asleep by the time he came in that night and in the morning, hardly any words were exchanged between them.

The pain he'd caused her might have been wiped out of her mind, but not from mine.

Probably the only plus side of memory loss is that mean and nasty exchanges could be lost within minutes, by the loser of memories. But for the other, anger, guilt and shame remained.

I let minutes pass, took another deep breath and went back out on the veranda where she was sitting, the damn bundle still at her feet. 'Mum,' I said.

She looked up at me, as if surprised, and tried to stand up, but quickly sat down, like someone had an invisible thread attached to her back, which they'd tugged at and reined her back onto her seat.

She tried again and this time stood up next to me.

'Eh-eh, *koté Frank*? Where is Frank?' she said.

'I don't know,' I said, still unable to disguise my irritation and anger. 'He's not here. He... he's gone out.'

'Where?' she said.

'To the shop.'

'Well, I will have to go home on my own.'

Exasperated, I went into the house and called Auntie.

'She doing dat again?' Auntie said. 'I coming. I sure is Frank spirit she seeing dere in de house.'

I had explained to Auntie that the people Mum thought she saw or had spoken to were imaginary. Hallucinations. What the psychiatrist said were false memories. They weren't spirits coming to get her to take her into the land of death with them. 'She just imagines seeing these people,' I'd told her. 'And she's forgotten they're dead.'

'You sure?'

'Yes, Auntie. That's what the experts say.'

'Experts? Huh. What dey know?' she'd replied. 'She even hearing dem talk.'

The old, engrained beliefs of people seeing the dead, when it was close to their turn to die; of the dead coming to escort them safely into their world, refused to leave Auntie's mind.

I rushed back to the veranda, but Mum was already on her way to the gate, dragging the bundle behind her.

'Mum?' She didn't even turn. I went after her. 'Where you going, Mum? Mum, come back inside.'

'Where's Frank?' She kissed her teeth again and stretched her neck looking right then left of the gate. 'I going without him.'

'Mum, come back inside,' I repeated, firm, but as quietly as possible, to avoid the neighbours or someone passing hearing, witnessing my mother's irrational behaviour. Reaffirming in their minds that their neighbour – the lady living in the cream house on Sweet Lime Grove, was unhinged, losing it.

She brushed off the hand I put out to her and shouted: 'Leave me alone!' then reached for the gate.

Too late, I realised. I hadn't locked it when I came in.

I couldn't let her go through it looking like a bag lady. But how could I stop her? The right words weren't coming in the right order for me to persuade her to give up her stupid, irrational mission. Yank the bundle from her hand and march her inside was what I wanted to do right now. That might work with a child, but Mum was a volatile adult, suffering from dementia and highly likely to put up a fight. Scream. Shout. Draw more attention to us.

'Mr Frank said you should wait for him inside,' I said, finally, certain that would work.

'I waiting here,' she said. Her eyes, daggers straight at me, then no eye contact as she slipped into a sulk. She stepped back to pull open the gate, then realising the bundle was too close to her leg, pushed it. Off it went rolling down the slope towards the lime tree in the far corner of the garden.

'What de hell?' She looked past me to the bundle settled at the foot of the tree, and took off after it, with quick short steps resembling a toddler who didn't yet understand the risks of falls.

I rushed after her. 'Mum!' She stumbled, leapt forward and fell flat on her stomach.

'*Bondyé*. My God,' she said.

'Mum, are you okay?' I leaned over to help her.

'Move.' She slapped my hand away.

'Come on.' I reached again.

She ignored me and sat up, looking bewildered.

I bent down behind her, put my arms under hers and lifted her up. 'Come and sit down, Mum,' I said, relieved to find no signs of bruises or scratches, only her right hand a bit red on the inside of the palm. I led her back inside.

The commotion seemed to have diverted her quest. We sat at the kitchen table.

'Where's Barbara?' she demanded.

'Auntie's coming.' I gave her a glass of water and sat in front of her scrutinising her face. 'Is anything hurting?'

'What's happening?' Auntie suddenly appeared in the kitchen, breathing heavily.

'She fell down,' I said.

'Ehh-ehh,' Auntie uttered, dragging the sound. 'Again?'

'The... a bundle – a sheet she had things wrapped up in – rolled away from her. She run after it...'

'*Bondyé.*'

'I don't think she's hurt, but...'

We both looked at Mum. 'Ione?' Auntie said, then turned to me. 'You want me to take her down with me?'

'I... I don't think so, Auntie,' I said. Mum didn't look hurt, but she had to be shaken up.

I left her with Mum and went to get the bundle, which wasn't as heavy as I'd anticipated.

'I will take her,' Auntie said, when I got back. 'She will be all right. Is jus' five minutes an' you can finish de cleaning an' everything. Come on, Ione. Let's go.'

'Where we going?' Mum said.

'To my home,' Auntie said.

'*Lakay mwen mwen vlé alé*. My home is where I want to go,' Mum said.

'Come by me for a little while first,' Auntie said.

'Well, okay.' Mum succumbed.

'You sure it'll be okay?' I asked Auntie.

'Of course.' She put an arm out to Mum. 'Let's go, Ione.'

Mum was already making her way out, handbag on her shoulder. 'I'll see you in a little while, Mum,' I said.

This violence towards me from Mum was new. Auntie had told me she'd thrown things at the carers before, but except for the threat the other night, she'd never targeted any of that at me.

'I'm sorry, Auntie,' I said.

'For what?'

'I didn't know how to... what to do.'

'Don't worry. Jus' come up when you finish doing what you have to do.' She turned to Mum.

Still unsettled, I saw them off, acknowledging how unprepared I was for what had happened. Why did I keep expecting normal behaviour from her, when I was fully aware of what she was suffering from? It threw me, each time I was confronted by something new from her. My emotions were getting in the way of the rational responses I should be making to stop her getting more upset and confused.

Letting her go with Auntie gave me the space I needed to try to get rid of the mice, but I also had to bear in mind that Auntie wasn't young. I shouldn't always agree to her rescuing me from Mum. That was why she'd called me saying it was all too much. It was why I was here.

Aggression and bitterness towards me, from Mum, was increasing. Alzheimer's was not only pushing me out of her memory but getting her to harbour bad thoughts about me.

Or had these bad thoughts been there before Alzheimer's, and the condition was simply allowing her to express them?

CHAPTER ELEVEN

Telling her I was pregnant brought a wall of semi-silence up between us. By then, Mr Frank's usual six-thirty dinner had been going cold on the stove and when he got in, he was often not hungry for it. I did my best to avoid Mum, staying in my room studying or sleeping. I'd disappointed her. Let her down. She had no idea of how much I was disappointed in myself. The pregnancy meant me having to drop out of uni. Postponing my career plans.

Having a baby to take care of was scary too. I wouldn't even have a proper job or my own home. Thank God I had Leo.

A week after that conversation with her, I walked into the kitchen.

Mr Frank was sitting at the table with a cup in his hand.

'Good morning,' I said.

He raised his eyebrows. 'You still here?'

'Lectures start late today,' I replied.

'Huh.' He emptied his cup in the sink and cleared his throat. 'I could have look after you good, if...' He looked over his shoulder. 'Instead you give it to a ram-goat-boy who caa do nothing for you?'

'What—?'

He walked out, leaving me trying to make sense of his comment. Was that a plan, a wish, a desire he had in his mind? It disgusted me.

I continued avoiding Mum and him, planning in my head how best to handle the growing mess. Then Sunday came. The front door had just shut. Mr Frank was probably off – according to him, at least – to collect some of his rent. Mum ambushed me in my room.

'Miss Erica,' she said.

I looked up from my pillow, half awake.

'I don't tell you your man will have to find a place for you to stay? Frank is not your father an' you make a sad mistake if you think you making him leave me because... because you go an' find your trouble.'

'I... I will,' I said. I'd taken her earlier threat as something she'd said in haste and anger, but after what Mr Frank had said to me in the kitchen, I didn't want to be anywhere near him, but my options were limited.

'Frank money not going to feed you an' your chile. Your man have to do dat.'

'Right, Mum,' I said, sitting up. 'I understand.' She was choosing him over me again. I got out of bed and faced her. 'Do you really know the kind of a man you're with, Mum?'

'What—?'

'Do you know what he said to me in the kitchen the other day?'

She said nothing, but the twitch at the corner of her mouth said she wanted to know.

'He made it clear that *he* wanted to be the one sleeping with me instead of Leo. Can you imagine that?'

'I... I don't believe Frank would tell you dat,' she said.

'So I'm lying?'

'Frank did feed you when you wasn' his chile. You cannot expect him to feed you now.'

'That's right change the subject. You'll have to face it one day. All he has to give you is money. And he's a dirty old man.'

She looked at me. 'I... I—'

'Never mind, Mum.' What was the point? 'I won't rock your boat. I'm going.'

'Is you bring dis on yourself an'... an' on me.' She disappeared, leaving the door ajar.

I scanned the room, mentally packing. Hating Mum, hating Mr Frank more, and dreading what lay ahead for me.

CHAPTER TWELVE

The tablets Mum got from that Dr Finch were well hidden away, but my concerns about her new behaviour made me think about the psychiatrist she used to see for regular reviews at the memory clinic when she was in England.

I searched through the phone book to find a psychiatrist here and took the earliest appointment they had – in three days' time.

Not a sound was coming from her room this morning. I took it as a good sign. There was no rush for her to get up. The longer she slept, the less confusion I'd have to deal with. I got rid of a couple of dead mice, replaced the traps, then made some porridge that I enjoyed sitting alone on the veranda. This was the kind of space I needed. Quiet. Me time.

A whiff of rotting mangoes flitted past as I leaned back on the chair, reminding me I had to get hold of the gardener. I turned and Mum was standing in the doorway, wearing her nightie.

'Oh, morning, Mum. You up now?'

'You eat already?' she said, her eyes falling on my empty plate on the table.

'I'll get yours, if you want, or do you want to get washed first?'

'I will eat,' she said, and followed me to the kitchen.

'Outside?' I said, holding her plate of porridge.

'I will eat it here.'

While she ate, I called Auntie for the gardener's number. She said she'd send him down.

Mum finished breakfast and went back to her room – to get washed and dressed, I hoped, but she could have been getting up to all sorts in there, moving clothes and stuff around. I let her, welcoming the space.

Later, she appeared fully dressed in the kitchen, handbag on her shoulder.

'Where're you going?' I asked, expecting her to say: 'To see Barbara.'

'Home,' she said, as if daring me to challenge her.

'Oh. I'll take you later.' I tried to sound casual.

'I'm going now.' She walked past me towards the kitchen door, turned the handle and stepped out.

'Mum.' I followed and stood beside her, watching her tug at the gate. 'I'll take you home later,' I said again.

'Why dis—' She dug in her bag, searching for her keys. Her house keys were on her bunch, but after the last incident, I'd taken the one for the gate off. She managed to get one into the lock, and started jiggling it. 'Why dis key not turning?' She shook the gate. The keys fell out of the keyhole. I bent to pick them up when a whack from her handbag knocked me off balance.

'Shi—Mum?' I'd landed on my bum.

'Leave my—'

'Mum! I'm trying to help you,' I said, rubbing where she'd hit my face. I got up and stepped back, closer to the veranda, to avoid another blow.

'I want to go!' she shouted. 'Open dis gate. Open it for me.'

I stood at the steps, a hand on my chest as she looked around, paced up and down before coming towards me. Should I open it and just let her go?

'I... I might as well kill myself,' she said, her eyes wet, perspiration dripping down the sides of her face.

I gulped, forcing images of how Mum could actually take her own life from my mind. 'Why would you say that, Mum?' I wasn't equipped for this. 'Mum,' I called out, hoping again to jolt her out of the world she'd been drawn into.

'I want to go home!' she shouted. 'Help!' she screamed, turning towards the gate. 'Somebody help!'

'Mum, stop shouting like that,' I said, stern, but close to tears, dreading what the neighbours must think. 'You need to calm down.' I was reasoning with Alzheimer's again. 'I'll take you.'

'Good,' she said, relief in her voice. 'Come on.'

I went back in, grabbed my bag and keys, unlocked the gate and started to walk up the road with her.

'Where?' I said. 'Show me where your home is.' We continued walking. 'Where is it? Where do you want to go?' I slowed our pace down to a stop and studied her puzzled face. 'Where's home?'

'Let's go an' see Barbara,' she said, smiling.

Mum's antics took me close to being on playground duty with four-year-olds. But you could reason with four-year-olds, while that was fast becoming a stranger in Mum's world.

The psychiatrist should be able to help.

Auntie suggested I leave Mum with her for a bit. 'Take a break,' she said.

'You sure?'

'Yes. Yes. Go. She all right here with me.'

My chest, every muscle in me began to unknot with the

prospect of a break from Mum. 'I'll be back for her soon,' I told Auntie.

Outside, I took a deep breath then a detour, bypassing Sweet Lime Grove, to the opposite side of the development. Strolling around the area, admiring the houses, trees and plants, brought a weightlessness I hadn't experienced since my arrival.

There was a 'Plot For Sale' sign on a large patch of land next to a house made from slats of a deep brown wood on the upper floor and concrete on the one below. A line of bay leaf trees formed a hedge demarcating the plot from the road. I picked a leaf, broke it in half and inhaled its citrusy scent. 'Mmm.' It sparked my senses. After another deep inhale, I tore off a small branch to take with me for a few more days of tea.

That night, I had just turned off my bedroom light ready for sleep, when a dragging sound drew me to the kitchen. Mum was wandering around it, pulling her wheeled shopping trolley behind her. Only she was dragging it with the wheels facing upwards, legs grating the floor.

'*Sa sé san mwen.* This is mine,' she said, taking a cup out of the kitchen cupboard and dropping it in the trolley. '*Sa sé san mwen*,' she repeated, picking up another.

'Mum? What are you doing?' I said. 'Mum, no.' I dashed towards her, but the second cup had landed in the trolley with a crash. 'Look, you're breaking them.'

She was off. Fixated. Deaf to my words, dragging the trolley into the front room.

'Mum. Mum! No!' I said, trying to take the trolley from her. But her grip was fierce.

'I have to take my things to go home,' she said.

'But you *are* home,' I shouted, unable to contain myself.

'*Sa sé san mwen*,' she continued, dropping one of her ceramic dogs in.

I sat down, chin in hand, watching her move around the room, picking up anything light and small enough to fit into her trolley.

'Fine,' I said, exasperated. If she wanted to pack all night long, I'd let her. She'd soon wear herself out. The whole episode was filling me with despair. Infuriated, I stomped off to my room. She couldn't help herself. She was ill and I, who was supposed to help her, couldn't. Alzheimer's was rendering me as helpless as Mum.

What's the point of me being here?

I lay across the bed, on my stomach, hands over my ears, eyes and jaws squeezed tight, insides fit to explode. Where was normality?

The dragging sound was coming my way. For a quick moment, I considered locking my door but, instead, I pulled myself further onto the bed, then turned onto my back to keep an eye on her. How much longer was this packing stuff going to go on for?

Humming, she entered my room, dragging her trolley past my bed. '*Sa sé san mwen,*' she said, between a hum, and picked up my deodorant. She walked further along. '*Sa sé san mwen.*' The pillow was dragged from under my head, forcing it to soft-land onto the mattress with a bump.

'Mum?' I sat up. 'What the hell? Mum, go back to your room. Go to sleep! That's mine,' I said, as she was about to lift something else off my dresser. 'Where you going with all that?'

'All of dis is mine. I am taking dem to my house.'

'For God's *sake,*' I shouted. '*This* is your frigging house.'

She stood still, giving the impression that she was considering what I'd said. 'Erica *woy*' she responded, kissing her teeth then giving me a look that suggested I was the confused one who didn't know what was what.

'That's mine,' I said, snatching my phone before her hand reached it.

'All right,' she said, in an almost jovial tone. 'Try an' steal my things.' She extended an arm towards my handbag.

'No.' I grabbed that too.

'Okay,' she said, like she'd surrendered. Accepted I was a strong rival.

'It's my handbag, Mum.' But nothing I said mattered.

She strolled out of the room, my pillow under her arm, the trolley still grating the floor, leaving black marks from the rubber on its legs. Through my opened door, I heard cupboard doors opening and shutting, Mum's faint mumblings, the drag from the trolley and a faint humming. I checked the time. After twelve. Why wasn't she tired? Where was she getting all of this energy from? There was no one I could call.

I went after her. Offered her a hot drink. Soursop tea might get her to sleep. The hot drink had worked twice already.

'I am not thirsty,' she said.

I should call the ambulance. Would I be expected to pay? If so, how much? Would it be worthwhile, even? They'd probably think me stupid for calling them out because an old lady with dementia wasn't sleepy.

But how could she not be tired when my eyelids felt like strips of dried leather too heavy for the muscles around my eyes to lift? I had to do something to calm her down. Get her to go to sleep. What drugs might she have in the house that could induce sleep? Cough syrup?

The bottle I found in her bathroom cabinet was exactly what I needed: *'Do not operate machinery when taking...'* Past its sell by date, but it wouldn't kill her, and might still get her drowsy enough to sleep. She swallowed down the two spoonfuls I gave her, but the pacing continued, with her pulling the trolley overflowing with things she'd picked up en route.

I followed her around for a bit, visualising strapping her to her bed whilst the drug took effect. A mosquito buzzed, *kouzeeeeeg*, past my ear. The itching sensation on my arm confirmed that it, or one of its relatives, had already helped themselves to some of my blood. Antihistamine. *That* was it. They claimed to be non-drowsy, but that wasn't for everyone. I'd give one to her. Between the syrup and the tablet, she was bound to fall asleep. And if I took one as well, we'd both get some rest.

I made her a cup of warm milk and honey, and got her to sit at the kitchen table to drink it with the little pill, mentally blessing her cooperativeness with medication.

She was starting to slow down. I made the trolley disappear and coaxed her back to her bed. Half an hour later, snoring woke me from where I was lying at the foot of her bed. I tiptoed to my room, locked the door and lay down, my arms for a pillow.

CHAPTER THIRTEEN

The phone was ringing. I got out of bed. Didn't make it in time, but knew it had to have been Auntie, so I called her back. 'Morning, Auntie.' I stretched and muffled a yawn.

'Morning, *ich mwen*.'

'Did you just call?'

'You-all still sleeping at dis time?'

'It's been a rough night,' I said.

'Ione couldn't sleep?'

'She was packing last night, saying she's going home.'

'Going home?' Auntie paused. 'Always, always going home. Dat's a really nasty sickness Ione have dere.'

I told her about giving Mum the honey and milk to help her sleep. Not a word about the antihistamine or cough syrup. 'I better go, Auntie,' I said, anxious now to go and check on Mum.

She was still asleep and, thankfully, breathing. How many of those antihistamines did I have left?

Our appointment to see the psychiatrist was two days away. Hopefully, I wouldn't have to give Mum any meds tonight, but if I did, I would. She needed to sleep as much as I did. I'd try her on one antihistamine tonight and see how that went.

. . .

My tracking suggested the mice were coming in through a rotting corner of the kitchen door. Cousin Headley volunteered to try fixing it, then said it would be better to replace the whole thing with a metal door. He took the measurements and said he'd arrange for someone to fit it.

I walked Mum up to Auntie Barbara's. They were getting the bus to Vieux Fort to do a bit of shopping. I'd offered to go with them, but Auntie said I'd be bored. 'We like to take our time an' I want to pass by de seamstress,' she said.

I suspected she was trying to make the most of having Mum's company on her shopping trips. Perhaps missing Mum already, like I had, when she was about to leave England for St Lucia.

I saw them off and walked back, enjoying the cool morning breeze, savouring the expectation of the hour or so I'd have to myself before they returned, but I hadn't been inside fifteen minutes before someone was shouting from the gate.

'Hey! Hi? Good morning!'

'Good morning,' I replied from the veranda. It was Claire, the neighbour I'd met in Vieux Fort. 'Oh, hi. Come in. It's open.'

'I saw you pass and told myself I should stop by and say hello,' she said, walking towards me, formally dressed like when I'd run into her in the mall. 'How is your mom – she sleeping?'

I told her Mum had gone out with Auntie.

'Oh, dat's nice. Those two always together. They well close.'

'Mmm.'

'So, you managing our hot sun?'

'Yeah. It's not too bad,' I said, smiling. She joined me on the veranda. 'Fancy a cold drink? I was about to have one.'

'I'm all right. I'm not stopping. Starting late, finishing late today.' She explained that she worked at a hotel close to the airport. 'You should come for a short stay. You can get a day pass, make use of everything, even the spa. You will enjoy it.'

'Thanks,' I said, but knew that would be near impossible.

'Enjoying your visit? Managing with your mom?'

Which should I answer first? Mum's antics didn't qualify as enjoyment, but being here to help take care of her was gratifying in a strange kind of way. 'It's... it's okay. Yes, I'm managing,' I said.

'She giving you trouble, I know. I hear, at times.'

'You do? From your house?'

'My bedroom facing you-all,' she said.

What had she heard? Me shouting at Mum or her at me? I was too afraid to ask.

'You need a lot of patience to manage ole people like dat,' Claire said.

'You not going to sit?'

'Oh, no. I tell you I jus' come to say hello.'

'Well, it's nice of you, anyway.'

She glanced around her, as if recalling something. 'If one Saturday you feel like going to the fish-fry let me know, eh? You have to have a break sometimes.'

The fish-fry was a seafood night that happened every Saturday, in Dennery, the next parish, a few minutes' drive from us. There were loads of food and drinks stalls, lively music that could be heard from a vast distance, laughter and dancing. Everyone enjoying themselves. Having no entry fee meant you could come and not spend a cent – just hang out and have a good time in the warm open air.

I'd enjoyed going there when I came on holiday. But how realistic was me getting a Saturday night to socialise, with Mum the way she was? 'I'll let you know. And thanks,' I said.

'Enjoy the rest of your day, eh?' She turned to go.

'You too.'

She said it was okay when I started following her to the gate, so I waved her off from the veranda feeling a little lifted from having a visitor and an invitation to go out somewhere. But her comment about hearing me and Mum at it left me anxious about other neighbours hearing everything as well.

This trip was supposed to have been straightforward, the biggest hurdle convincing Mum to leave with me. But no. Now we had to deal with something else. Her behaviour. Sleeplessness. Roaming at night, not wanting to or forgetting to shower.

The psychiatrist was bound to give her something to help with all of that.

CHAPTER FOURTEEN

Dr Peres' surgery was in the north of the island, past Castries. Cousin Headley had agreed to take us.

'I wouldn't ask,' I'd said, 'but it's such a long way. It would be too much for Mum and I don't know if I'll be able to find it.'

'It's all right, all right,' he said.

Auntie had suggested coming with us, but I told her it wasn't necessary.

'You'll let me know how things go,' she said.

'Of course, Auntie.'

I got Mum up early and to help put her in a good mood, gave her breakfast before mentioning the shower. I'd also got her clothes ready the night before, to help speed things along.

'Good morning, cuz.' Cousin Headley was early.

Good excuse to hurry Mum up.

'Morning, Headley,' she shouted to him from the kitchen, before turning back to her tea.

'Morning,' I echoed.

He replied, saying he'd wait on the veranda.

'Let's hurry up,' I told Mum, quietly. 'We don't want to keep him waiting. We can both have a quick shower, then—'

'*Ki mannyè*, how is it,' she began, drawing her eyebrows in, '*ou toujou adant jou moi épi* – you always in my arse with, "shower, shower, shower"? Erica, you are not my mother,' she shouted.

'I know that, Mum, but I'm just... we both have to shower, don't we?'

Cousin Headley appeared in the kitchen. 'You-all all right?' he said.

Mum kissed her teeth as she got up from the table and toddled off to her room.

'This is what she's like.' I shrugged. 'Oh, I forgot to offer you a drink.'

'I'm all right, you know,' he said.

I picked the cups and plates from the table, then Mum reappeared.

'Erica,' she said.

'Yes?' She had what resembled a piece of cloth in her hand.

'Look.' She came towards me, apparently blind to Cousin Headley's presence. 'Look.' She lifted the cloth closer to my face. 'You see?'

I looked down at the crotch of a pair of knickers in her hand. 'Ugh. Mum!' Nose turned up, I leaned away. 'Mum! No! Cousin Headley's here, you know.'

'Eh-eh, Cousin Ione,' Cousin Headley said.

'I don't take man,' Mum continued, ignoring both intrusions. 'You see? My knickers clean. Is you dat does take man,' she snarled. 'You dat need to shower. Shower... shower... shower.' She disappeared, muttering to herself.

Shame froze me to the spot. How could she have done that? Planting ideas of me having sex with a man in Cousin Headley's head. Displaying her dirty knickers like that, in his presence. I wanted to disappear. 'Sorry,' I said to Cousin

Headley, unable to look at his face. 'I... I'm so sorry – I don't know why she has such a problem with having a shower.'

'Is not your fault,' he said. 'I going back outside, eh?'

I spent the next few minutes washing up, hoping in that space and time the memory of what she'd just said and done would have faded from her mind. *What have I come back to?*

I went into her room, entering cautiously.

She was brushing her teeth. I didn't dare mention the word 'shower' again. I'd have to accept what was what for now. That she'd at least washed her underarms, and privates over the bidet.

'Your clothes are here, Mum,' I said, still cautious. No pushiness or instructions to aggravate the disagreeable mood she seemed to be in this morning. The thought of her not having a proper wash, especially before seeing the doctor, and that incident with the knickers, had me ruffled. More arguments wouldn't help. I didn't want to think about how sweaty the rest of her body might be, but went close enough for a sniff. Smelling powder and lipstick helped.

'Okay,' she replied.

I helped her to get ready, at her own pace. She dabbed on some powder and I fixed her earrings.

This journey up north was a whole hour and a half, in traffic. Cousin Headley lowered the volume on the radio to ask if it would be okay to fit the door tomorrow. I told him that would be fine and he turned the volume back up. The music, in between the presenter's babble, was up-beat – nice enough to boogie to, but my mind kept going to other things, like how this appointment might go. What help would this psychiatrist be to Mum?

I didn't feel comfortable discussing Mum's condition with Cousin Headley. With Auntie it was straightforward, automatic. I was brought up with her. There was an emotional bond that made her part of my inner circle. As fond as I was of Cousin Headley, he was a cousin I wasn't brought up with. I hadn't met him until I started visiting St Lucia and my visits weren't usually more than three weeks at a time. He hadn't asked me anything about Mum's condition either but, no doubt, Auntie would have filled him in on some things. The fact that something was wrong with Mum was obvious. Everyone close enough to her knew that – even the neighbours now.

I'd seen the sadness on his face sometimes when he looked at her, but never fear. I hated the thought of people seeing her as being mentally ill, without the understanding. That stigma wasn't nice.

'Thanks for all this ferrying us around, Cousin,' I said. He was fast becoming our regular personal cabbie and was still refusing to take any money from me. I'd mentioned it to Auntie. She said not to worry about it, but I suspected she might be compensating him on Mum's behalf.

Today the journey seemed long and given what Mum had put us both through with the dirty knickers thing this morning, I felt an extra show of appreciation was needed. 'You've been so helpful,' I said. 'Sorry about all of that this morning.'

'Well.' He shrugged, hesitating. 'Cousin Ione is Cousin Ione. Both she an' Cousin Barbara are like aunties to me, you know. Dey used to take good care of me when I was small, even take me to school. I tell you dat already?'

'Yeah. But that's nice.'

'My mother did tell me I even used to refuse to go to de toilet if it wasn't dem taking me.'

'That's sweet.'

'Uh-huh.' He nodded. He was proud of that story.

I didn't know him well enough to start spilling my guts about how Mum's condition was affecting me. The worry it was causing. 'Really nice,' I said.

The woman running the radio programme stopped playing

the music to read a problem letter from a listener. A few words in, Mum interrupted from her usual seat in the back.

'Where we going?'

Cousin Headley gave me a quick glance.

'We're going to see a doctor?' I said, turning to look at her.

'A doctor? For what?'

'We're going to talk about medication for you,' I said.

'Ohhh,' she replied, her voice trailing off.

I tried to refocus on what the presenter was reading out, but switched off again. The more I thought about Mum's condition and where we were likely to end up with it, the bigger the problem felt.

We entered the town, driving past the port with the calm turquoise Caribbean Sea on our left and slum-like dwellings on the right. Further in, school children walked, huddled together. Girls in their green, blue, purple skirts or dresses, all complimented with white ribbons in their hair. Boys in their trousers and shirt. Rucksacks on their backs.

Three cruise ships were docked in the harbour across the road. Tourists were trickling out from them, to be waylaid by tour guides and taxi drivers eager for the promise of revenue the engagement might bring.

Cousin Headley's voice redirected my thoughts as we drove across the bridge, passing houses and supermarkets.

'De place is not far from here,' he said, bending his head down to scan his side of the road.

I scanned mine. 'I think it's here,' I said, spotting a small building with 'Dr Peres' written over the top of tinted glass windows that you couldn't see through from the outside.

Cousin Headley pulled into a bus stop just past it and dropped us off. 'I'll be back in a while,' he said. 'I have a few things to pick up down de road.' He nodded at me and drove off leaving a cloud of exhaust fumes.

· · ·

'Good morning.' The receptionist, a dark-skinned middle-aged woman, greeted us with a smile when we walked through the door. She handed me a clipboard with sheets of paper on it. 'You can fill it out for her in here,' she said, and showed us into the waiting room behind her. It was empty, except for the wicker chairs, water cooler and a medium-sized fish tank with small, pretty fishes pecking at the algae on the glass.

Like zoos, the whole idea of fish tanks was cruel and selfish to me. Especially in the Caribbean, when all you needed to do was snorkel to see these beautiful creatures in their natural habitats.

The windows were wide enough to give patients the opportunity to temporarily abandon their worries and focus instead on the breath-taking view of the same peaceful blue Caribbean Sea we'd passed when we entered the town. I walked over and took a deep breath, forgetting about the forms for a while, letting the calmness wash over me.

'You not sitting down?' Mum's voice tripped me back into the reason I – we – were here. I sat down next to her.

No, no, no and *no* I ticked for the health conditions they asked whether she had. *No* to all, except she had Alzheimer's. I got Mum to sign the form and took it back to the receptionist.

'Want some?' I said, helping myself to a cup of water, when I returned.

'No, thank you,' Mum said.

'Go on. You should.'

She shrugged. 'Well, all right.'

Ten or fifteen minutes later, I was in the midst of watching the fishes in the tank gliding through the water, when the receptionist said we could go in. She pointed the door out to us.

Dr Peres was a young doctor. Maybe mid-thirties. Unlike any doctor I'd seen, she wore lipstick, foundation and high heels. She greeted us in English at first, then asked Mum in

Kwéyòl how she was. Mum seemed more at ease with her after that.

She tried to engage Mum in conversation, asking her where in St Lucia she was born, how long she'd spent in England and if she was pleased she'd come back.

I explained to Dr Peres why we'd come. She checked Mum's blood pressure, her eyes, tongue and hands. I gave her a copy of the letter, from England, confirming Mum's diagnosis, and she proceeded to give Mum yet another memory test. I'd been through so many of these tests with Mum. The pain they brought made me want to leave the room, or ask the doctor if it was necessary to put her through this – the reconfirmation of her inabilities; diagnose her all over again.

Wasn't the letter I'd given her enough?

'Diagnosed 2010,' Dr Peres said, putting the test results aside. 'So you must know quite a bit about the condition.'

'Yes.' I nodded. Despite the number of years Mum had had Alzheimer's, and the number of appointments I'd been to with her because of it, discussing it brought me to the brink of tears, which I was currently doing my best to suppress. Relief came when she stopped to address Mum.

'How have you been feeling, Mrs Joseph?'

I'd long stopped pointing out that Mum was a 'Miss' and not a 'Mrs'. Especially knowing that 'Mrs' was what she preferred.

Mum looked at me. 'I don't know,' she told the doctor.

'She's been falling over,' I said, trying to choose my words to spare Mum any discomfort or embarrassment. 'Her behaviour has changed a lot since... since I was here three months ago.'

'I see,' Dr Peres said.

'And she doesn't sleep well at nights,' I added, hesitating then glancing at Mum. 'She' – I lowered my voice – 'threatened me with a knife one night. She didn't recognise me.'

Dr Peres gave me a lingering look, then turned to Mum.

'You finding it hard to sleep?' she asked, then switched back to me. 'Is she?'

I turned to Mum. 'You do find it hard to sleep at nights sometimes, don't you, Mum?' then brought my attention back to the doctor. 'Sometimes she gets up, wandering around, late at night. The other day she said she saw a baby and a cat, when there's only me and her in the house.'

'Mmm.' Dr Peres made some notes. 'Eating, drinking, toileting okay?'

'Yes. But she's becoming violent. Kicking – lashing out as well.' I considered mentioning the shower, but compared to that attack the other night, it seemed minor.

'So... violent? Has she ever suffered from depression?'

'No... well, not as far as I know,' I said. 'But maybe. Especially when her partner – my... kind-of stepfather died. They'd been together a long time.'

'And how long ago was that? That he died?'

'Six years.'

'Oh. A while. You live with her?'

'No. I live in England. I've come to take her back with me, but thought while I was here – in England she used to see a psychiatrist, so I thought – especially because of her behaviour and not sleeping, I'd take her to see a psychiatrist here.'

'Mmm. Did the psychiatrist in England prescribe anything for her?'

'Only something to slow down the progression. But she's off those now.'

'Mmm.' Dr Peres nodded. 'Any threats to take her own life?'

'No. Er... yes,' I said. 'Only once – the other day, when she was frustrated that she couldn't get through the gate to go home. She always wants to go home, even though she is at home. Then she said, she might as well kill herself,' I added.

'Still, we have to watch that,' Dr Peres said. I shuddered inside. 'We'll also do a urine and blood tests to make sure she doesn't have any infections. I can give you something to help with the behaviour – the psychotic *episodes* – to reduce the distress for her, and help her mood.'

The doctor glanced at Mum's notes. 'Mrs Joseph,' she said. 'I am going to give you something to help you sleep and to bring you a little calm.'

'Psychotic?' I repeated. This mental-ill-health language was a shift from the 'cognitive impairment' term the psychiatrist in England had used to described Mum's condition.

The doctor looked at me and lowered her voice. 'I'm afraid we have to use the same drugs we use for persons suffering from other mental health conditions. It's all we have.'

'What stage would you say she is in?' I asked Dr Peres, to see if she'd confirm what I'd read on the internet.

'Four to five,' she said, nodded and glanced at Mum.

Only two more stages to go. How long will that be in time? Where should she be to get the best care and for us to make the most of the time she has left?

'We will start her on a low dose with the drugs and see how it goes,' Dr Peres said. 'There are some side effects, of course.' She shrugged. 'Come back and see me in a couple of weeks. We'll see how she's managing. We'll have the results of the tests by then, too. And can try something else if there are problems. Okay, Mrs Joseph?' She looked at Mum, lips pursed.

'Okay. Thank you,' Mum responded, a hint of hope in her eyes.

I thanked her too, relieved at the prospect of Mum having less of the extreme confusion, stopping seeing who and what wasn't there, and having her sleeping through the night. I wanted those bags and dark stains under her eyes gone, and for Mum to look more like her old self. But an anti-psychotic drug?

'Do you *have* to take her back to England?' Dr Peres asked.

'Well... It's hard to find carers for her here. People find her behaviour hard to manage. And I have to go to work.'

'That may be so,' Dr Peres hesitated, 'but I wouldn't advise taking her on a long-haul flight, at least not right now. It will not help her condition. Maybe in a few weeks, if we can get the psychotic episodes under control.' Her tone was stern. Concerning.

'Oh, but—'

'There's also managing her on the flight itself. The stress it could put on her.'

'Flight? What flight is dat?' Mum interjected, her gaze flitting from mine to the doctor's face.

'It's okay, Mum,' I said, touching her before addressing the doctor again. 'Wouldn't these... these tablets calm her down enough?'

'It's your decision to make,' Dr Peres said, a perturbed look on her face. 'But I wouldn't advise it. Not right now, at least.'

I stared at her. There had to be a way around this new problem she'd presented me with.

I took the prescription she was holding out.

'Thank you,' I said.

Mum thanked her again and we went to reception to pay.

'No,' Mum said, as I got my purse out. 'I have to pay.'

'It's your card.' I showed her the bank card I'd been holding on to since my last visit. It was safe with me.

'Ohhh. Well, okay.' She stepped back.

Cousin Headley came out of the waiting room. I suggested Mum used the toilet. 'It's a long drive back.'

We stepped out of the cool, air-conditioned building into morning sun.

'What's dis med'cine de doctor give me, dere?' she asked, as I took her hand.

'Something to help you to sleep and help you stay calm.'

'Calm? So I am not calm?'

'You get very upset and angry at times,' I said, aware that that description could just as well have applied to me. It was always awkward discussing these things with Mum. I feared saying the wrong thing in the wrong way and setting her off.

Cousin Headley pointed to where he'd parked the minibus – it was just a short walk away on a side road – and helped Mum into her usual seat behind us. I slid into mine and sighed.

'Everything okay?' he asked, buckling up.

'Not great,' I said, 'but we'll see. The doctor's given her some medication.' I asked if he could stop at a pharmacy along the way.

'Of course,' he said.

Dr Peres' advice not to take Mum back to England was threatening to blow a hole in my plans, but the psychiatrist in England had advised against Mum coming back here three years ago too and we'd gone ahead with it anyway, because Mum had insisted. It hadn't killed her, and nor had I seen a particular deterioration in her condition when she arrived. But it might be different now, with her being much further into the disease.

A quiet panic mounted in me. Not only was I scared of these psychotic episodes, and what else was along the road with this disease, but the thought of having to manage any of it on the plane petrified me. I couldn't know what to expect.

The mid-morning journey back was faster than the earlier rush-hour drive, and it was quite soothing meandering through the mountains, taking in spectacular views of rain forests from above and around us; watching people in the villages we passed going about their daily lives.

'Straight home?' Cousin Headley asked, when we passed the turning for Aux Leon.

'Yes, please,' I said.

Cousin Headley declined staying for lunch. I was sure he was popping down to Auntie to give her as much of an update as he could on the morning's events.

'Why we caa eat inside?' Mum said, as I walked past the kitchen table.

'It's nicer outside. There's more breeze.'

She relented.

While we ate, as part of my strategy to keep the conversation away from the doctor's visit and her health, I asked if she fancied taking a walk up to Auntie's later.

'Maybe,' she said.

'If you're not too tired.'

'Dat sun does get so hot.'

'It will be cooler later. We can take our time and use the umbrella. I'm sure Auntie would love the visit.'

'What's going to happen to me?' she asked, halfway through her meal.

That question again, that no one could fully answer. 'What do you mean?'

'Who's going to stay with me when you go?'

'I... I want you to come with me,' I said.

'Where?'

'To England, of course, but... but the doctor says we might have to wait a bit longer.'

'Englan'?' She put her fork down. 'Englan' you want to take me?'

'What else can we do, Mum? You don't like the carers and I... I have to go to work.'

'I have no place in Englan'. I'm not going dere.'

'You – you'd stay with *me*,' I said.

'Eh-eh.'

I was at a brick wall, again. Should I ignore the doctor's advice, like I had before? Mum wasn't that far gone for me to get away with conning her into taking a flight to England. But,

as the doctor had said, how would I manage her on the plane?
I'd find a way.

'Let's eat, Mum,' I said.

'I'm not hungry.' She left the table.

'Mum?' I went after her. But she slammed her door in my
face. 'Mum?' I called from the outside.

She didn't answer.

CHAPTER FIFTEEN

Closed doors.

Closed bedroom doors became a thing when we moved in with Mr Frank. Everyone needed privacy, he'd said. His and Mum's bedroom was a place for only the two of them. When I'd tried to wander in there after Mum, she'd looked jittery. 'You want something?' she'd ask.

'Not really,' I said.

'Well, I'll see you downstairs. You know Frank don't like people in his bedroom.'

'Oh.' I'd become 'people'. Not her daughter, her only child. So I took the first opportunity I found to enter freely. Though I've regretted it to this day.

Their bedroom was the first you'd see as you hit the landing after coming up stairs. Luckily – or unluckily – that day, one of them had left their key in the lock, and I'd spotted it. Mum had been due home in under an hour and I had to wash and put the rice on before she arrived. I'd have to be quick, if I wanted to have a nose inside.

It wasn't that I expected to get some revelation from the snoop. I knew how the furniture was organised cos I'd glanced inside when one of them, especially Mum, was going in or coming out, and I'd been in there briefly to talk to Mum when he wasn't around. But it was clear that it wasn't a place either of them wanted me lingering in.

I turned the handle. It opened despite the key being in the lock. First, I sat on their firm bed, bounced up and down and glanced around at the double wardrobe – one side for Mum, the other for him. The tall dresser with neat clusters of toiletries: perfumes, aftershave, body cream, talcum powder and Vaseline. Sinking my feet into the thick shag-pile carpet, I got up and opened his wardrobe door, which sent the smell of clean clothes towards me. On the wardrobe floor, to my left, were shoes, laid neatly in pairs. An old suitcase was propped up on the opposite side next to a stack of magazines. Magazines? Mr Frank often came home with a rolled-up *Sun* newspaper, but never a magazine. I picked one up and a centre page immediately opened onto a large, glossy, colour picture of a naked woman holding an erect penis – larger than I'd ever imagined one could be – to her mouth.

'Ah!' I gasped, dropping it like it might contaminate me. 'My God.' Dirty magazines? I picked it up and folded the page back in, but as I was about to drop it on the pile, the front door slam shut. Someone was coming. I had to get out. I tossed the magazine onto the pile.

'Ione?'

Mr Frank. I couldn't answer. Not until I was where it was okay to be.

'Who is here?' he shouted up the stairs.

'Me,' I responded, clicking their bedroom door shut behind me before facing him on the landing.

'Where you was?' he said.

'I... I was just going to put on the rice for Mum,' I said, cringing past him to make my way downstairs.

'Ione leave her key in the door?'

'Sorry? What?' I said, dragging as much innocence as possible into my voice.

'Don't worry,' he said.

But there were raised voices in their bedroom that night. *Sorry, Mum.*

The stain of that pornographic image stayed in my head and I never went snooping in there again.

I paid and said good-bye to the handy-man who'd fitted the new kitchen door, then went over the fifty-plus listed side effects of the anti-psychotic drug Dr Peres had prescribed for Mum. Restlessness, agitation and anxiety were concerning, but seizures was the most worrying one. Was it really worth it?

The dosage for both tablets were low, but I'd held off starting her on them. My efforts to tackle one problem could end up bringing a multitude of them. In the depths of reading up on the sleeping pill, I'd planned to start tonight, I heard a crash, then Mum shouting: '*I-gas. I-salòp. Adan tjou.*'

She was cursing. Swearing at someone. A crashing sound sent me racing to her bedroom. *Please let her not have hurt herself.*

'What's happened? What's...?' I said. A heavy scent of bay rum whipped at my nostrils. 'Er... What's happened here? Mum?'

The mirror attached to her dressing table was broken in half. Bits of glass were scattered over the surface and the floor.

'Somebody!' Mum shouted. 'A man. A man was trying to come in through de window. I hit him. De bastard. Peeping... trying to come inside my house.'

'Where?' I stepped around the broken glass and leaned out of the window to take a look. 'I don't see anyone, Mum. And nobody could reach up here without a ladder. There's no one there.'

'Not dere. *Dere.*' She pointed at what was left of the mirror attached to her dressing table.

'Well, that's not a window, Mum. It's a mirror. Come and see.' She moved warily, unsure, towards me. 'Look.' I pointed at her reflection in what was left of the mirror. She flinched and stepped back. 'It's you, Mum. That was you in the mirror. It's not a window.'

Why was I trying to explain this to her? She'd mistaken the mirror for a window and her own reflection for somebody else. A stranger. She hadn't recognised her own face.

'Come, Mum.' Accepting the risk of her wandering around, and possibly creating another problem for me to sort out, I took her arm and led her to sit in the front room.

How was I going to make sure her room was free from glass? The tiniest bit could be anywhere.

I threw everything left on the dresser onto the throw on her bed, bundled everything up and put it outside for cleaning later. Then I pulled the drawers out of the dresser, left them on the bed and lifted the casing outside.

Mum began following me around. I tried to keep her behind me. Got a dust pan and broom, picked up the larger bits of glass from the floor and bagged them. When the vacuum cleaner started humming too loud for her, she scurried back into the front room, where I preferred her to be. One stray piece of glass could cut through anyone's foot.

Satisfied that I'd done the best I could with the floor, I set to sorting the things I had outside.

This room was going to have to be made Mum-friendly. Meaning barely furnished. Mirrors out of her sight.

Drenched in sweat, and on the verge of clawing out my hair, I headed outside, where I paused for a few breaths of fresh air before beginning to tackle the task of making the dresser safe enough to take back to her room.

'Hey, what's going on there?' Claire was at the gate. This

wasn't a good time for visitors, but I let her in and explained what had happened.

'My God,' she said. 'She break all the mirror?'

'Yep. I'll have to go over the room with the vacuum cleaner again, before I let her in there,' I said. 'You never know where a tiny piece of glass could be.'

'Where she now?'

'I left her in the front room.'

'I'll go an' check on her for you.'

'Thanks,' I said, then got on with brushing and wiping the glass off the dresser.

A minute later, Claire was back. 'She's okay.' Then: 'Here, let me help you.'

'You'll need gloves,' I said.

'Tell me where.'

I sent her to look under the kitchen sink.

She also got the outdoor broom, swept under and around the dresser some more to get rid of the tiny bits, then to reduce the likelihood of anyone bringing a piece of glass in the house under their shoes, swept the outside area.

'Careful you don't cut yourself,' I said.

Two hands really do make light work, and having Claire to talk to whilst doing all this released some of my frustration. She helped me carry the bed throw to the back of the garden, empty it out and shake as many particles off as possible.

'Bes' to hang it on the line to let the wind shake off what we cannot see,' she said. After that, she ran the vacuum cleaner over Mum's room again for me, and we took the dresser back in, minus the mirror.

'Girl, what you really going to do about all of this? You don't think you could put her in dat ole people home, in town?'

'Old people's...? Oh, no. I couldn't do that.' I shook my head. 'She's coming back to England with me.'

'But I hear it's a nice place. They looking after the ole

people in there good. Keeping her here is like – this is danger-ous. You don't think?'

Until the other day, when Mrs Andrews had mentioned the care home in town to me, I'd been under the impression that there were only charitable care homes here.

I'd been to one, not too far from Cherry Orchard, with Mum, to take some of Mr Frank's old clothes, after he died. I'd almost cried seeing the buckets on the floor to catch the rain coming in through the leaky roof; the worn lino, and pails in place of toilets for residents. The only good thing about the experience was that the old people looked clean and the staff couldn't have thanked me and Mum enough for what we'd brought.

'Can't they fix the place?' I'd asked Mum, when we'd left.

'It's for paupers. De Church is running it an' say dey have no money.'

'The Catholic Church is loaded, Mum. Why can't they send some of that money down here to help these old people?'

Mum had shrugged.

'It cannot be easy for you, managing your mom,' Claire said. 'Remember, I know.'

A reminder wasn't needed. 'How much do you hear?'

'A lot. Voice travel far, you know.'

Her look of sympathy deepened, causing me to feel more exposed.

'Mmm.'

But who could manage Mum's behaviour now? She'd become a special-needs child. The tablets would be our only hope.

After Claire left, my mind returned to what she'd said about the care home. Later, after putting Mum to bed with her first dose of sleeping pill, I called Claire.

'I was just about to call you,' she said. 'You on your own?'

'Yes,' I said.

'You want some company? We didn't even get a chance to sit and talk.'

Was Claire feeling sorry for me? Whether she was or not, I welcomed the company.

'Oh, that would be nice.' My alternative evening would be sitting on the veranda, or in my room, trying to find ways to distract myself from over-thinking.

'Well, I will see you in a while,' she said.

How sad was it that a visit from a neighbour I'd seen a few hours ago would excite me in this way?

I missed my honest and open talks with Delia, but couldn't keep interrupting her at work. Access to her was hit and miss at the best of times, and the time difference didn't help. Claire's visit would give me a chance to unwind, with sensible company, and there'd be no Mum to see to.

There wasn't much by way of drinks in the cupboard. If she didn't drink rum, she'd have to have the sweet ginger wine Mum had there, or something non-alcoholic.

I needn't have been concerned about that because after I told her what was on offer, she said she wasn't a big drinker. 'My head can't take it. The most I would have is a little wine or shandy.'

'There's wine,' I said. 'But I'm not sure if you'd like it or how long it's been opened.'

She settled for some of the guava juice Mrs Andrews had brought over. 'Plenty ice, please,' she said.

I had my usual. A glass of wine after work was routine for me back in England. Here, rum and Coke had replaced that.

Once seated, I thanked her again for her help earlier.

'It's not a problem,' she said.

Going straight for the jugular, I asked if she knew the name of the care home she'd told me about earlier.

'I... I'm not sure, on. You thinking about it?'

'Maybe. I think it might be the same one Mrs Andrews

mentioned to me, the other day. But I'm not sure if I could put Mum in a home.'

'They say it's nice. A lot of people does put themself in there, when they ready.'

'That's what Mrs Andrew said.' I asked Claire if she knew the size of the place, where it was and what the cost was likely to be.

'I cannot tell you how much it cost, but I know it cannot be cheap because is only people who have sufficient amount of money does put themself in there.'

I couldn't see the costs being a problem for Mum. Her pension was sure to cover it. It wouldn't do any harm to take a look.

'So, you live on your own in that big house?' I asked Claire, changing the subject.

'You could say dat,' she said. 'The owners in Englan'. They don't come down dat often. I stay there for them.'

'So you're house-sitting?'

'Dat's what you-all call it?'

'You get reduced rent?'

'No. No rent, I just pay the electricity and water when I'm there. And the owners pay me a little something every month. When they come down, I stay with my sister in Micoud.'

'Sounds good,' I said.

'But I cannot sit in the house all day. So I work too.'

'Of course.'

'You think you might put your mother in the home?' She dragged me back to my Mum issue.

'I might go and have a look and see. See how it looks,' I said. 'I want to take Mum back to England with me, but we went to see a doctor yesterday and she says I might not be able to, at least not for now.'

'So you might have to leave her?'

'Maybe.' I hesitated. 'I'll see.' I talked about the position I was in with work, and financial loss implication of taking my pension too early. 'I never imagined my mother would end up with a disease like this.'

Alzheimer's, the uninvited sitting-tenant in Mum's brain that we couldn't get to leave, was destroying her life and messing mine up. And it wouldn't leave, either, without taking Mum.

Claire's voice cut into my thoughts. 'It's a big problem.'

I told her about the new drugs the doctor had prescribed.

'I hope they work,' she said.

'Me too.'

'She was always such a nice lady. Always giving people fruits an' things.'

'That was Mum – but this disease is definitely changing her. You never know where you are with her. What to expect. One minute things are okay, then... God knows.' I sighed.

'Mmm.'

'Funny thing is, she's not mean to Auntie.'

'Maybe it's because it's her big sister.'

'Maybe.'

'It's a shame you don't have a sister yourself, or even a brother to help you with her.'

'Yeah. Wouldn't that be great?' I said.

There had been times, in my childhood, when the idea of having a brother or sister thrilled me. And along with wishing for a nice man for Mum, I'd longed for a sibling. Having Mum all to myself had been great, but so was the idea of having someone to play with and do things with; have another person to love and be loved by. Maybe even share some resemblance with. Mr Frank came in the guise of a nice man, but I never got that sibling. I'd remained the only child. I hadn't wanted that for Millie, either, but after losing Shane, and Leo disappearing to Africa, I never met anyone I wanted to have another child with, and kept myself well protected from that. Mum had probably done the same. Now Millie too was an only child. Though it had occurred to me that she may have half-siblings somewhere in Africa, who might not have known anything about her, and she didn't know existed.

'Do you have any children?' I asked Claire.

'No. No. Not me,' she said.

'Still waiting for the right man?'

'The right man?' Claire laughed. 'No. I'm sure you must have heard. It's women I prefer.'

'Oh,' I said. 'So you're—'

'A lesbian. Gay. Whatever you prefer to call it.'

'I see. I didn't realise.'

'I hope you don't feel uncomfortable with me now.'

'Oh, no,' I said.

'You sure?'

'Yeah.' The number of gay people I'd worked with? Her sexuality was not an issue for me.

'You didn't want to have more children, yourself?' she said.

'I did... but...' The memory of Mum's hallucination the other night – her thinking she'd seen and heard a crying baby in the living room, returned to me. 'I mean I had a son, but I lost him. He died,' I said, swallowing through the tightness at the back of my throat.

'Oh. Dat's so sad. A boy?'

'Uh-huh... Shane.'

'Dat sound bad. He was big?'

'Six months. Only six months. Hard to believe, sometimes...'

'All of dat you go through already?'

I nodded, my mind taking me back to the hospital, staring at Shane's still, soft body. Desperate to hear a whimper, a movement, have back the incessant crying that had made me bring him in. 'By the time I took him to the hospital, it was too late,' I said.

'I'm so, so sorry.' Claire's hand on my arm came in time to halt the tears. I looked away. 'It's okay.'

'You still have your lovely daughter. She resembles you a lot.'

'I know.'

'She couldn't come down with you?'

I told her it was a busy time for Millie.

'Well, maybe the next time,' she said.

'Maybe.' When would that be?

I was considering a third drink, when Claire said she'd better head back home.

'You can come by me anytime you like,' she said.

'If I can get someone to stay with Mum.'

'You have your auntie. Or we can go to the fish-fry,' she reminded me.

'Oh, yes. I really need to do that before I go back.'

For the first time, we hugged lightly when saying goodbye. I locked the gate behind her and the faint scent of castor oil from her hair.

Back in my room, suppressed memories of my last few hours with Shane came to me.

Millie's voice message was a great distraction: '*Hi, Mum. How's it all going? Hope things are—*' But here my data ran out, so I couldn't listen to the rest of her message, nor respond. Not having internet in the house was starting to be a real pain.

The top-up would have to wait until tomorrow. I poured myself that third drink, and sat on the veranda again, a new plan taking shape in my head. There was no harm in looking at the care home. If it was as nice as everyone seemed to be saying it was, it could save me battling the hurdles of taking Mum back to England with me.

CHAPTER SIXTEEN

The mellow feeling that third rum and Coke had delivered last
night came at a price: broken sleep from hot sweats and dehy-
dration, and sluggishness for most of the morning.

Before getting breakfast, I sneaked into Mum's room, like I
had before, to allay my tiny fears that the sleeping pill might
have put her to sleep for ever.

Reassured, I called the care home, spoke to a Mrs Paul and
arranged a visit for Monday morning. After that, questions
began banging about in my brain again. Like, how or why we'd
got to where we were. Mum wasn't even that old and deserved
to live deep into her eighties – nineties, even, like some of her
other siblings. And, like Auntie Barbara, they'd had high blood
pressure. Auntie Sim had had diabetes as well. If Alzheimer's
hadn't claimed Mum's brain, she would be completely healthy
and we'd live the life I'd foreseen her old age bringing. A second
bonding for us, without Mr Frank.

How often did dementia hunt around for innocent, healthy
bodies? Why had it picked my mother's?

I'd had all of these thoughts before, of course, since diagnosis. And despite not finding any satisfactory answers, the ques-

tions kept returning. The new and pressing question, this time, was whether a care home in St Lucia would be a good alternative that would get us around the complications of taking her back, finding carers and me being able to go back to work. But more importantly, would I be okay with leaving her there?

After breakfast and getting dressed, I went to check in on her again. This time she stirred. 'Frank?'

'It's me. Erica,' I said.

'Mmm.' She lifted her head, looked around and flopped it back on the pillow.

I leaned over her. 'You okay?'

'Al—all right. *Las*. Tired,' she said.

'Breakfast is ready, if you want to get up. But you can rest here for a bit, if you like.'

She mumbled a reply. I put down a cup of the cinnamon tea I'd made earlier, and left her to it.

'Barbara?' she said, when I went to check whether she'd finished her tea. 'You'll have to stay with Auntie for a bit today,' I said, taking her empty cup. 'I have to go down the road.'

'You going out? I coming with you.' She made to get out of bed.

'I'm just going to top up my phone,' I said. 'Won't be long.'

She took off to the bathroom. Straight to the sink to brush her teeth.

I'd started on lunch when she came out, still wearing her night dress and deliberately ignored her when she asked for Mr Frank. His name left a sour taste in my mouth, as it should in hers. 'Auntie Barbara's coming down soon,' I said.

'What is going on in here?' she demanded, her tone aggressive and deliberate.

I continued chopping onions. 'I'm getting our lunch ready,' I said. 'We're having a stir-fry. Ready for your breakfast?'

'Let me pass, you hear?' She moved towards the stove.

'I've made porridge,' I said. 'Oats.'

'Eh-eh. I don't want oats. She glared at me. 'In my own house you want to tell me what I have to eat? *Sa ki wivé ou?* What happen to you?'

Weary of what might come next, I stepped aside so she could reach the stove. *Should have started her on the antipsychotic drug yesterday*, a small voice whispered in my head. Regret couldn't help me now. Delaying the start of the meds was delaying a possible change that could benefit everyone.

What was wrong with me? Every episode of aggression, anger and confusion I went through with Mum frightened and worried me, but after they passed, I'd slip into a state of false hope; half convincing myself that things were or would be manageable and not so bad, after all. Now I was shivering inside at the fear of this episode escalating. The knife I'd been using was still in my hand. I put it in the bowl with the vegetables and walked away from the sink with it.

She took the milk pan off the drainer, filled it with water and put it on the stove. Then she tottered towards the fridge. I guessed it would be boiled eggs for her.

'I've made porridge, Mum,' I said again.

'I don't want your focking porridge,' she screamed, slamming the fridge door closed and dropping one of the eggs in her hand.

I shuddered, cowered to the front room and perched on the edge of the sofa with a view into the kitchen.

The ugly side of her that had turned its back on me, years ago, when I'd needed her, was confronting me again.

CHAPTER SEVENTEEN

I didn't completely move out on that Sunday she'd told me I had to go, but I did go to Leo's. The guy he shared his flat with didn't mind me staying there for a while.

The following day, when I was sure both Mum and Mr Frank would be out, I went round to get my things.

From that first night, not a day passed without me crying. Leo would comfort me, telling me things would work out all right.

'Why don't you go and see her?' he'd ask.

Through tears, I'd reply: 'She doesn't want me. Don't you understand? She told me to leave.'

Her need to keep Mr Frank was stronger than her love for me, and the need to have me in her life.

Months went by with no contact from her. I couldn't bring myself to contact her either. Her rejection had cut a cord. Set me adrift. I did my best to adjust to my new living arrangements. My stabiliser wasn't just the love from Leo, but the flourishing love for Millie, the little human growing inside me.

Between Leo's job at an advice centre and mine at the

library, we managed. But, as desperate as I was to have my mum in my life again, I maintained my vow not to contact her.

I *had* to believe Alzheimer's was the only reason behind Mum's animosity towards me. *It* was the demon presenting me as the enemy in her life, and not the resurrection of buried resentment she'd been harbouring for years because I didn't like nor approve of her staying with Mr Frank.

She took a small creole loaf out of the sealed container and went back to the fridge for the butter. '*Wi*. Yes,' she said, cutting her eyes at me, before turning towards the stove again. '*Véyé mwen*. Watch me.'

I got up, slipped into the kitchen, dropped the bowl with the knife on the table and rushed to my room for my handbag. I wouldn't stay another second in this house. She could burn the pot all she liked. Burn the whole frigging house. I didn't want to be there any more than she wanted me to be.

'*Koté ou*? Where are you?' she shouted, coming towards me, as I stepped out of my bedroom.

'Leave me alone,' I shouted back, hurt and anger welling up in me. 'You need me. *You* need me. I don't need you!'

I marched through the gate, tears filling my eyes, chest tight, everything coiling up inside me. I wanted to scream. Shout some more. Every step I took intensified my need to get away from her.

'Hey.'

I ignored the voice calling from behind me.

'Hey!'

Whoever it was, I didn't want to know. Peace was all I wanted and needed. Quick, soft, steps were getting closer, but I kept walking until a hand touched my shoulder. 'Erica?'

I glanced back at Claire panting as she jogged alongside me.

'Where... where you going in such a haste?'

I couldn't stop walking. Couldn't speak. Wished she hadn't caught up with me.

'Erica. You all right?'

I didn't answer.

'Slow down, nuh?'

'Hi,' I said under my breath, so as not to appear rude.

'What happen? What happen to you?' she asked, her stare fixed on the side of my face. 'Something upset you? What... what have you so vex?'

'My mother,' I blurted out, anger and pain still raging through me.

'Listen. Slow down.'

I ignored her.

'Come on.' She took my hand. 'Let's sit down. Sit down somewhere.'

'I... I have to...' I kept walking. Afraid that if I slowed down or stopped, I'd collapse and start bawling my problems out to someone I shouldn't be exposing that much of myself to. 'I... I'll be okay,' I said, hoping she'd concede and go on her way.

'I know you will be okay,' Claire said, 'but right now – come.' She took my hand.

I slowed down and let her lead me, a few yards on, to a metal bench shaded by a huge moringa tree. She brushed some dried pods and leaves off it and sat down. 'Let's take a res' here,' she said, still holding my hand. 'Something happen?'

Warm metal under my bum, I nodded, afraid to let any more words than were necessary out. Words that would expose the pain my mother's tongue and actions caused me. Force me to face the fact that I wasn't sure of my mother's love.

'You don't have to tell me, if you don't want to,' she said after a pause, 'but I tell you already I know it's not easy to take care of a person with dat thing your mother have.'

'She can be so hurtful,' I heard myself say. 'Says such horrible things, that make me feel...' I sniffed, lost for words. 'I don't know where I am with her sometimes. Scares me... Makes me so... I... I can't take it. It's too much.'

'I can imagine,' Claire said. 'I know she said the lady you had here helping her was taking her things. And she cursed her so bad. Made her leave.'

I nodded. Mum had told me lots of bad things about Mrs Pierre. And had almost convinced me, until I spoke to Auntie Barbara and Mrs Pierre herself.

'She doing the same thing to you?' Claire said, sitting with her upper body turned to me

'No. Not that. She's being mean. This Alzheimer's has her – it's like she hates me.'

'Dat sickness is bad.' Claire shook her head.

'I feel like... sometimes, I don't know her. We've had our problems, but... I thought... I still love her and she's... I don't understand why she's so horrible to me.' I took a deep breath and wiped my eyes.

'You have to have a lot of patience to manage people with dat kind of thing.'

'I know. And I don't think I have it,' I said. 'I'm gonna look at that care home. That will probably be the best thing.'

'They should know all about how to manage people with dat dementia.'

'Mmm.'

'Well, you know I am here if you want a friend to talk to.'

'Thanks.' I wiped my eyes again and sniffed. 'I... I can't take it when she treats me like this. In... in this hateful way. I wish things could be different.'

'It's the sickness. She must love you, deep inside. You are her only child.'

'Doesn't feel like it, sometimes. She's already forgetting who I am.'

Claire took in a breath. 'For true?'

I nodded, my mind flashing back to my first night, when she'd threatened to stab me.

'So she's there – in the house, on her own right now?'

'Mmm. I had to get out.'

'The little break will help both of you.'

'I'm all right now.' I sniffed and stood up. 'I'll walk around for a bit. I'll be fine.'

'Be sure you don't get lost, eh?' she said, still seated. 'Joke, I joking.' She smiled. 'You cannot get lost in here.'

'Sorry for holding you up.'

'It's not a problem. They owe me so much time in dat place already.'

'Right,' I said.

'I'll check on you later.'

I thanked her and forced a smile.

CHAPTER EIGHTEEN

Mum wasn't there when I got back to the house. She'd left a mess in the kitchen, and in her bathroom, but no evidence of burnt pots. It was odd that I hadn't run into her or seen her out there.

I remembered what Auntie Barbara had said about her giving the wrong money to people, forgetting where the bus stop was. She could make all sorts of boo-boos if she went out shopping on her own. I called Auntie.

'Is here she is,' Auntie confirmed. I took a deep breath, relieved that Mum was safe. 'You want to talk to her?'

'I just wondered where she was,' I said, my voice shaky. 'I have to go to the shops now, anyway.'

'I will bring her when she ready.'

That suited me. As I tidied up, I considered the situation around Mum's behaviour and the tablets. The sooner she started taking the anti-psychotic one the sooner we were likely to see a change. The few weeks I had left should be enough time to monitor the side effects and feed them back to Dr Peres.

Pain from the morning's altercation and my sense of inadequacy continued simmering. By the time I'd finished cleaning up her mess, resentment had clawed its way in, nudging me as I passed Auntie's road on my way to the bus stop, imagining Mum, the unpredictable one, sitting up there with Auntie. Doing what? Asking to come home? Being calm and reasonable and loving towards her sister? Had the memory of what took place between her and me this morning already been quashed by Alzheimer's?

To find peace, I tried to put all of it aside. I should make the most of this time away from her.

Buses were frequent on this route, but often full. The first one flew past. The second had room for two. I could have gone closer to home for my top-up, but headed further out to Vieux Fort instead.

When the bus took the bend, past the sea front before entering the centre of the town, I glanced at the hotel where Claire worked, imagining how much more pleasant this trip would be if I was simply a tourist. Then my thoughts catapulted back to Mum.

After topping up, I finished listening to Millie's message, asking for an update, then texted her back with one, adding: *Talk soon.*

There was no hurry in getting back home. I wandered through the supermarket, picked up some groceries and other bits and pieces, including a notebook and pen to log any effects the drug might have on Mum. Then it was off to one of the bars by the sea front, for a cold drink.

I paid, thanked the bar tender and, with my shoes off, strolled towards the shoreline.

This side of the Atlantic could almost have been mistaken for the Caribbean Sea today. Waves calm. Not their normal roaring and frothy self. I sat close to the veiny roots of a coconut tree, the bar a short distance behind me. A few tourists were paragliding, skimming over the water, the wind in their face, gannets flying overhead. What freedom.

Looking across at the ocean brought thoughts of England, many miles of water from there. Cold England, not often as warm or as hot as here. But there I had a sense of worth: friends and family who loved me; a great career, access to things I loved: theatres, restaurants, art galleries, great TV, shopping and quality goods. I had many more years of that fulfilment ahead of me.

Reggae music blasted from somewhere behind me. An old favourite – 'Money in my Pocket,' by Dennis Brown, reminding me again of the good times I hadn't had enough of.

Taking the last swig of my drink, I got up, dusted off the back of my trousers, picked up my shopping bag and strolled to the main road to get the bus back up to Mum's.

I took my time, though, as I wasn't in any particular hurry to see her.

Their voices alerted me. Auntie had brought Mum back.

'*Koté i?* Where is she?' I heard her saying to Mum. 'Hello? Erica?'

'Here. I'm here,' I replied, coming out to meet them in the passage way. 'You're back. Hi, Auntie. Hi, Mum—?' I glanced at her face, afraid of what a good look at it might stir in me.

'Hello,' Mum said. 'Where you was?'

'At the shops,' I said.

'Oh.' She walked past me to her room.

'I don't see dat tablet doing nothing for Ione yet, *on,*' Auntie said, after the back of Mum disappeared.

I took her arm and led her out to the veranda. 'I've only given her the sleeping pill,' I whispered.

'What you mean?'

'The other one has scary side effects, Auntie. I... I wasn't sure.'

'Eh-eh.' Auntie glared at me. 'I don't understan'.'

'I was a bit scared.'

'So you think you know better dan de doctor?'

'It's not that, Auntie.' I tutted. 'I just... was a bit worried.'

'Give Ione de me'cine, you hear?'

'I plan to. From tomorrow.'

'Tomorrow? Why you caa give it to her today? You take Ione quite Castries to see a psy—special doctor, an' now you afraid to give her de med'cine dey give you for her?'

'She's supposed to take it in the morning. It's too late to start it now.'

'Well in de morning. Make sure you give it to her, eh?'

'I will, Auntie. I will.'

'Good.' Her tone softened. 'So why you din come up with her earlier?'

'I needed to top up my phone,' I said.

'But you know you din have to go far for dat. You can do it jus' dere by George – in Micoud.'

'I needed to clear my head.'

'Clear your head?'

'It's not easy, Auntie.' I didn't want to go into it. 'How was she with you?'

'She was quiet, den start to ask for everybody. I don't understan' why she always want to go home so.'

'She's never sure where she is, I suppose.'

Mum joined us. 'What you-all doing out here?'

'I'm just going,' Auntie said. 'I'll see you tomorrow, Ione.'

'All right,' Mum replied.

I hesitated, then suggested I walked Auntie down.

'Walk me?' Auntie said. 'I will be home by de time you walk to de kitchen,' she said. Though it would take her a little longer than that.

'Call me when you get in,' I said.

'For what? You think dis is London? I will see you-all,' she said, heading off.

I tried to make the most of the rest of the day with Mum by walking around the garden with her, getting her to hold the carrier bag while I picked mangoes using what they called a *kali* – a long stick with a flour bag secured to the end of it by a metal ring with hooks. You tug at the stalk the mango is hanging from with the hooks and the mango falls into the bag.

'Take care, Erica,' Mum kept repeating.

'I am, Mum.' What was there to be careful about a mango landing on my head or face?

'Dat's enough mangoes now, Erica. De bag almos' full,' she said, after a while.

I stopped and took the bag from her.

'Let's see how your orchids are going,' I said, putting the *kali* to stand nearby. 'Ooo, something's happening,' I said. A purply spike was shooting out of two of the leafy parts.

'I don't worry with dem, you know,' Mum said. 'Dey does do what dey want. But when dey send flowers, I'm happy.' She smiled.

I'd often made her smile with flowers.

We walked past the lime tree and she insisted we collected the yellow limes that had fallen under and around it. We weren't allowed to pick the green ones on the tree. Folklore or fact, the tree would stop producing if we did.

After our fruit picking, I cut some summer flowers Mum had grown from seeds I'd brought her from England. We took them inside where I placed them in an enamel cup on the kitchen table.

'Dat look nice, eh?' she said.

'Does, doesn't it?' We both smiled.

I craved for times like this with Mum. When things were relaxed and we blended well together. It was what I'd expected it would be like in her old age, especially with Mr Frank gone. Her in her own home, me keeping an eye on things, helping when she needed it. Me and her doing fun things together, like we used to. But someone, something, had other plans.

We ate the chow mein I'd cooked, on the veranda, with a small salad.

'It's a long time I don't eat Chinese,' she said.

'Yeah, but it's not even close to that nice takeaway on the high street near me, where we used to get our crispy duck and pancakes, is it?'

'Duck. Where you going to find duck here?'

We laughed. I soaked in her smile. Wished there was more of it, instead of the deep frown and half-dazed expression Alzheimer's had introduced to her persona.

'I bought you something today,' I said, remembering the small jigsaw puzzles I'd picked up in the supermarket earlier.

'What...? For me? What's dat?'

'Nothing much – just a couple of puzzles to help you pass the time, when you're bored.'

When I'd spotted them in the supermarket my mind had flashed back to work at Rushmede Primary. Then to me and Mum on the floor, soon after we'd moved in with Mr Frank. Two hundred pieces we'd tackled in those days, not bothered about how long it might take to finish. We'd move the sofa up against the wall to make space in the middle of the room to accommodate it, and us. Mr Frank would edge past it to get to his favourite seat close to the television. He'd look at us and shake his head.

'Ione, you don't think you too big for them kind of things? Dat's for children, man,' he'd say.

'I din get dis when I was a chile,' was Mum's reply, 'so I'm taking my turn now.'

Those moments belonged only to us. Me and her.

The few hours of peace and semi-lucid conversations made the morning's clash pale into the background, but anxiety started creeping in on me when she yawned and said she was tired. If she lay down at all, it would be after a rummage through everything in her room. Changing things around, putting things where they didn't belong. I'd tried to keep it minimalistic in there, but it was hopeless expecting her to leave things alone.

Thankfully, that night, the sleeping pill got her to skip the activity. After taking it and getting washed, she said she was tired and went off to bed.

I sat on the veranda and gave Millie a call.

'At last,' she said. 'How's it going?'

I told her about the care home I planned to visit.

'Thought they didn't have any,' she said.

'That's what I thought too, but apparently there is. One, I'm told, only people with a bit of money can afford.'

'Oh, gosh. That's great. You think you'll put Nannie in there?'

'Maybe. If it's good, I could leave her there for a couple of years or so – until I draw down my pension. We'll see. Auntie Barbara won't be pleased,' I added, after a pause. 'But I'll have to deal with that.'

'It's worth having a look.'

I updated her on the meds and the visit to the psychiatrist.

'So she's saying you can't bring Nannie back?'

'Well, not exactly,' I said. 'We'll have to see how the meds go. Just a bit concerned about the side effects.'

'Everything has side effects, Mum,' she said. 'Best not to worry about them.'

'Yeah. Let's hope she doesn't get any of them.'

'Anyway, from what you've said about her behaviour, she definitely needs calming down.'

'But I've seen some people on those drugs, Millie. They look so dopey.'

'You have to at least try it.'

'Mmm. And at least Auntie Barbara agrees with her taking them.'

'Good you're agreeing on something.' Millie chuckled, then sighed. 'I'm gonna head to bed now.' It was late for her.

'You and Adwin okay?'

'Yeah, course.'

'Good.' I was doing my best not to mention the test again. 'Give him my love.'

'Okay. Love you, Mum.'

I said goodbye and got up to choose my clothes for tomorrow's appointment at the care home.

CHAPTER NINETEEN

Asking Cousin Headley to take me to visit the care home would mean declaring everything to Auntie. I didn't want to do that, so I'd hired a car.

Auntie was fine with having Mum at hers or being between hers and Mum's while I was gone. She assumed I was doing the usual – shopping. There was no need to tell her any different.

I wasn't sure what to expect St Patrick's to look like, except that it would be nothing like the one Mum and I had given some of Mr Frank's old clothes to. Claire had said this care home was where people who didn't have a live-in carer signed up for when they couldn't manage on their own any more. It was up north too, the fanciest part of the island. I read that as promising.

I'd seen care homes on television in England, heard reports of what went on in bad ones. But in England there was a government monitoring and inspection system. I doubted they had that here, judging by the condition of that pauper's home.

The prospect of finding a nice care home for Mum in the country she loved and wanted to end her days in, reduced the guilt I would have had if it was a care home in England. It would mean me being able to go back to England, for a couple more years, at least, with the satisfaction of knowing that Mum was okay. She could communicate in English or Kwéyòl, like she was used to doing, still be in the sun, have meals she was familiar with and be in the culture she felt at home in.

That aside, the misgivings beginning to load on me as I drove along the main road wasn't all to do with the idea of putting Mum in a home, but also about the secrecy around the visit. Why was I doing this? Hadn't I agreed – promised Mum, in her most lucid days – that I wouldn't put her in a home? With strangers? So what was this visit all about? It wasn't mere curiosity. If this care home turned out to be nice, given my choices, it would be difficult not to put her in there.

My mind flashed back to a couple of brochures Millie had given me to look at after we'd talked about the pros and cons of putting Mum in a home in England.

'What's the problem,' she'd said, 'if it's a nice place?' She'd been trying to stop me feeling guilty or bad for putting Mum in one. 'You're gonna have to go to work and she can't stay at home on her own for the next five years or however long you've got left to work.'

The places in the brochures had looked clean, and the staff had welcoming smiles. Maybe Millie had a point – but she was young. Not brought up like I was. She belonged more to the culture where it was the norm to put old people in a home. She couldn't fully understand how it felt for me.

I switched on the radio for some music to lift my mood.

Following the instructions Mrs Paul had given me, I turned into a side road full of potholes and craters that gave the impression I was on a bumpy funfair ride. Another right turn took me up a steep hill to huge black gates, which started sliding open as I was about to get out. Beyond it was a circular white building with a continuous veranda on each of the two levels.

An officious-looking woman wearing a fitted navy skirt with matching jacket and high heels came out of an adjacent building to my right. 'Good morning,' she said, walking towards me.

I slammed the car door. 'Good morning.'

'You must be Miss Joseph?' she said. 'I am Mrs Paul. We spoke on the telephone.'

'Oh, that was you? Nice to meet you.'

We exchanged smiles and a light handshake.

'Shall we talk first? Then I can show you around,' she said, and led me through the door she'd just come out of. We walked down a small hallway then into an office. The temperature in there explained why she was wearing a jacket. 'Please take a seat.' She pointed to a chair positioned at an angle in front of a large desk. A computer screen glowed, facing her.

'Thank you,' I said, sitting down.

She went straight to the point. 'For your mother, wasn't it? The place you are looking for?'

'Yes,' I confirmed, tension bulging in me.

'You're from England?'

'Yes.'

'You still living there?'

'Yes. That's why I'm looking for care for my mother. I think I told you on the phone. She has Alzheimer's.'

'I have to say.' She smiled, and lowered her voice. 'I thought you was a fancy white lady, over the phone.'

'Oh. Oh, really?' I chuckled. People often made that comment about my telephone voice here.

'I hope you will find St Patrick's suitable for her.'

'I hope so.'

'We're not a very large care home, but you will see we have plenty of room for expansion.' She went on to tell me more about the facility. How many rooms they had, the age range of residents, and the kind of care they provided. Then she picked up her pen. 'How old is your mother?'

I told her, and explained what kind of support Mum would

need, her habits, moods, level of confusion and short-term memory span. Doubt started to spread inside me as I listed them.

'I see,' she kept repeating, jotting the occasional word down as I spoke. Then when I came to a stop: 'What kind of room would you want for her? Own bathroom, or shared?'

Making Mum share a bathroom when she'd spent so many years with her own would have amounted to lowering her standard of living. Like taking her back to our rented room in Haringey. I couldn't do that to her. 'Oh. Own bathroom,' I said.

'Okay. Well, let's take a look around, uh?' Mrs Paul grabbed a set of keys off her desk.

'I... I have a few questions I'd like to ask,' I said.

'That's not a problem,' she said, the keys still in her hand.

I pulled out the piece of paper on which I'd written a list of questions I'd got off the internet, plus a couple of my own.

'As I said on the phone, my mother has Alzheimer's – dementia,' I said, and asked if there were any other residents there with the condition.

'Aamm... dementia? Yes, of course.'

I continued going through my list.

'And my last one,' I said, 'is about the fees.'

'For a room with shower and toilet, it would work out as $2,300.'

'EC?'

'Yes. Eastern Caribbean.' Mrs Paul straightened her back. 'And you would need to pay it monthly. In advance.'

'Right.' I quietly exhaled, mentally calculating what that would translate to in pounds. 'Okay.' Close to six hundred, at the current exchange rate.

'You ready to see the rooms now?'

'Er... Uh-huh.' I nodded and stood up to follow her.

'We'll start at the top.'

The anticipation as we walked out of her office to begin

the tour around the building took me back years, to when I was going through my list of primary schools, then later secondary, in search of the best one for Millie. A place where my chatty, creative, and sometimes bossy daughter would fit in, make friends and learn in a safe and happy environment. The same anxiety I'd experienced then, was stirring in me now.

Mrs Paul and I stepped outside and I glanced at the grassy lawn on each side of the building, thick shrubs on the outskirts of the grounds.

Was I really doing this? Considering a care home for Mum? Would they be able to manage her craziness and extreme behaviour? Would she be happy here?

'There are eight rooms on each floor,' Mrs Paul explained, as we took the stairs. 'But only two of the units currently available have their own bathroom and toilet.'

'Is there a lift?' I asked, noticing a ramp on the side of the building.

She said there wasn't. 'None of our residents need it and we manage well with the ramp.' At the top of the stairs, she unlocked a metal door.

Most of the rooms were open, but the majority of the residents were inactive. Sitting on a chair close to the entrance of their rooms, by their beds or lying down.

I asked if there was a communal area.

'You mean the dining room?'

'Where they can socialise with each other,' I said.

'Yes, but we find they prefer to be close to their rooms.'

'And what kinds of group activities do they do?'

'If they show a special interest in something, like drawing, painting and such, we would ask families to bring those in for them.'

What I'd had in mind were group activities – games to help residents have an idea of what day it was, be reminded of who,

and maybe where they were, who each other were. Gardening –
planting seeds and watering them.

All residents sitting outside their rooms were alone. Only
one was talking to another, who was sitting close by her on the
balcony.

'Here's one of the available units,' Mrs Paul said, after we
passed a very elderly lady, seemingly asleep in a chair.

She pushed the door open and began to apologise for the
damp, musty smell inside. The furniture in there was a wooden
bed frame and chair painted in a dark glossy stain. It was hard
to imagine Mum in there. In a little room. A cell of her own.

'This one has been empty for a while,' Mrs Paul said.

I peered into the toilet and shower area, where a mop was
sitting in a metal bucket.

'Dat shouldn't be there,' she said, from behind me.

Someone, maybe Mrs Paul, should have checked the rooms
before I arrived. Mould was growing between some of the tiles.
If Mum was going to be in here, I'd insist on the walls and floor
being steamed cleaned. But the view from the window was the
Caribbean Sea in full display. It was a lovely spot for any kind
of home.

Mrs Paul informed me that some residents chose to bring
their own curtains or blinds.

'That's nice,' I said.

She locked the door behind us and stopped in front of a
very elderly lady sitting in a chair, whose eyes flicked open
when Mrs Paul, in a voice I might use to use to engage a shy
four-year-old, said: 'Hello. Good morning, Mrs Emanuel.'

Mrs Emanuel stared up at her impassively.

'Well,' Mrs Paul turned her attention back to me, 'let's take
a look at the next unit.'

I glanced back at Mrs Emanuel. Eyes closed again.

We passed the kitchen, where two members of staff parted,
abandoning the conversation they'd been having.

'Can I see the communal area?' I asked Mrs Paul.

'You mean the dining room?'

'Where everyone gets together for things,' I said.

'Oh, yes. It's just here.'

It was a light room, close to the kitchen with yellow walls, cream floor tiles, wall lights and armchairs arranged against the wall. The dining table and chairs were set to the right. A few more seats were dotted around the veranda with a truly soothing view of the sea.

We moved on to the second room on offer to Mum. The only difference I could see between this one and the one on the level above was the smell, which was of wet concrete.

Mrs Paul had mentioned, before opening the door, that they'd recently had some work done in there. 'The painter is due in next week, but I am showing it to you just so you can see the difference in size from the one upstairs,' she said. 'You said your mother was mobile? She's able to walk – move around?'

'Yes.' I nodded. If only she knew how active Mum could be.

The view from this side of the building were layers of hills, vegetation and houses in the distance. Still beautiful. But how long, after painting, would it take for the mustiness to leave?

The occupied rooms I'd glanced into had looked drab, with faded pastel-coloured walls and dark dull furniture. And when answering the questions from my list, Mrs Paul had said their staffing levels were roughly one to every three residents, but I didn't see any evidence of that.

Do most of the residents come here to die?

Mrs Paul said some were taken out on day trips – to the beach or shopping, and to spend short spells visiting family. A touching idea, that would mean Mum being able to see and be with Auntie outside of visiting hours. Cousin Headley could pick her up, take her to spend a night or a couple of days with her. And I could arrange to have care for both of them on those days so it would be easier on Auntie. We could do the same when I came down.

Given Mum's track record, leaving her in St Patrick's would be easier than arranging for her to have care at home. There'd be fewer risks of arrangements breaking down. Mum might give the carers in the home a hard time, but she couldn't send them packing, like she'd done with the last two I'd arranged for her.

'Well, what do you think?' Mrs Paul said, after we'd walked around the lovely grounds.

I couldn't lie nor be too honest. 'It's... it's not bad,' I said, though I wished I could be a fly on the wall to get a better sense of everything. Had I come at a bad time? Or was this how it always was with the residents? 'I'll discuss it with the family.'

'Of course. Call me if you have any more questions.'

I thought of nothing else on the way home. Problem was, I couldn't even discuss it with Auntie. At least not right away. My guilt over not telling her about today's visit would have to stay with me until I'd made my final decision, which wasn't going to be straightforward.

CHAPTER TWENTY

'So, what was it like?' Millie's voice was brisk.

I'd called her when I got back to fill her in on the visit. 'Not too bad, I suppose,' I said, hesitating.

'Is it good enough for Nannie? That's what we need to decide.'

'I don't know. It's hard.'

'What would you give it out of ten?'

'Mmm.' I hadn't been assessing it through numbers. 'Er... seven – maybe.'

'No higher?' Her tone told me she was disappointed, but I'd be lying if I'd said an eight or above.

'Don't think so,' I said, visualising the little rooms Mrs Paul had shown me.

'It's not a lot.'

'But it's the best on the island.'

'And not quite good enough.'

'I'd put her there if I needed to.'

'But don't you?'

'Well...' I reflected, briefly, on the word 'need'. 'Not quite yet. Let's see how things go.'

'Pity you couldn't take pictures.'

'Doubt they would have allowed me,' I said, though I hadn't thought of that.

'That's true. This is one of the times when I feel I'm in the wrong business. They need decent homes – really good care homes, down there.'

'Telling me.'

'So what're you going to do?'

'We'll leave it for now.' I was tired of talking about it. 'See how things go. At least I know it's there and what it's like.'

'It's up to you, at the end of the day.'

She was right. Mum, nor Auntie, got to choose. It was all on me. Unfair, really, on many levels, but we couldn't change that.

'It's not what she would have wanted,' I said.

'But situations change, don't they, Mum? Plus, this home's in St Lucia. Not here, in England. You hadn't discussed that bit with her.'

'I know.' It was a depressing subject.

'And I don't want to be mean, but Nannie's old. She's had her life and you've got your job and everything.'

'I'll have to think about it.'

'It's either that, get new carers in, or hope the tablets will work and she'll be able to travel.'

'Mmm.' I sighed.

'Nannie's lucky to have you there for her. Someone who loves her, and who'll make the best decision for her.'

'I know,' I said.

Millie paused. 'What's your gut feeling?'

'Well... ideally, I'd like to be able to leave her in the home for a year or so. And get back to work. I could monitor things – you know...'

'That sounds—'

My bedroom door pushed open. 'Hold on, Millie.'

Auntie Barbara was standing in the doorway, glaring at me.

'So dat's what you-all planning? To put Ione – your mudder – in a home?'

'Is that Auntie?' Millie asked, lowering her voice as if Auntie could hear her.

'Yeah… Let me… I'll have to call you back,' I said, my quivering fingers breaking the connection, as I faced Auntie Barbara's rage. How much had she heard?

'You mean to say in dat little time you here, you already go an' find a home to put Ione in?'

'I only wanted to see what it was like, Auntie,' I said.

'A home?' Auntie's voice rose to a scream. Mum wasn't with her, so she had to be somewhere inside. 'A *home*, Erica? You would put Ione in a home? *Mé ou sa visyèze*. But you're such a hypocrite. *Mésyé!*' she added the Kwéyòl word for surprise.

'What is going on here?' Mum was at the door.

I stared at Auntie, eyes begging her to let it go. 'It's all right, Mum,' I said. 'Me and Auntie are just talking.'

'I don't believe dis. *Mésyé!*' Auntie paused, before looking at Mum. 'She planning to put you in a home, Ione.'

'I… I was just—'

Auntie walked out onto the veranda, Mum following behind her.

'You know yourself dat Englan' is de best place for Ione,' Auntie shouted. 'An' in dat little time you reach here, you already planning how you can leave her in a home.'

Mum looked at me, startled and confused. 'Englan'?' she said. 'I not going to Englan'.'

'You would rather go in a home, Ione?' Auntie's voice broke off as if she was close to tears.

'I might not be able to take her to England, Auntie. The doctor said.'

'When? When de doctor tell you dat?'

'What you-all—'

'Don't listen to her, Mum. You're upsetting her,' I told Auntie.

'I know what I hear! What you planning!' Auntie headed out of the gate, still shouting.

'What's going on?' Mum said. I stepped off the veranda. 'Where you going?'

'Nowhere. Just in...' I fought against the urge to bolt out of there. Past Auntie. Escape from the confusion find clarity – a way to calm things down. But Mum. I couldn't leave her there – not like this. 'Just in the garden,' I said.

'I coming. We picking mangoes?' she said.

'If you like.' I wiped my eyes and walked towards the *kali*.

Tears trickled down my face as I yanked each mango from its stalk.

'What happen to you an' your auntie?' Mum asked, taking another mango from me to add to the pile on the ground. 'Why you-all quarrelling like dat?'

'It's just a misunderstanding,' I said.

'About me?'

'Yes.'

'I'm not going to England, eh,' she warned.

'I know, Mum. You said.'

'We can't eat all of dese mangoes. We can give some to de girl living over dere.'

'Claire,' I said, glad she'd changed the subject.

'An' dat lady dere.' She pointed at the Wilsons' house. We took the mangoes inside. I washed them and Mum picked a couple to eat. 'We'll eat outside?'

'If you like.' I shrugged.

'How many you want?'

I'm not hungry,' I said.

'How you mean? Since when you have to be hungry to eat mango Pal Louis? Dat's your favourite mango. Why you think I plant it?'

'Because of me?'

'Of course.'

I fought back more tears. She hadn't told me this before.

The full stomach sent Mum off to her room to rest, leaving me time to get back to Millie, who'd texted to ask if things were all right.

It's fine, I texted back. *I'll sort it.*

But the earlier annoyance hadn't left me. I called Delia and relayed the whole thing to her.

'Oh, no,' she said. 'Can't you just go up there and speak to her? Explain that you hadn't made a decision yet?'

I told her I didn't see the point and didn't want to end up having another row. 'She's annoyed that I'm even considering putting Mum into a care home. The fact that I've found one's made it even worse.'

'Oh, dear.'

'You know how that generation can be stuck in their ways.'

'So you haven't heard anything from her since she stormed off?'

'No.'

'But you will. You've got your mum, who you both love, in your care. She has to have contact with you, if she wants to see her sister. I know how that works.'

Delia had been through a horrible separation from her husband. It had taken years before they had settled into an agreed routine allowing him access to their two boys.

How weird, that Mum had become this child... and one I hadn't given birth to.

It was just me and Mum for the rest of the day. All the self-reassurances after my conversation with Delia didn't stop me from imagining what Auntie must have been thinking about me: I was a big, fat, let-down to her sister. A daughter with no heart. But *she* was the one being unreasonable by expecting me to give up everything that mattered to me, aside from Mum, just like that, because Mum had Alzheimer's.

After Mum's diagnosis, I'd promised to be there for her. That we'd face the challenge together. But I hadn't anticipated these complications: her being in St Lucia and not able to travel; nor had I expected her condition to bring on this scary, unpredictable stuff – behaviour she couldn't help and I couldn't manage.

But she had been more amicable today. Maybe the new tablets were already calming her down.

I kissed her cheek. 'Goodnight, Mum.'

'Good night, *ich mwen*,' she replied.

'I love you.' The unplanned words spilled from my mouth.

'I love you too, *ich mwen*,' she replied, her voice soft and endearing.

With Mum in bed, I got the notebook and pen I'd bought earlier from my bag, and instead of the observation notes I'd planned, began writing, 'Mum...'

I took a deep breath and put the book away. Fixed my usual drink and went to sit outside. All lights were out in Claire's house. A rhythm was floating through the air. Where could it be coming from? A bar, across the bay, in Micoud? Friday night limes, hook-ups with friends. I could be part of something like that. Take Millie's advice and Claire's offer to go to the fish-fry. And stop sitting here alone, every night watching over Mum.

I focused on the beat, my hips moving from side to side on the seat as I tried to place the song perforating the air. I'd have to carve out a space for a little fun.

CHAPTER TWENTY-ONE

The anti-psychotic drug gave Mum a daytime drowsiness; made her movements and processing slower. She seemed less with us than before, more childlike. Dependent. Confused. But every time I thought about stopping it, fear of the alternative – what we'd had to manage before – convinced me it was for the best.

But was it a price worth paying in the hope that she'd stop being aggressive towards me? Cooperate? Stop asking for and seeing people who weren't there? Stop packing to leave and wanting to go 'home'? Were my hopes and expectations too high?

'Morning.' Her eyes met mine, peeking at her in the bathroom.

'You getting washed?' I said.

'Mmm.' It was easier to get her in the shower now.

I made her bed, put an outfit on it for her, and told her to come for breakfast when she was ready. It was cornflakes today.

She came out looking like she could do with more sleep and sat sipping her tea. I poured warm milk in the bowl of cereal. She thanked me and started to eat.

'Fancy going for a drive today?' I said, walking to the sink.

'Okay.'

Auntie hadn't called yet today. No doubt still off with me, but Delia was right. She couldn't avoid me if she wanted contact with Mum.

'We can go after lunch,' I said.

'Mmm. I...'

'What?' I looked at her. An odd expression was forming on her face. I leaned in closer to her, unnerved by the sight of her eyelids flicking rapidly up and down, the build-up of sweat on her cheeks and forehead. 'Mum? Mum? You okay?' Her head became floppy, eyes half-closed. 'Mum? Mum?' I repeated, tapping her cheeks and holding her.

She took three gasping breaths. Each one threatening to be her last.

Panic gripped my insides. 'Oh, my God! Mum!' I looked around, unsure what to do. How could I best help her? If these were her last breaths, I wanted to be with her. If they weren't, I needed to get help. She gasped, again and again. Her skin turned pale and clammy. Her head slumped to the side. What was happening? *An ambulance. I need to call an ambulance.* But what was the damn number? I hadn't a clue. *No. No.* What I feared couldn't happen. Not again.

Each breath she took sounded more shallow.

Don't leave me, Mum. Please don't. Not like this.

'Mum?' I repositioned myself to get a better look as her. She straightened up. Yellow liquid dotted with the cornflakes she'd already swallowed spewed from her mouth onto her lap and the floor. 'Oh, my God, Mum?' More liquid dripped from her mouth. Her head flopped to the side again. The balls of her eyes moved slowly from right to left. Her face became cold, body slightly rigid. 'Mum? Mum?' She was alive. Still breathing.

Trembling, I rushed to the phone to call Auntie. 'I think Mum's just had a stroke,' I said.

'A stroke?'

'She passed out. Fainted.'

'She fall?'

'No, but I have to take her to the hospital. What's the number? For an ambulance, Auntie?'

'Nine, one, one,' Auntie said. Then, more emphatically: 'Nine, one, one. I coming.'

Another ten minutes, and Mum seemed almost back, though too weak to stand on her own, so I shouldered most of her weight. As I walked her to her bedroom, I noticed she'd wet herself. In the middle of me washing and changing her, the ambulance men called, asking for specific instructions to the house. Twenty minutes later, when Auntie arrived and I was toying with the idea of getting a cab, they pulled in through the gates.

'Ione?' Auntie was saying, as I explained what had happened to the ambulance men.

Mum looked drawn and weak.

The men said only one person could come in the ambulance with her, so Auntie stayed behind.

All I could think of all the way to the hospital was whether the anti-psychotic tablet had had anything to do with this. God, Mum could have died.

The hospital was a state, by English standards: the floor and chairs were grimy; it was in dire need of renovation. *What sort of care would Mum get in here?*

After triage, they showed us into a cubicle with rusty taps. Mum was lying on a threadbare sheet that made me wonder how clean it was. A nursing assistant came in, made three attempts at hooking Mum up to an ECG machine then left, saying it wasn't working. I looked at Mum, relieved she was alive, but having second thoughts about having brought her here.

She started to shiver from the cold air coming through the AC unit above our heads. 'You cold, Mum?' I asked.

She nodded.

I apprehended a nurse and asked for something to cover Mum with. The sheet she brought was worn as well, but would have to do.

I looked around the room, not wanting to touch anything for fear of germs. My inclination was to get us both out of there, but to where? It was best to at least get Mum seen to, get confirmation of what she'd had. A stroke, seizure, or had she just passed out? I hoped someone would be able to explain.

Another nurse got the machine to work and, an hour later, I saw a Dr Fredrick, who explained that Mum had indeed had a small stroke. He couldn't tell me if it was because of the Alzheimer's or the medication she was on and suggested I discussed it with the doctor who'd prescribed it.

'This might not have been the first,' he said, 'but only a brain scan could confirm that. Small strokes can lead to major ones,' he reminded me.

I got a cab to take us home, put Mum in the shower and while she was getting dressed, called Auntie to tell her we were back.

'Dey sen' her home?' she asked.

'Yeah. There wasn't much they could do,' I said.

'*Pòdjab*, poor devil, Ione. But why all dese things happening to her?'

'I don't know, Auntie. The doctor said it might be the condition.'

'Where dat condition – Alsymuss sickness, come from?'

'God knows, Auntie. Wish we could send it back.'

After so many years in a crappy relationship with Mr Frank,

why couldn't Mum be allowed a peaceful old age? It was hard to believe that all of the strain and pressure of staying with him hadn't contributed to her ending up with dementia.

Signs of her unhappiness after they moved to St Lucia had been obvious, way before Auntie had filled me in on what she called Mr Frank's 'nasty ways'.

The dampening of Mum's excitement, had coincided with a change in Mr Frank's behaviour. The first few times Millie and I had visited, he'd occasionally invite Mum and us along with him to bars and beach events. But in the last few years before he became ill, he'd take off on his own, leaving Mum to activities with us, which didn't bother me until I saw the disappointment on her face when he went off, dressed up smelling sweetly of aftershave.

And it was no surprise to me when I learnt that he'd found it impossible to resist, or fell victim to, the young women searching for someone – anyone – who could alleviate their hardships.

Older returnee men, with their foreign currencies were ideal candidates for exchanges of sex for a good time and cash. And what an ego boost for Mr Frank, and the others like him, who would normally never have got pretty young women showing that kind of interest in them. Age, marital status or life partners meant nothing to these young women; their focus was on fun and finances. And what started off for Mr Frank as offers of a few drinks and a chicken meal to a twenty-two-year-old he'd met in a bar, evidently developed into a full-blown affair.

'De chile can pass for his own – even gran-chile,' Auntie had said, when she'd filled me in on his antics. '*Pòdjab*, Ione.'

'She should leave him,' I said.

'I tired talking to Ione,' Auntie said. 'An' a ole man like Frank cannot see de... de way he an' de rest of dose ole men behaving – dat kind of involvement with chil'ren is nasty. I tell

Ione long ago, he can bring any kind of sickness for her. Nasty.'
She pursed her lips.

Mum hadn't got the fresh start she'd hoped coming back home with Mr Frank would have brought.

CHAPTER TWENTY-TWO

I made some fresh cinnamon and ginger tea for Mum and encouraged her to have a lie-down.

Even in this short space of time, her health needs had been mounting. Moving from Alzheimer's with no underlying health issues, into a world of antipsychotic drugs, strokes, alongside decline. A mini nightmare was materialising in my head.

Knots began forming in my chest, at the sound of Auntie's voice outside. Was she here to cast more blame, or simply anxious to see her sister? She'd brought us some lunch, which I took as a peace offering.

'I say you won't have time to cook with all dat up an' down you been doing with Ione,' she said, entering the kitchen.

I thanked her and took the bag.

'It's nothing. Rice an' chicken. It's jus' for you an' Ione. I eat a little already.'

The smell set my stomach rumbling.

'Mum's lying down.' I didn't much like the idea of eating in the bedrooms, but Mum had been through enough, so I told Auntie I'd bring the meal in for Mum.

I didn't care what the doctor in the hospital had said. I'd

make an appointment to see Dr Peres to see if she could put Mum on something else, and wasn't going to give Mum any more of those anti-psychotic drugs. But I didn't say anything to Auntie about it.

She kept us company for most of what was left of the afternoon, and to satisfy my need for adult conversation with someone who understood the real me, after she left, I texted Delia asking if she was free to talk.

Ten minutes passed. And whilst I was preparing our supper, the phone rang.

'Hi, Mum.' Millie's voice sounded lifted. 'He's done it,' she said. 'The test.'

'Oh, great! When do you get the results?'

'I'm not sure. Think it's next week.'

'Let's hope it comes up negative.'

With the phone lodged between my ear and shoulder, so I could continue cooking, we chatted a bit about what was going on with Millie, then I filled her in on the last event.

'Gosh, poor Nannie,' she said. 'That had to be scary for both of you.'

'I swear I thought she was going to die.'

'Don't suppose you've decided on the care home yet?'

'No, but I can't see me getting twenty-four-hour care for her anywhere else but in a home.' I paused. 'Hold on. I think she's coming.' I glanced down the corridor, thinking I'd heard a hum, but didn't see anyone.

'You can only do the best you can.'

'I know.' *The best I can* and *the right decision*. The two statements repeated in my head. We said goodbye and I went straight to Mum's room, to check on her.

She wasn't there. 'Mum?' I called out, then doubled back to my bedroom. The door was wide open, but she wasn't in there either. Nor on the veranda. 'Mum?' I called out again, this time directing my call out towards the garden. There was a rustle of wind through the trees, bird songs, a faint sound of traffic in the distance, but no sight of Mum or response to my calls.

I went back inside, searched through the house again, putting my head in the spare room, but Mum wasn't there.

Searching around the garden was fruitless. She was nowhere.

The gate. Shit. I hadn't locked it after Auntie left. I stepped out of it, looked up and down the road, then ran up to the cross-road at the brow of the hill. No sign of Mum. Only a grey cat sauntering from one side of the road to the shade under a palm tree.

If she's gone far beyond the gate, she's probably taking a familiar route. Maybe to Auntie's.

I hurried back to the house, heart pounding, clothes damp with sweat, thoughts pinging this way and that in my head. Where could she be? I prayed she'd be there when I got in and called her name again, running through the house, checking behind wardrobe doors and bathrooms again. Nothing.

I grabbed the phone. 'Auntie!' Panic and fear had done away with my manners. 'Is Mum with you? I can't find her. She's gone,' I said, stifling the urge to cry. 'I don't know where she is.' I couldn't breathe.

'What you mean?'

'Is she with you?' I let out a breath as a tear slid down my face.

'No.' The word stretched long and heavy against my ear. 'But how you mean, you don't know where she is?'

'I don't.' This couldn't be happening. Neighbours? Except for Mrs Andrews, Mum only exchanged pleasantries with them, especially now that her condition had deteriorated. I'd only told Mrs Andrews and Claire about her diagnosis. Others would get to find out in time, I was sure, although they would have already heard the screaming and shouting coming from here, seen some of the commotion when she became persistent with 'going home'. They'd definitely know things weren't right with her and that *that* 'thing' was to do with her brain. If she'd gone to any of them, they'd be polite, but would have seen her back home. 'I'll see you later,' I said, and hung up.

I locked the house and went across to the Wilsons'. The dogs barked until I went away. No one came out so there wasn't likely to be anyone there.

Old Mrs Humphrey's gate was locked. I shouted a few, 'Good afternoons.' No one responded.

Mrs Andrews hadn't seen Mum either, but said she'd let me know if she came across her.

A glimpse of someone approaching the gate stilled me to a skipped heartbeat. Then hope shrivelled in my chest. It was Auntie.

She bustled towards me. 'You still don't see her?'

I shook my head. 'I'll have to report it to the police.' Where could Mum be? Soon it would be getting dark.

'I call Headley an' leave message for him. But how Ione manage to leave de house without you know?' Auntie looked me.

'I... I left her in her bedroom. I... I was just there in the kitchen talking to Millie.'

'You din lock de gate after me?'

I shook my head. 'I didn't think.'

'You din hear me shout for you to lock it?'

'No.'

'Erica – you know already you have to make sure de gate always lock.'

'Auntie, I told you I—'

'So what we going to do?'

'I just said, I have to call the police. Right now.'

'*Bondyé*,' Auntie said, as I walked away.

The person who answered the phone gave me a name I didn't grasp. 'How long has she been missing?' she asked.

'I'm not exactly sure,' I said. 'About an hour or so, I think.'

'But that's short.'

I explained that Mum had dementia, her level of confusion, and the likelihood that she might get lost. 'That's why I'm worried.'

'And you're sure you don't know where she could be.'

'I've looked everywhere I could think of right now,' I said.

'It would be better if you come in an' made an official report.'

The indifference in her voice agitated me, fuelled my frustration and sense of powerlessness gnawing at me.

I asked Auntie to stay at the house. 'Just in case she comes home.'

She suggested I waited for Cousin Headley. 'It will be quicker if he drop you.'

But I couldn't. Every second that passed with me not knowing where Mum was, cultivated more fear, more agonising thoughts of where she might be; and the risk increased that something terrible would happen to her. I had to be active – doing something about finding her.

I hastened along to the police station, my stomach churning. *It will turn out fine. It will turn out fine*, I told myself, thoughts taking me back to that day in England, when she was staying with me and I'd come in late from work and found she wasn't there.

She loved a window-shopping spree, visiting markets, looking at trinkets, clothes. That kind of thing gave her pleasure. So I'd assumed that was where she'd gone. But it was late. I'd called her phone and heard it ringing in her bedroom. I called her friend, Mrs Gooding, but Mum wasn't with her. At minutes to seven, I started to panic.

Mum wasn't likely to be with her, without me knowing, but to be sure, I'd called Millie.

'Where could she be?' Millie said.

'No idea. She couldn't still be looking around the shops.'

'No. Not at this time. She hates being out at night on her own.'

'I know,' I said.

'I'm coming over.'

I had called other relatives in case Mum had gone to visit them. No one had seen her.

Frantic, I'd called the police. Millie arrived just before them. They asked for a description of Mum, things to help them recognise her. I told them about the calls I'd already made and they left, promising to do the best they could to find her.

Visions of Mum being raped, attacked and left for dead somewhere raced through my mind. Was this how her life was going to end?

Not long after the police left, the phone rang. 'Hello,' a man at the end of the phone said. He was calling from Paddington station. 'We have a lady here. Name's Ione – Ione Joseph.'

'My mum. She's my mum. She's with you?' I exhaled.

I couldn't get there fast enough.

'This can't ever happen again,' I'd told Millie.

But four years on, here we were again.

She couldn't have been alone for more than ten minutes and I'd stayed close to her room the whole time. How could she, in that short time, have managed to slip out without me noticing? If only I'd locked that blasted gate. But I hadn't heard Auntie ask me to lock it – she had keys to everywhere too, and I'd assumed she'd do it. Why hadn't *she*?

If the gate had been locked, Mum would be safe at home and everything would be normal.

Alzheimer's normal.

I'd filled out the tedious Missing Person's form in triplicate, reiterating what I'd explained to the officer over the phone. Put crosses in boxes, described her: height, eyes, complexion, hair length and what she was probably wearing.

'We will call you as soon as we have any news, but in the meantime,' the officer said, 'keep asking the neighbours and looking around. The more people we have looking for her, the more it's likely we'll find her.'

I was thanking the sergeant when Cousin Headley and Auntie walked into the station.

'Do your bes' to find her for us, please,' Auntie told the sergeant.

'Of course,' she replied.

We drove around Micoud first, asking whether anyone had seen Mum. Popped into shops, where the local shop-keepers actually knew her, but no one had seen her. Not that day. We did the same in Dennery, asking people hanging around the fish market, bars, on the streets. No one had seen her.

'What if she caught a bus to Vieux Fort?' I said, perturbed.

'What she going an' do in Vieux Fort?' Auntie said.

'You never know.' My mind took me back to the time in England when she'd mistaken her stop and hadn't a clue where she was or how to make her way to me. 'You just never know,' I repeated.

'She could have go to Castries too,' Cousin Headley said, his voice low and sad. 'But it getting late already. Let us check Vieux Fort. We will have to do Castries tomorrow, if nobody find her by dat time.'

We hadn't covered everywhere in Vieux Fort, but the shops were closing now. Most of the people we asked had eyed us sceptically, then shook their heads. Everyone saying no, they hadn't seen her.

Back in Cousin Headley's bus, we sat in silence, tired, drained. Worried. The smell of the salt from the sea as we drove along the main road, before passing the airport, planted more frightening thoughts in my mind. Could Mum have wandered close to there?

Heading to Castries in the morning in the hope of finding her was a long shot. How likely was she to be walking about for all of that time? Castries was the main town, but pretty dead late at night, after the shops were shut and stall holders were gone.

'We better take Auntie home,' I said. 'Eh, Auntie.' I rubbed her shoulder. 'You must be tired.'

'I'm all right,' she said.

I wished I could console her, say something that would give her a smidgen of hope. I was trying to find and hold on to that myself.

She was probably still blaming me for all of this.

'You want to stay over with me tonight, Auntie?'

'Uh-uh.' She shook her head.

'I will stay with her,' Cousin Headley said, glancing at Auntie Barbara. I'd given her the front seat and taken Mum's usual spot, directly behind her. 'Dat's all right, Cousin?'

'Yes, because I don't think I will sleep tonight,' Auntie said, her voice fading into a murmur.

'You can come an' stay with us too.' Cousin Headley turned slightly to address me. 'Eh?' he asked Auntie.

'No. No,' I said, before she could respond. 'I'll stay home in case... in case Mum comes home.'

Silence sat rigidly with us for the rest of the journey. We approached the house, and I searched for signs of light. Nothing. I sighed.

'We will see you in the morning, eh?' Cousin Headley said, pulling up outside the gate.

I slide the door open and got out.

'Let's pray we find her tomorrow,' he said.

Tomorrow? 'Mmm,' I said, my hand still on the door. *Why wait until then?* 'What about if we went to Castries now?'

Cousin Headley hesitated and glanced at Auntie. 'Now?'

'Now?' she echoed, leaning forward.

'Anything can happen to her out there between now and tomorrow.'

'I.... You think she would find herself quite in Castries?' Auntie said.

'She'd only have to take one bus ride,' I said.

'Let me drop Cousin Barbara first. Eh, Cousin?'

The disappointment and gloom on Auntie's face nudged at my guilt.

'I'm so sorry, Auntie,' I said. 'I should have... I—'

'Go inside an' check she hasn' come back,' Cousin Headley said. 'When you finish, phone me an' I will come an' meet you for us to go.'

Auntie leaned back in her seat.

'Thanks,' I told Cousin Headley.

The gate was ajar – the way I'd left it for Mum, in the hope that she might find her way home. A vision of her sitting on the veranda waiting for me to let her in fleeted through my mind. The disquieting darkness told me those visions were fantasies. All in vain. But I searched through the house again anyway, switching on every light, exposing every corner.

Minutes later, Cousin Headley was at the gate.

'You still want to go?' he said, before I got in.

Castries would be around an hour's drive, if the traffic was light. But it was six-thirty. Rush hour wasn't over yet.

'You... you don't think it's worth it?' I said.

'I'm not saying dat, but – come on. Let's go.' He beckoned me with his head.

I got in. 'You're not too tired, are you?' I was desperate to find Mum, but didn't want to force him to drive all that way tired.

'Who me? No.'

His eyes said different. He was going for the same reason as me – to be doing something to help find Mum. His beloved cousin.

'It's a bit heavy, isn't it?' I said, as we joined the traffic heading north.

'What to do?' He shrugged.

'I feel so bad about all of this.'

'Mistakes does happen. Especially when we have too much on our mind.'

'And we've left Auntie there on her own, when she really needs company.'

'It's too late for her to come with us,' he said.

'She's annoyed with me. I wasn't in her good books even before all of this.' I told him about our clash over me visiting the care home. 'She thinks I intend to put Mum in there, but I just wanted to see what was possible. And now, Mum's gone missing, all because of me.'

I prattled on, with Cousin Headley giving the odd response, to confirm that he was listening.

Finally, maybe to shut me up, he said, 'Don't worry so much about what other people think. God alone can judge your actions. An' as long as you know you don't intend any wrong in your heart for your mudder. As for me, I find you doing everything you can for her.'

'I am – I mean, I do,' I said, nodding.

'Let's pray we find her safe, eh?'

'Mmm.' All I was doing was clinging to hope.

"Welcome to Denier Riviere", the roadside sign said. Traffic was thinning, but we still had a way to go.

The last time I made this journey, I was in this very seat next to Cousin Headley with Mum sitting safely behind us. My concerns then had been about the new medication the doctor had prescribed for her.

Her disappearance had left a gaping hole. A worry that

grew deeper with each minute, hour that passed without a sign or word of where she might be.

We followed the traffic around the mountain at Barre de L'isle. Views I'd taken pleasure in over and over again. Looking down into the dense darkening forest now unnerved me. Where could Mum be?

'You think we'll find her?' I said. The thought was pressing on my brain.

'Who can say? We trying.'

'Mmm.'

We drove along the bouncy two-lane road they called the Millennium High Way, central Castries now minutes ahead of us.

'Start to look out for her,' Cousin Headley said.

Shouldn't we have been doing that earlier? She could have got off a bus on route to Castries. Why hadn't I thought of that?

Outside the light was dim, unlike when we'd searched for her in Vieux Fort.

Cousin Headley drove to all the bus stands first. I jumped out, peering inside buses, checking everyone's face, heart sinking when someone I imagined might be her turned out not to be.

Each time I returned, head hanging.

'No?'

I shook my head and got back in.

We drove on, parked by Derek Walcott Square and walked around the nearby streets. Drunks and vagrants put their hands out for 'change'. We ignored them. The market was closed, but we went in anyway. Our only encounter was a rat running out of a dark corner, forcing me to shriek and grab Cousin Headley's arm.

By the time we got back to the car and started driving around again, there were less people about. We passed eating places and bars all closed up for the day. One, Cousin Headley told me was a popular rum shop, was still open. A group of men ranging from mine to Cousin Headley's age stood close to three long wooden tables and benches by the entrance.

'Is mainly drunk people you will find in dere,' he said. 'But you stay here. Let me take a look.'

I watched him make his way past the tables, throwing a glance at the two people slouched over one of them, heads face-down over their arm. He disappeared inside.

Mum wouldn't be in that kind of place, but it was worth a look. Cousin Headley reappeared, hands in his pockets. He glanced up and down the road, then took his time getting back to the minibus. I didn't need to ask any questions.

We drove on passed three young men hanging out on the corner of a street, jesting, laughing, sipping from bottles of local beer.

'What you think?' Cousin Headley said.

It was minutes before nine.

'What about up there?' I said, pointing towards a bridge on our right.

'Dat taking us out of town.'

I sighed. 'Might as well go home then.' Though, for me, the search wasn't over. Every sighting of anyone I thought might be Mum, brought an inkling of hope.

We drove the bulk of the journey home in silence until a bump in the road jolted me. 'Huh.'

'You sleeping?' Cousin Headley said.

'Not really.' But I had nodded off.

'We will soon be home.'

I wiped the side of my mouth. 'Thank you so much for taking me.'

'We try our bes'. An' we can look again tomorrow, but by then, I hope de police already find her.'

'Me too. You still going back to Auntie's?'

'Yes. I have a key,' Cousin Headley said.

CHAPTER TWENTY-THREE

He dropped me off. The dark house confirming, once again, that Mum wasn't back. I wandered around, less expectant. Sinking deeper into sadness, I fingered small things in her bedroom: her comb, the headscarf she tied her head with before going to bed, face cream, the coconut oil she rubbed on her skin after a shower. The engrained scent of joss sticks she believed cleansed her home, that I'd tried and failed to air from her room. Everything was as it had been when I left. I sat on her bed. Glanced around the space I struggled to keep tidy and that she continuously rummaged through looking for things she believed were missing. 'Where are you, Mum?'

Pushing back frightful thoughts worming their way into my head, I gave way to tears.

Minutes slipped by. I sighed and left her room pulling the door shut behind me.

After a long, warm shower, I fixed myself a snack and was staring out of the window in my room again. At Micoud, beyond the dark patch over the bay. Could Mum be down there, in the village somewhere, unnoticed? Undetected? Wherever she was, she could have a lucid moment where she'd know what she needed to do. Ask someone for help. She knew how to do that.

My half-nibbled snack of crackers and cheese and glass of rum and Coke was doing little to comfort me. I went to sit on the veranda.

In the distance, dogs barked. Whistling frogs screeched.

It was mid-week. After ten here. England being five hours ahead of us meant Millie, Delia, pretty much everyone, would be in the depths of sleep.

No lights in Claire's house suggested she was at work or out with friends. I wouldn't intrude.

A strong breeze made me shudder. I sniffed, was about to lean back in my seat, when I heard a rattle at the gate, which was still open. *She's back.* 'Mum—?' I stood up.

'Good night. Good night. Erica? It's me.'

My anticipation that the rattling sound marked an end to the nightmare I was in abruptly left, but Claire's voice and presence brought a different kind of relief. I had company.

'Hey,' she said. 'I hear about your mom.' Then she asked the painful question: 'You-all find her yet?'

'No.' I shook my head.

She joined me on the veranda, sat down and I told her what happened.

'It's my fault. If I'd shut that bloody gate,' I said.

'You mean to say your auntie couldn't jus' lock the gate behind her instead of calling you to come and do it? I don't see dat it's your fault, *on*. And if you forgot, you are only human.'

She was trying to make me feel better, but I had played a part – I had meant to check the gate, but forgot. No matter what logical explanations I, or anyone else, came up with, I'd been irresponsible. If a member of staff let a child slip out of his or her class and that child ended up going through the gates and onto the streets, there'd be hell to pay and I'd be part of that disciplining.

'I just hope the police find her by morning,' I said.

Going over it again with Claire and not being able to think of anything but where Mum could be was draining.

'I hear what you say about the police,' she said, 'but don't let nobody fool you. Try and look for your mother as much as you can.'

'I plan to,' I said.

'Because,' – Claire hesitated – 'I... I don't want to worry you, but St Lucia don't have enough police to spend any long length of time looking for your mom.'

'But—'

'They don't even have enough police vehicles to do what they should be doing.'

'What?' God. Were the services really that bad here? Why couldn't I go to sleep and wake up to find none of this had ever happened?

'I would help you to look, but I have work tomorrow.'

'It's okay,' I said, eyes falling on my plate and glass on the table. 'Do you want something... something to – a drink?'

She settled for water and followed me inside to get it. 'But try not to worry – not many people here would do something bad to a ole lady.'

After she left, I locked up. Lay on my bed with misery and loneliness for company again. Closing my eyes brought more anxiety. When the house phone started ringing, I sprang up. *Please God, let that be the police station.*

'Good evening—?' I said.

'Nothing, eh?'

'Oh, it's you, Cousin.' I couldn't disguise my disappointment.

'Cousin Barbara ask me to check with you, before we go to sleep.'

'Oh. No. Nothing. She's still awake?'

'Yes. Well.' He hesitated. 'We will see tomorrow.'

'Yeah.' I said good night.

Two a.m. And I couldn't stop conjuring up more bad images, sinister thoughts of dangerous places where Mum could be. An old lady wandering around on her own in the dark, unsure of where she was, maybe trying to find her way to that place she considered 'home'. Add to that her vulnerability, confusion, possibility of having a stroke. As much as there were nice people out there, bad ones were in the mix. Thieves, vagrants, drunks like some of those we'd seen in Castries. People like that could harm her. Claire had said it was unlikely that anyone would, but there were always people who might not think twice about taking advantage of others. Especially someone like Mum.

CHAPTER TWENTY-FOUR

A massive roar, I soon realised was thunder, bolted me out of sleep. I opened my eyes into darkness, trying to locate myself. Bad things happened when the weather was like this. Tangled visions from the past and present began to surface.

Memories of the night my little boy died.

Wind rattled the windows. A second blast of thunder came with a charge of lightning so eerie that, on impulse, I reached for something to steady me. I got up, switched on the light, squinting to alleviate the discomfort in my eyes then went to the window. *Ugh.* I was standing in a puddle.

Heavy droplets of water splattered my arms, chest and face as I reached to pull the windows in, shutting out as much as I could of the menace outside.

Mum. Was she somewhere safe from this? My watch said five o'clock. I must have slept because it was almost half three the last time I checked. Then, this whirling wind had only been a shimmering whisper, which must have lulled me to sleep.

I walked around checking other windows. Water had come in through Mum's as well. How long would this weather last? Might it escalate into something more sinister? Dangerous and scary? If a hurricane was coming, surely someone would have told me.

Wet and shivering, I tiptoed back to my room and sat on the bed.

'Where are you, Mum?'

She had to be alive. To be safe.

I needed *her*.

I grew up with no memory of my father, just the knowledge that he'd died when I was ten years old. He never visited. A clear message that he wasn't interested in me. So I didn't miss him as a person.

With Mum, it was different. The cosiness of just me and her, when I was a child brought a close reciprocated love that anchored me.

I'd experienced the pain and anguish the rift between us had caused. I needed her love. She filled a special space in my life that no one else could. Dementia was threatening that now, but I still needed her.

I had to find her. But what could I do at this time? And this weather would make it impossible without a car. I had to sit tight for a few more hours – until I thought Cousin Headley would be up.

I sent a message to Delia. *We can't find Mum*, and lay there, eyes shut, listening for her reply.

She called. 'What were you saying in that text?' she said. 'What's going on?'

'She's missing,' I replied, tears of guilt filling my eyes.

'She went out on her own?'

'Yes.' I sat up, squinting, my back resting on the headboard. 'I was supposed to be watching her, but forgot to lock the gate.' Voicing what had happened intensified again the failure I couldn't suppress or put to bed.

'Oh, God,' Delia said.

'I feel so stupid. What's wrong with me? I keep getting it

wrong.'

'What? What do you mean?'

'Big, important things – life and death things.'

'You're not the only one who makes mistakes. There's always room for error in judgments.'

'I failed Shane. And now I'm doing it again with—'

'Children get sick, Erica,' Delia said, exasperation in her voice. 'And old people with dementia wander off all the time, even in care homes. You have to stop beating yourself up.'

'But it's *my* actions. My actions that make disasters happen, to people I love, when they don't have to. My son. Now my mother. I was in charge – it was a staff ratio of one-to-one, and still I messed up.' I stopped talking so I could breathe.

'Come on, Erica, you know very well that what happened to Shane also happened to many other babies. And they probably all had caring parents who loved them, like you. And with Shane there could have also been that awful sickle cell trait no one knew about. You can't keep blaming yourself for that. I've told you. It wasn't your fault.'

I'd repeated those words in my head, and out loud, for so long. Years go by when I manage to convince myself I'm fine and am over that nightmare. Then something happens: a storm, a thought, an incident like this.

'You've looked everywhere for her?' Delia asked.

'Yes... yes. Almost.' Tears were trickling down my face. 'And now we're in the middle of a... what looks like a storm. Can she survive that – if she's outside – out there, somewhere?'

'You'll find her. Somebody will find her.'

'Alive?' The word left my mouth like a soft breath.

'Of course,' Delia said. 'You have to stay positive, Erica. You have to.'

Delia was always coming up with this positive mind set. Convinced it affected reality. 'Promise me you will.'

'But—'

'She's not likely to be dead after just one night out.'

I wanted to hold on to that thought, but that positive mind-set thing was a challenge for me. 'The storm,' I said. 'If she's—'

'Erica, she might be a little... I don't know, need some caring for, when you find her. But you must believe she'll be alive.'

'Okay. Okay.'

'Listen. I've got to go. I'm out on site. The others are waiting for me.'

'Okay.'

'Good luck with the search. I'll call you later. But call me if you find out anything. Right? Anything.'

'Mmm. I will.'

Delia was the smarter of the two of us. More level-headed, I'd say, despite this mind-set thing. She'd excelled in the sciences, whilst I leaned more towards the arts. She'd graduated in mechanical engineering. There were times when I wished I was more like her.

'Not every cloud is a rain cloud, Erica. Sometimes it's just passing. The sun's hiding just behind it,' she'd often told me. But I found thinking about the downside helped me to prepare for the bad things they bring, before they arrive. It lightens the blow of a horrible surprise.

I reached for a hanky.

'I'll call you later,' Delia repeated. 'Make sure you pick up.'

A streak of light at the window drew me out of bed. I looked up at the bulb in the ceiling. *Are you supposed to keep lights off or on during lightning?*

I left the bedroom and headed for the kitchen to get some soursop tea to help calm my nerves.

I hadn't consciously planned on making the call, but I did: a different sergeant answered and asked when I'd made the report.

'Yesterday,' I said.

'That is only one day. Not even a whole twenty-four hours, from what I'm seeing on the form,' he said.

'I realise that. But I wanted to ask where you'd looked – which areas. And if you're even able to look?'

'Able to look?'

'Yes. Do you have the capacity – the staff? And look at the weather!' I shouted over the sound of unrelenting rainfall and blasts of thunder outside.

'Well, madam, it's our job to look,' the sergeant said. 'But I cannot tell you exactly where officers in the patrol team have looked. Not at this time.'

'So you do have a patrol team?' I asked, aiming to dispel Claire's suggestion that they were too under-resourced to look for Mum.

'Well, of course.'

'And you promise they will be looking, even in this weather? She's been gone all night. Anything could have happened to her. How would she stay out of this rain? There's wind, lightning—' Another clash of thunder roared. 'Did you hear that? She's outside. Out there. Probably scared,' I said.

'We will do our best to find your mother, madam. Even in this weather,' the officer said.

I wanted to believe it. But rain was like snow to Caribbean people – weather they didn't want to be out in for fear of catching a cold.

'It should be in the paper later today or tomorrow too. People will be on the lookout,' the sergeant said.

'Tomorrow?' The tinge of optimism he'd given me was quickly snatched away. 'Well... thank you,' I said.

We *were* going to have to do our own searching.

I called Millie, but she didn't pick up, so I left a message asking her to call. This kind of news couldn't be given through a text or voice message.

The rain hadn't stopped, but it was lighter than earlier. Grey clouds spread over the sky. There wasn't a hint of sun. The wind hadn't completely let up, either. Hopes of Mum making her way home flickered in my mind, even during my hurried shower where a fresh idea presented itself to me: I wasn't going to drive around with Auntie and Cousin Headley. That would add to my guilt. And one accusing comment or look from Auntie might trigger another clash between me and her.

I called Cousin Headley on his mobile and told him I wouldn't be coming with them. 'It would be better if we spread our search. You go one place and I go another.'

'Well, okay,' he said. 'But you see all dat rain an' bad weather outside?'

'I know,' I said, choosing to ignore the negative thoughts his words were conjuring up. 'I'll do Vieux Fort and the local areas.'

'By bus?'

'I've hired a car.'

'Oh...oh. Okay. Well I – me and Cousin Barbara will go Castries way.'

'Great. Thanks,' I said. 'I better get going. Tell Auntie... say good morning for me.'

'Okay. We will let you know if we... if anything.'

'I will too.'

'God is good. We bound to find her today.'

'I hope so,' I said.

CHAPTER TWENTY-FIVE

Stepping out into the sunless gloom, made it difficult to hold onto the positivity I'd promised myself and Delia to nurture.

I sat in a half-empty bus, holding one of Mum's umbrellas dripping on the floor between my legs, the bottom part of me partially soaked.

The car I hired was from the same company I'd used for the visit to the care home. After picking it up, I began the drive around Vieux Fort. The storm had broken branches off trees, created deeper potholes in the roads and forced most people to stay indoors. Those who needed to be out were in a hurry to get back in.

Everyone I asked gave me a curious look as I approached them, their eyes, facial expressions questioning, some with added irritation. Like before, no one had seen Mum.

'A ole lady?' one man replied, when I explained that my mother hadn't come home last night. 'You sure she don' go an' stay with fam'ly or a frien'?'

'No,' I said. 'She gets confused.' I tried to explain about the dementia.

'No, sorry,' he said, bluntly. 'I haven't seen her.' He moved past me.

The weather, and scarcity of people around, filled me with more doubt. Forced images and thoughts of Mum stuck somewhere, harmed, raped – even killed, found their way to the forefront of my mind. What was the point? This search was futile. *But what if she's still alive? In a place where I can find her?*

Dead or alive, I had to find her. No matter what, she needed help. I had to keep searching.

Within two hours, I'd driven through much of the main areas. I parked up again and headed for the sandy parts. The sea was grey. Choppy. Its angry, Atlantic self. Palm trees swayed in whatever direction the wind dictated. All the bars were closed, but I walked around anyway, determined to find her.

Time gobbled up the morning. Still no Mum. Miserable and dispirited, I started the walk back to the car, my eyes on the ground in front of me, when I heard a voice, calling out to someone. I looked up. Couldn't see the person's face because of the umbrella she was carrying, but her shoes suggested a woman. I quickened my pace to catch up with her. 'Excuse me! Excuse me!' I said.

She slowed down and looked towards me as her fluffy dog lifted its hind leg and squirted pee at the roots of a sea grape tree.

I asked her the question I'd been asking total strangers since yesterday, and gave a brief description of Mum.

'I see,' she said. 'You're English?'

That wasn't answering my question and I was in no mood for a discussion on nationality or identity. 'I live in England,' I said.

'And you've lost your mother?'

'Yes. She has dementia.'

'Ah. That's sad,' she replied. 'But I'm sorry, I haven't come across her.' She tugged at the dog's lead.

'Thanks, anyway,' I said, and turned to go.

'I used to live in England too, a long time ago. Elephant and Castle,' she said, almost behind me now. 'You know there?'

I glanced back at her. 'Yes.'

'Keep her close, when you find her. Your mother.'

'I will,' I said, quickening my pace.

'Come on, Trudy.'

This whole experience was becoming surreal. At least when Mum had got lost in England, worries for her safety had been short-lived: within hours, she'd been located, and I'd been on my way to her.

I'd covered the main parts of Vieux Fort. Micoud too. Cousin Headley hadn't called which meant they'd had no joy. I called to find out how it was going.

It was as I'd expected. Nothing.

'De police don't call you yet?'

'No,' I confirmed. 'How's Auntie?'

'She lying down. We jus' come back. She din sleep good at all last night.'

My get-out clause. I couldn't manage Auntie, not right now. 'Tell her I said hello.'

'All right.'

'I'll call her later.'

Millie's call caught me sitting in my regular spot on the veranda, hope dissipating, positive thinking trailing close behind it.

'Mum?' she said. 'I got your message.'

'Mum's missing,' I said. 'I forgot to lock the gate and she slipped out without me noticing.'

'My God. When?'

'Yesterday, when we were talking.'

'Oh, no.'

'I feel like crap. I'm so scared something bad has happened to her and all because of me. I came here to make sure she was okay and—'

'I suppose you've looked everywhere you can and asked around.'

'Yeah. Done all of that. Reported it to the police. I don't know...' I sighed.

'It's not the first time Nannie's gone missing. It'll be all right.'

'But she's never been missing for this long. Overnight, Millie.'

'Mum, it's a little island. Somebody's bound to find her.'

'What if something's happened to her? She's been having mini strokes – passing out. You don't understand. Nobody understands... how I... what this feels like. If—'

'You can't realistically watch her twenty-four-seven! Who could?'

'I should've been paying attention. And Auntie, she's blaming me. I know it.'

'Aww, Mum, please don't let Auntie make you feel worse.'

'I can't help it.'

'Didn't Nannie leave the shop without Auntie noticing? Don't take her on. Everybody knows you love Nannie, Mum.'

'I know. I know,' I said. 'But I can't see how... it's hard to imagine her being okay after being lost – gone for such a long time. And the weather... last night we had a storm and it's only now easing off. She would have been out in all of that.'

'Why didn't you call me last night?'

'And wake you up? I know you. You'd never get back to sleep.' I sighed. 'I was also hoping I wouldn't have to tell you until after we'd found her, or she came back home. Didn't expect she'd be lost for this long. It's killing me.'

'Oh, Mum. Wish I was there with you.'

Hearing Millie's voice was heartening.

'I'm not gonna tell you to try not to worry,' she said, 'cos I know you will. I'll be worrying myself, but try not to think the worse, eh? Can't you get some marijuana from anyone? Something to help you relax?'

'Millie!'

'You could have it as a tea. It would help you to feel... you know, *irie*. Chilled.'

'*Irie?* This isn't a time to get high, Millie.'

'I know.' She gave a slight giggle. 'It's just so you can relax. God, I wish I was there.'

'I'll be okay. *It* will all be fine,' I added, for myself more than for her. 'We'll talk tomorrow. Must be getting late for you.'

'Yeah, but that's all right.'

'I'll let you know when we get any news.' I did my best to sound lifted. Positive.

'Yeah. Call me when you do.'

I was grateful for her support, and the idea of a marijuana tea sounded half appealing, after we'd said good-bye. But that was out of the question.

Passing Mum's bedroom, on the way to the kitchen, out of nowhere, a whirl of feelings gathered in my chest. I put a hand over my mouth and sat at the kitchen table stifling the urge to cry. 'It's okay' – I forced the words out – '... okay to cry.' Sobs gave way to whining tears. 'Please, let her be found. Alive and well. Please... oh, Mum... let her be okay.'

I sat in the semi-darkness, drained, my mind a blank, until a sound coming from my phone stirred me into a kind of reality. Sniffing, I wiped my nose. Where was it? I glanced around, dragged myself up and headed back to my room.

There were two missed calls from Delia and a text, asking if there was any news.

No, I texted back. *Too tired to talk. Maybe later.*

I put the phone down and got under the sheets.

CHAPTER TWENTY-SIX

I hadn't a clue what time it was, but my phone was ringing. I tried to open my eyes, then reached out blindly, tapping my hand in the direction my ears lead me to. A touch knocked the phone to the floor. I reached again, sliding off the bed, then grabbed it.

'Hello?' I croaked. The person had rung off. I stood up, rubbing my sore hip. 'Mmm.' My stomach didn't feel right. I squeezed my eyes shut, opened them and pressed the call history button. It wasn't a number I recognised, but it was local. I dialled it back.

'Good morning, Micoud police station,' a deep, dull voice said.

'Hello. Did you say Micoud police station?' Though I was sure it was what I'd heard.

'Yes.'

'Someone just called me from this number. My name's Erica.' I took a breath. 'Erica Joseph. Is this about my mother? Mrs Joseph?' It had to be.

'Yes. Miss Joseph. I am Sergeant Hippolyte.'

'Sorry, good morning.' I recovered my manners.

'Good morning. You filed a missing person's report?'

'Yes. My mum. She's missing.' I tightened my grip on the phone to steady my hand. 'Have you found her? You've found her?' I asked, petrified of the answer.

'We think so,' the officer said.

'Where? Are you sure? Is she... is she all right? Is she with you?'

'She's in Gros Islet.'

'Where?'

'The police station there. Her name is Ione Joseph?'

'Yes. Ione Joseph. Where...? Where did you find her? Is she all right?'

'Somebody found her in Gros Islet. She is at the station there.'

'Gros Islet?' I sat on the bed. That was up north, close to where Dr Peres' office was. How had Mum got all the way up there?

'Is she okay? She's not hurt in any way, is she?'

'I... I'm not sure. I don't believe so. In any case, they will be taking her to the hospital to check for those things. Is just proce-dure,' the officer said.

His casual manner took the edge off my fears, but I hadn't forgotten the condition of the hospital I'd taken Mum to when she'd had the mini stroke.

'Can... can I ask that they take her to the private hospital, please?' I said.

'The Oriole?'

I wasn't sure about the name, but: 'Yes,' I said. 'The Oriole. Please ask them to take her there. Not to the regular one.'

'All right.'

Relief streamed through me.

I got the number for the Gros Islet police station from him, hoping I could at least hear Mum's voice. Gauge how all right she was. Then I thanked him and disconnected the call.

Mum's been found. She is alive and safe.

I called Gros Islet station. 'My name's Erica Joseph,' I said. 'I understand you have my mother there? Mrs Ione Joseph?'

'Oh. Dat – de lady dat was lost? You are her daughter?'

'Yes. Is she there? She okay? Can I speak to her, please?'

'Dey jus' take her to de hospital,' the woman on the phone said.

'Oh. Was she okay? Did she look okay? Did she say anything?'

'Er. Yes, I believe... You will have to meet her at de hospital.'

'Would you know – where... where – where she was found?'

'Just a minute. Let me check.'

Heart pounding I waited, anxious to head off. To make sure it really was Mum. To reassure her, let her feel safe again.

'At de back of a Gros Islet bus,' the woman said. 'The driver found her lying down dere dis morning and brought her.'

'The back of a bus?' I gasped. 'My God.' A chill ran through me, as I processed what the officer was saying.

'Say thanks God she is safe now.'

She was safe, but more unnerving questions started piling into my mind, like how long she'd been on the bus for and what condition was she was in when they found her.

'Thank you,' I said again and made a dash for the bathroom, tripping over myself, my thoughts. I couldn't leave the house fast enough, but needed to give Auntie the good news and put an end to her worrying. Thank God, I still had the car.

She answered with the usual, 'Good morning.'

'Morning, Auntie,' I said. 'Auntie, they've found her. They've found Mum.' My voice rose to a tiny screech.

'Wha—You sure? Where?'

'In Gros Islet. This morning.'

'Eh-eh. How Ione find herself quite Gros Islet?'

'They... they've taken her to the hospital. I'm on my way there now.'

'Why? What – Something happen to her?'

'They said it's procedure – to give her a check-up. I'll call you as soon as I get there, as soon as I see her, Auntie. And then I can come back and get you, if you like.'

'But—'

'I can't wait, Auntie. Mum's probably worried – not sure what's going on. She'll feel better once she sees me.'

'But I want to come.'

'I know, but I can't wait. I have to go now.' I'd suspected calling her would make things messy like this. 'Maybe Cousin Headley can bring you? I'm happy to come back and get you, once Mum's settled, cos by the time you get ready – you know what the morning traffic is like going into town. I have to go now.'

'Well...'

I looked at the clock. I totally understood why she wanted to come, but knew how long it would take to get her out of her front door. I had to get going. And all this talking was holding me back.

'All right. I will call Headley,' she said.

'I'm sure he won't mind.' It was most probably pushing me further into her bad books, but I didn't care much about that right now. 'I have to get going, Auntie. I'll call you as soon as I see her.'

'All right,' she said. 'Call me as soon as you see her, eh?'

I raised my eyebrows in exasperation. She was delaying me, repeating what I'd already told her. 'Yes. And I'll come back for you, if Cousin Headley can't bring you.'

I sent a quick text to Delia and Millie, made a necessary stop for petrol — and, forty-five minutes later, I was negotiating the one-way system leading to the hospital.

I parked the car and walked briskly to reception, desperate to see Mum.

CHAPTER TWENTY-SEVEN

The ward was on the first floor. I pushed the door open and approached a small nurses' station. A board behind the desk had a list of names, which I assumed were the patients', but Mum's name wasn't there.

'Yes. Can I help you?' One of the nurses drew my attention.

I told her who I was looking for.

A younger-looking nurse sitting next to her whispered something to her. 'Mrs Joseph?' she said. 'The elderly lady who was missing?'

It jarred me slightly, hearing someone refer to Mum as 'the elderly lady'. Whatever her age, she was just Mum to me. My mother. Plus, she wasn't frail, seriously wrinkled, only seventy-eight. All she had was Alzheimer's, but yes... I supposed in the eyes of most people, she was 'an elderly lady'.

'Yes. She's my mother,' I told the older nurse, who came out from behind the desk with a sheaf of papers in her hand.

'I'm Nurse Whitley,' she said. 'Come with me. The police brought her in not too long ago. She is in bed nine.'

I followed Nurse Whitley, each one of my breaths shorter than the last. Through a heavy wooden door not too far from the nurses' station was the smallest ward I'd ever seen, with only four beds in it.

'Mrs Joseph's daughter is here,' Nurse Whitley said, putting her head in at a curtain drawn around what I assumed was Mum's bed. 'Come in.' She looked over her shoulder at me then widened the opening in the curtain.

My eyes leapt to the bed, desperate to confirm that the person on it was really Mum.

She was lying on her side with another nurse securing a drip on a silver pole next to her. A monitor was flashing lights behind her bed.

'Mum?' Going closer, I scanned her face, arms – the places that were exposed – looking for signs of possible injuries, scratches or bruising.

'Uh?' she responded, shifting to locate my voice.

I touched her arm. It was her. She was safe, within grasp. In front of me. 'It's me. Erica. I'm here,' I said.

'Uh? Erica?' She looked up at me. 'It's you, *ich mwen?*' she said, in a soft, light voice.

'Yes. I'm here, Mum. How are you feeling? We've been so worried, Mum.'

'Mmm. Okay.'

'We've given her something to relax her,' Nurse Whitley said, giving a sympathetic smile.

'She wandered off. Out of the house. I didn't even notice. Then it was too late. She has Alzheimer's.'

'Oh,' the nurse fixing the drip said. 'So how long was it before they found her?'

'Nearly two days,' I said, almost choking on the words.

'Oh, dear,' the nurse said.

'We will need to collect some information about your mother from you,' Nurse Whitley said, handing the papers she'd been carrying to me, with a pen. 'Just drop them back to the desk when you've finished.'

'Okay.' I nodded. 'Mum? Mum, you sure you're okay?' I said, as soon as they left us alone. 'Where've you been? We've been going crazy looking for you. Where did you go?'

'I'm in de hospital,' she said, dragging the words. '*Koté* Barbara? Where's Barbara? Frank?'

'Fr—' *Of all the people she could have asked for...* 'He... they're coming,' I said.

I called Auntie. 'I'm with her,' I said.

'She all right?' Auntie asked.

I moved away from the bed and lowered my voice. 'She seems a bit out of it. They've got her on a drip and given her something to relax her. But it's her, Auntie. I'm so glad she's all right.'

'Me too. Headley say he will bring me. I can say hello to her?'

'Mum?' I said, stepping closer to her bed.

'Mmm?' Her eyes were closed.

'Auntie wants to say hello. Auntie Barbara,' I said.

'Baaaa...?' Mum murmured.

I spoke back into my phone: 'I think she's sleeping, Auntie.'

'All right. I will see you in a while.' The space between Auntie's words and her tone of voice made me think she was welled up, but at least we had good news.

'I'm sorry about all of this, Auntie,' I said. 'I really am. But I think she's fine. She'll be okay.'

'God is with us. De police find her. Let's pray for her to get better.'

Did she mean from Alzheimer's, or recover from this episode in the hospital?

I texted Millie and Delia again, letting them know I was with Mum and promised to call them later.

It was pure joy to see her, be with her again, knowing she was safe.

I began taking in her face. She wasn't wearing the little wig that had become her go-to hairstyle. Her own hair was untidy, with loose, flyaway curls escaping from her plaits. I wanted to comb it out, but had nothing to do that with. Instead, I stroked some of the strands, trying to tuck them in to make the plait I could access a little neater.

She moaned. 'Sorry, Mum,' I said, stroking her hair then running my hand over my own because I didn't know what else to do.

When I was little, she'd often plait my hair for school, with me half-asleep, my head on her lap. She'd tell me how soft and lovely it was. 'You get dat from your father,' she'd say. 'You have Indian in your fam'ly.'

'Who, Mum,' I asked. 'Who was Indian?'

'Your grandmother, I believe,' she'd say, and my mind would take me to an imaginary old lady, with long, grey, straight hair all the way down to her bottom. Then sad thoughts of the father I never knew would slip into my mind and I'd wonder why he didn't like me enough to want to see me.

Mum's comforting words made thoughts of him become unimportant.

I had *her*.

CHAPTER TWENTY-EIGHT

'Ione?'

Auntie's voice startled me. I lifted my head from the foot of Mum's bed, and stood up to give her my seat. 'Hi. Hi, Auntie, Cousin Headley,' I said.

Auntie went straight to Mum, with Cousin Headley peering over her shoulder.

'Think she's still sleeping,' I said.

'Oh, Ione. We find you. Thanks be to God,' Auntie said, a hand on Mum's shoulder.

'Where dey find her?' Cousin Headley asked me.

'At the back of a bus. She was asleep, I think,' I said.

'Sleeping?' Cousin Headley frowned and shook his head. 'In Gros Islet, Cousin Barbara tell me.'

'Yeah.'

Auntie turned to me. 'But who find her?'

'The driver, they said. In the morning.'

'*Mésyé*,' Cousin Headley said. 'De bus driver dat find her?'

I nodded. 'Luckily.' I hoped I'd be able to thank him.

'She safe now. Dat's de important thing,' Auntie said, her attention back on Mum, who'd began to stir.

Sister Whitley came in. 'Excuse me,' she said, and informed me that a Dr Medouze was here, to speak to me.

'Oh. Thank you. I'll be back in a minute,' I told everyone, and left.

Dr Medouze was standing at the nurses' station. He wasn't bad-looking. Dark, slim, medium height, wearing black trousers with a light-blue shirt. Nurse Whitley introduced me.

'Pleased to meet you,' he said. 'We can talk over here.'

He led me to a nearby area with soft seats and I explained again what had happened with Mum.

'That sort of thing is more common than you might think,' he said. 'But I imagine it must have been very worrying for you and the family. Thank goodness, she's safe now.'

'Yeah.' I sighed. 'I'm so relieved.'

He went on to tell me a story about a woman who'd 'escaped' from a care home. 'She had actually gone into a rum shop, ordered a drink and charged it to the home. Would you believe that?'

I forced a smile. *Could that have been St Patrick's?*

'Oh, boy,' he said, shaking his head. 'But all's well that ends well. Isn't that what you-all say in England?'

'Yeah. Some people do.'

'You were born in England?'

'No,' I said.

'I did my training there. Bristol.'

'Oh.' I hadn't been to Bristol.

'They offered me a job too, but I couldn't wait to get out of the cold.'

'You could have got used to it,' I said.

'Oh, never. You're still living there?'

'Yes. I came down to take my mother back with me, but the psychiatrist we saw the other day said it might not be possible.'

'She's a very healthy lady, for her age.'

'Apart from Alzheimer's,' I said, hating the reminder.

'How long ago was she diagnosed?'

'Four years now. In England,' I said, and gave him a bit of history about Mum's path to diagnosis.

'I see she's on zopiclone and risperidone. Did you bring them with you?'

'No. Sorry,' I said. 'I was in such a rush. But I've stopped giving her the risperidone.'

'I see. Can I ask why?'

'It was making her dopey and...' I told him about the stroke the doctor in the other hospital had said Mum had had.

'I can prescribe something else while she's here, if I have your agreement. And I would like to run some tests, just to make sure there's nothing else we need to be treating. UTIs are quite common with the elderly and can add to their level of confusion too – your mother might not have the awareness to tell you she's experiencing anything. That might be why she wandered off.'

My own suspicion for what had made Mum walk off was her hearing talks about care homes. Dr Medouze's suggestion sat better with me.

I told him she'd had blood tests just over a week ago and they were all clear. 'But she's always trying to go home,' I said. 'We're never sure where that means to her.'

'Yes. That's common too.'

'She wouldn't usually be able to just walk off, but I forgot to lock the gate that day.'

'I see,' he said, pausing. 'How would you feel about us doing a brain scan? From what you've said about her having mini strokes—'

'I wasn't sure if that was due to some side effect of the drugs,' I said. 'That's why I stopped it.'

'I see. Then that might be a good reason to go ahead with a scan. We could get a clearer picture of what's going on in her brain and the extent of degeneration.'

'Oh,' I said.

'In England you have the National Health Service, but remember here there's a cost. Brain scans aren't cheap, and I'm assuming she doesn't have insurance?'

'No, she doesn't.' I asked how much it would cost.

'Accounts will give you the full price. But I would recommend it, if it's affordable.'

I agreed to check the price with Accounts and let him know via the sister on duty. When Mum had finally had her brain scan in England, to confirm her diagnosis, it had taken a lot of persuading and coaxing. She'd been scared to go into the machine. Now, with her Alzheimer's worsened, she might not be able to manage it at all.

'Bear in mind it would be easier to do it while she's an in-patient than to have to take her home and bring her back again for it,' Dr Medouze added.

'Right.'

'We'll go ahead with the other tests, for now, then?' He gave me an empathetic smile. 'I think it's best she stayed at least for tonight, for observation.'

'Okay.' I nodded.

I went straight to Accounts to pay the necessary deposit. The final bill, they said, would depend on how long she stayed in for and any tests and medication they would have to give her. If she had the scan it could cost an extra $1,500 dollars. I gasped when the young woman told me the price.

Auntie was sitting alone at Mum's bedside. She told me Cousin Headley had gone to the canteen.

'De doctor say she all right?' she asked.

'Yeah. She might have a brain scan to see how advanced the Alzheimer's is,' I said.

'Erica?'

It was Mum. I moved past Auntie to get closer to her. 'I'm here, Mum,' I said.

Her eyes opened, highlighting the ashen tone of her skin, dark stain and bags under her eyes – stark reminders of the irreversible condition she was battling. Attributes that marred the beautiful face I used to admire. *Could she have had another mini stroke at the back of that bus?*

'Where you going?' she asked.

'Nowhere,' I said.

'Where Barbara?'

'Look me.' Auntie stood up for Mum to see her.

'*Pa babyé*. Don't quarrel,' Mum said. 'You-all mustn' fight. You hear?'

Auntie and I looked at each other. 'We're not, Mum,' I said.

Had Mum and Cousin Headley said something in my absence that had led to Mum saying this, or was she remembering the clash between me and Auntie?

'Nobody not fighting here,' Auntie said.

'*Bon*. Good,' Mum said.

A slim, mature woman wearing a pale green nun's habit came in carrying a tray with a sandwich and tea for Mum. Cousin Headley was behind her, and handed me and Mum a small bottle of water. 'I din know if you did want anything else,' he said to me. I thanked him and said I was fine.

A couple of hours later, Auntie was falling asleep in the chair.

'You should take her home,' I whispered to Cousin Headley. He looked tired as well.

'You say dey keeping her here tonight?' he said.

'Yeah.' I was in no hurry to go home myself. 'I'll give you a call later.'

Mum slept for most of the time I was there and I was

surprised when one of the nurses came to get me saying Dr Medouze wanted to discuss the test results with me.

Mum had a UTI and her iron levels were slightly low.

'Not too low to worry about it,' Dr Medouze said.

I told him she'd had this low iron problem for years. 'We've been trying to manage it through her diet.'

'A course of antibiotics should sort out the UTI. We'll monitor the iron.'

'Okay. Thank you, Doctor,' I said, sighing.

'Your mother is becoming a child again,' he said.

'Mmm.' That sad reality I couldn't miss.

'Once a man, they say—'

'I know.' I interrupted before he could say, 'twice a child'.

'If we manage to live long enough.'

'I suppose.'

Mum was more alert when I got back, sitting up in bed, with a smile that said she was pleased to see me.

I smiled back. 'How are you feeling?'

'Not too bad,' she said. 'How are you?'

How am I? This glimpse of the real Mum warmed me. I yearned for more of it.

'I've... we've all been worried about you. You've been gone almost two days, Mum,' I said, perching myself on the side of her bed. 'I was so worried. We searched everywhere for you. I'm so glad somebody found you. And you're safe.' I rubbed her hand. 'Can you remember... any of it? Where you went or anything?'

She frowned and stared ahead of her. 'No.' She shook her head. 'I don't remember.'

'Nothing? Nothing at all?' I waited, hoping her fixed gaze would help summon up a memory, no matter how small, that would give me a clue about what she'd experienced in the last two days. 'You remember the man – the bus driver, who found you?'

She shook her head. 'No.'

'Don't worry,' I said, swallowing my disappointment.

She turned her attention to me. 'My daughter,' she said, and put a hand out to touch me. 'He told me you was nice-looking. That you resemble me.'

'Nice-looking? Who?' My mind fell on Dr Medouze. I glanced over my shoulder. 'The... the doctor?'

'Frank,' she said, sighed and looked away.

'Mr Frank?'

'But you was so young.'

The thought of Mr Frank telling Mum he found me attractive brought up past incidences of his inappropriate comments and suggestions to me. It repulsed, and angered me. But she was confirming, to my face, what she'd been too afraid to do before: that instead of Mr Frank having fatherly, nurturing feelings for me, what he'd wanted was to get me in bed.

'He did like you in the wrong way,' Mum said.

Her admittance drew me even closer to her. 'What woman didn't he want to get in bed with, Mum?'

She looked away. Shut down again. Through shame? Or to lessen her pain?

I'd heard them arguing the night after I'd told her I was pregnant, and had knocked on the bathroom door when I heard her quiet sobs in there.

'Mum? You okay?'

'I'll finish in a minute,' she'd said, seconds later.

I waited for her to come out. It was clear from her face that she'd been crying, but she insisted she was okay when I asked her again.

'It's about me, isn't it?' I'd said, quietly.

She didn't answer, but went straight back into the bedroom.

'So when you taking me home?' Her voice brought me back to the present.

'What?'

'When dey say I can go home?'

'Oh... the... the doctor – you have to stay for the night to make sure everything's okay with you. They might do more tests.'

'Tests? For what? Nothing will never be okay with me.'

'Why d'you say that?'

'You know. You know – everybody know something is wrong with me and nobody cannot fix it.'

Mum hadn't spoken like this for ages. I hated having to discuss her condition, but valued and wished for more lucid moments with her.

'Everyone's doing the best they can for you, Mum,' I said.

Hearing her acknowledge the fatality of her condition took me back to four years ago, when we'd arrived home, after her diagnosis.

She'd walked through the front door ahead of me and straight upstairs.

I'd left Millie making the tea and went up her. 'You okay?' I'd asked, sitting beside her on her bed.

'So... so what is this sickness dey say I have?' she said.

I paused, trying to work out where to start. How to explain, without scaring her or letting her know how gutted and scared I was too. 'Alzheimer's,' I said. 'It's... it's a type of dementia—'

'Dementia?' she repeated.

'It's something that's affecting your memory and how you understand things, Mum. It's why you forgot the pot on the stove... forget things, get confused about things all, a lot of the time.'

'But everybody does forget things sometimes.' She fiddled with the pretend wedding ring on her finger.

'People with dementia forget more than normal,' I said, looking away, hating having to explain it, to help her fully understand.

'*Bondyé*, my God,' she said quietly, looking at the floor. 'Dementia.'

I was trying to stop myself from breaking, as I was doing now. Make the uncharted road ahead seem smoother, less problematic for her – at least for now. 'You'll be okay, Mum,' I said.

'They will give me med'cine for it?' she'd asked.

'Yes. But... but it won't take it away.'

'It won't take it away?' She'd raised her eyebrows at me. 'So what it going to do?'

'Slow it down. Stop it getting worse too soon.'

'You mean it's going to get worse? Worse how?'

'Well... you'll forget more, get more confused and...'

'*Bondyé*.' She sighed. 'So I'm going to die.'

'Oh, Mum!' I hugged her. 'We're all going to die,' was all I could say, at the time.

We'd held each other. I couldn't stop the tears. 'Don't cry, *ich mwen*,' she'd said. 'Don't cry.'

And here we were four years on. 'So what use is it them have me here?' She kicked at the sheet covering her legs.

'You were gone for almost two days,' I reminded her. 'No one knows what happened to you during that time.'

'I just' want to go home,' she snapped.

'I know, Mum.' I stood up and hugged her. 'You can probably come home tomorrow. Let's be happy that you're safe.' Blinking tears away, I let her go and sat down, eyes still on her.

'Frank did like too much woman.'

'I know, Mum. But it's over now. He's gone.'

'Where?'

'He's dead, Mum?'

'Who say dat?'

Alzheimer's had kicked lucidity aside. I offered her a drink.

·   ·   ·

After her supper and medication, Nurse Whitley advised me to let her sleep.

'I love you, Mum,' I said, kissing her forehead before leaving.

'I love you too, *ich mwen*,' a small, feeble voice replied.

'See you tomorrow. Sleep well.' I stroked her arm, picked up the bag they'd given me, with her personal things in, and left.

Outside, the air was dank, but I welcomed it after being inside for so long. My immediate worries about Mum were over, or at least being addressed. But as I hitched the bag onto my shoulder, I couldn't get rid of what I'd learned that day. She'd known all along that Mr Frank's roving eye hadn't excluded me, her daughter. And still she'd stayed with him.

CHAPTER TWENTY-NINE

I took the bag with Mum's things straight to the washing machine, opened it and an acidic odour filled the air around me. Mum's dress was soiled. She'd vomited at some point whilst she was missing. I put everything to wash and texted Millie and Delia: *Back from the hospital. Mum's doing ok. I'm fine. Talk tomorrow.*

After that I texted Claire, who replied saying she was at work: *Will catch up with you tomorrow*

Mum wasn't home, but I knew where she was, I reminded myself, as I moved around the house. She was safe and in good hands, but I was missing her.

I went into her room. Opened drawers, the contents reflecting the disarray her mind and life was in. The small prayer book I'd put on the shelf in her wardrobe, lipsticks I'd secured in a toiletries bag, body cream and more loose photographs were all mixed up again with clothes in the drawer.

I pulled the whole thing out and tipped the contents onto the bed. 'How...?' The gold necklace with the 'Mum' pendant I'd been searching for to put with the rest of her valuables was stuck in one of the corner joints of the drawer. Has this been here on all of the many occasions I've been through her things, looking for it? With added care, I prised out the gift I'd given her on her fiftieth. The day I'd picked her up under the guise of taking her for a birthday meal.

'It's a special treat, Mum. For me and you. Not even Millie's coming,' I'd told her. Then played the usual trick of pretending I'd forgotten something at home that I needed to drive back for, knowing the whole family, including Millie, Auntie Barbara, Mrs Gooding, even Mr Frank, were already at my house, under the strict instructions that went with organising a surprise birthday party.

She'd suggested waiting in the car for me, but I encouraged her to come in. The look on her face when everyone shouted, 'SURPRISE!' and what was really happening dawned on her, was a joyful picture I'd kept in my mind ever since.

She was still pretty then. All made up with lipstick, powder, a fancy wig, fitted blue and white dress and kitten heels. Nothing like the face I'd seen in the hospital bed earlier.

'Oh, Mum,' I said, to the sense of her in the room.

I had to shake off this ache and loneliness. Be close to the next best person to Mum.

'Auntie,' I said, when she answered the phone. I was sure she'd be getting ready for bed now. 'Can I come over?'

'Of course,' she said. 'You have to ask me dat?'

She was looking out for me from her veranda, waited until I came through her gate then said: 'You must be so tired. But happy, eh?

'Aren't you?' I said.

'Of course. I'm very happy my sister is all right. You eat yet?'

'I'll have something when I get back.'

'Come.'

After a peck on the cheek, I followed her to the kitchen

where stewed saltfish with ground provisions was waiting on the stove.

'Ah, Auntie. That looks great.' I smiled.

'Take what you want.' She handed me a plate. 'Dere's cucumber salad in de fridge.'

I thanked her and dished up a plate from the pots.

'I will meet you outside, eh?'

'Mmm. How have you been?' I asked, joining her with my meal.

'Well.' She took a deep breath. 'I hope I can get a good sleep tonight.'

'I'm never gonna forget to lock that gate again.'

'Huh. Not only you. I not leaving der gate for nobody to lock again, when I have a key. I was feeling like when I did lose her in town.'

'At least that was only for a short time, Auntie. Not nearly two days.'

Coming clean with our feelings lightened some of the guilt I'd been carrying.

'How she was when you leave her?'

'She was okay. Sleepy.' I paused. 'Auntie, I just don't know why she can't stop going on about Mr Frank.' I told her what Mum had said about him earlier.

Auntie frowned. 'He did ever disrespect you? You know – in dat way?' She dropped her gaze.

'Sometimes.' I told her about the time when I'd accidentally walked into the bathroom and he was standing there with no clothes on, then abruptly shut down the image in my head.

Auntie gasped. 'An' how ole you was?'

'Fourteen – I did tell Mum.'

'An' what she say?'

'She said I needed to make sure nobody was in the bathroom or toilet before I went in.'

'But is he dat should have locked de door.'

'Anyway, it never happened again. After that, I made sure to knock and call out before going in.' I slipped another forkful of food into my mouth.

'Frank was a nasty man. Is for his money Ione stay with him.'

'Not love?'

'Love?' Auntie gave me an extra-long glare.

It was sad and disappointing that Mum's fear of being hard-up or having to scrape like she used to, had made her stick with a man like Mr Frank.

'She chose him over me,' I said. 'And stayed with him despite everything.'

'He is dead.'

'I know, Auntie.'

'An' now she sick.'

'Those two things aren't connected, to me, Auntie. None of it made me stop loving her. None of it.'

'I see dat, but now, she need *you*, Erica. She don't have nobody else who can do what you can do for her. You think it's right for you to put her in a home?' Auntie said, less accusing, this time.

'I... I didn't say it was. What... the conversation you over-heard was me exploring, trying to work out the best thing to do.'

'Understan' me, eh? Everybody know Ione is lucky she have you.'

Was I the unlucky one, landing with all of this?

'Dey tell you when dey letting her come home?'

'Tomorrow, hopefully.'

She started warning me about them not keeping Mum there for no reason, apart from getting more money out of us. 'Dey better dan de government hospital, but dey charging you for every day she in dere, you know. Every piece of cotton, every glove, every needle, every pin,' Auntie said.

'Cotton?'

'Yes, I'm telling you.' Auntie's voice sprang up a couple of decibels, her words stumbling over each other, like when she was edging on anger. 'You will see when you get de bill. You have to put your money out when you go to Oriole, you know. An' I don't see why dey must charge so much money.'

'They have good nurses and doctors.'

'Some of dose nurses have no right calling demself nurse. Dey mean an' hard. What time you going an' see her tomorrow?'

I put my fork down. 'Oh, early.' The question of the brain scan came to mind.

'Mmm.'

The gap in our conversation gave the shrilling chirps of whistling frogs and crickets busying themselves in amongst the vegetation and soil, a space to be heard. I sighed. 'Who wants to get old, eh, Auntie?'

'Huh,' she replied. 'Ione mus' say thank God you come, wherever you decide to put her.'

Auntie had lost her only child, Sylvie, years ago. Hers was the first funeral I'd ever attended. She was thirteen when she died from a blood disorder. *God's work*, the grown-ups – including Auntie and Mum – told me it was when I'd questioned the fairness of it all. There'd be no more giggles or games with my closest cousin. I wouldn't hear her voice, touch her or have any conversations with her again.

'Why would God do such a bad thing?' I'd asked Mum.

'Only He knows,' Mum had replied, holding my hand. 'Only God.'

I quizzed myself over it, questioned God's motives. Little did I know at twelve years old that questioning God's motives had no end – hardly a day goes by without me questioning the logic, the reasons, why I'd had to lose Shane.

'Are you not lonely here on your own, Auntie?' I said.

'Well...' Auntie hesitated. 'Sometimes, especially now I one not too good. We used to give each other plenty of company, even before Frank die. We was always close, you know.'

'I know.'

'The others used to be jealous sometimes, but we was jus' close.' She sighed. There was a glitter in her eyes. 'Me an' I one.'

I hadn't given a lot of thought to what all of this meant to Auntie and how much it was affecting her. She was hell-bent on me taking Mum back to England, even though it would mean her being more alone. A part of her must have been secretly relieved that the doctors had advised against it.

'What do you think you'll do when you get too old to manage, Auntie?'

'Me?' She paused. 'I don't know. I have Headley to help me out with some things.' She shrugged.

'And me,' I said, meeting her eyes with a reassuring smile.

'I... I have you too?'

There was reservation in her voice. From what she could see I was about to let Mum down. Why not her? Could she really rely on me?

'Of course,' I said. 'I... I want to do the right thing, you know, Auntie. For Mum. But it's hard.'

'Mmm,' she said, shifting her gaze.

'I'm gonna try to get more time off so I can stay longer to sort things out.'

'Oh. Good.'

My phone started to ring. 'Sorry, Auntie. It's Millie,' I said, pressing the green button. 'Hi, darling.'

'How's Nannie doing?'

'She's doing okay. I'm at Auntie Barbara's.' I glanced at Auntie sitting opposite me and considered telling Millie I'd call her back, but it was already late for her.

'Poor old Nannie,' she said. 'You sure you don't want me to come down and give you a hand?'

Auntie disappeared inside.

I reminded Millie she was running a business.

'Yeah, but—'

'You can't work from here. I'll manage just fine,' I said, though I would have been more than happy to have her with me.

'But—'

'Millie, I love you. It's good that you're offering to be here for me and your nan, but it will be fine.'

'You sure? She all right with you now? Auntie?' Millie lowered her voice.

'Oh, yeah. Yeah,' I said, trying to locate Auntie Barbara.

'Well, let me know if you change your mind.'

'I will. Listen, I'd better go. Say hello to Adwin, and don't forget to let me know the test results.'

'I won't.'

'And be good to yourself.'

'Be good to myself? I should be telling you that. Okay. I'll call tomorrow.'

'I love you.'

'Me too, Mum.' She lowered her voice. 'Better say hello to Auntie, innit?'

'Yeah. Fill Auntie Delia in for me, okay?'

Auntie was clearing the stove. 'Millie wants to say hello,' I said, handing the phone to her.

Talking to Millie, she sounded like the aunt I'd known as a child. I took over the clearing up while they talked.

'Thank you *ich mwen*,' Auntie said after the conversation with Millie. It was still light, but past her closing-up time. I told her I was leaving.

'I was glad for de company,' she said, when I apologised for delaying her.

'Hopefully you'll sleep better tonight,' I said, hugging and kissing her.

That night, like ice to water, I melted reassuringly into sleep.

CHAPTER THIRTY

At six o'clock the following morning, I sent an email off to Phillipa asking for more extended leave, then set about tidying the house and getting Mum's room ready for her return. Later, I called the hospital and gave my okay for the brain scan.

'Morning. Morning!' Claire shouted from the gate.

I rushed out to her. 'Morning, Claire. How are you?'

'It's me should be asking you dat,' she said.

'Come in. Come in!' I stood aside to let her through the gate.

'I don't want to stop you from what you doing,' she said. 'I don't even reach home from work yet, but I say let me pass to check how everything is with you. Your mom doing okay?'

'Well… yeah. You know they found her at the back of a bus?'

'A bus? Dat's where they found her? I don't understand…' She sat on one of the veranda chairs. 'But how long she was in dat bus for?'

'Not sure. At least one night. But the driver took her to the police station, when he found her.'

'An' he – the driver – didn't check his bus when he finish—? *Bondyé.*'

'She could have had a stroke or something back there, but I'm just grateful he found her. And, so far, she seems okay.'

'Of course. Dat's good,' Claire said.

I offered her a drink, but she was keen to get home. 'Which hospital she in?'

'The Oriole,' I said.

'Oh. Okay.' She seemed distracted for a moment. 'An' you don't know how long she will be there for?'

'They might let her home today.'

'Let me know, eh? I'll come and see her as soon as I can.' She stood up.

'Oh, okay.' I thanked her for coming.

She tutted. 'People don't know how much trouble this kind of sickness can give.'

'You're telling me.'

'You still plan to take her back to Englan' with you?' she asked on our walk to the gate. I told her what the doctors had said. 'So I'm not sure yet.' But I was running out of options.

'Erica, girl, we'll talk again soon,' she said, after a pause. 'Give my love to your mom.'

'Okay.'

I closed the gate and prepared to make my way to the hospital.

On the journey, I reflected again on my conversation with Auntie yesterday. I'd taken what Mum had told me as a confession. One that made me glad, despite the pain at the time, that she'd made me leave Mr Frank's house.

After moving out, I'd kept the promise I'd made to myself not to contact her. And at the time I believed that her not contacting me was confirmation that she didn't care about me or her grand-child that I was carrying.

She was disappointed in me. I got that. I was disappointed too, but things happen. It had happened to her. She didn't have to sever ties with me because Mr Frank had said he wanted me out. She was right, I wasn't his daughter.

But I was *hers*.

Throughout the whole pregnancy, I'd managed to avoid all the places I might run into her. But I couldn't bring myself to send her away when she turned up at the hospital a day after Millie was born.

Delia was with me at the time. 'It's your mum,' she'd said.

We both watched Mum approaching my bed. A short glass vase with a display of orchids in one hand, a bag in the other.

'Hello, Erica,' she said. 'So how are you? How are you, Delia?'

Delia gave a polite response.

'I'm fine,' I said.

'I... I brought you dis.' Delia helped to make space for her to put the vase next to the fruit bowl. 'An' some food. I know how hospital food is.'

Emotions had me tongue-tied.

'This is my grandchild?' She walked round my bed, smiling, and leaned over the hospital cot Millie was lying in, tightly wrapped up and fast asleep.

I was pleased to have proved her to be wrong about Leo. He'd stuck by me through the whole of the pregnancy and not aban-doned me and the baby, like she'd said – and had done herself. He'd been away from my bedside when Mum arrived, but had returned offering her the opened arms I couldn't yet bring myself to give her, something that continued for a while after that visit.

Leo gave Mum the address of the new council place we'd got just before Millie was born and the day after I was discharged from hospital she visited, bringing toys, clothes and whatever she thought I could do with for Millie.

I thanked her and told her it wasn't necessary.

'I'm jus' trying to help,' she said. 'It's my gran'chile. My first.'

But each visit from her made the strain of pretending things were all right between us more unbearable.

'Don't you feel strange, Mum?' I asked one day, after putting Millie to lie in her travel cot, next to my chair in the front room.

'About what?' she said.

'About us. We haven't seen each other or spoken for months. The last time you saw me, I wasn't even properly showing. I mean, it's been almost a year, since we've... we've spoken or anything. Now you're visiting me, telling my daughter you love her, buying her gifts and everything... but what about before? Before, when I was carrying her and... and you didn't want to know me.'

'I did want to know you.'

'You threw me out,' I said.

'I tell you is Frank—'

'You blaming him? Did he force you not to have contact with me?'

'You... I—'

'Let me see if I've got this right. He told you he didn't want me in the house because I was pregnant and not his child. You said okay and told me I had to go. And as if that wasn't enough, you didn't even lift a finger to contact me to see if I was lying in a ditch. If I was okay.'

'In a ditch, Erica?'

'How would you know?'

'You had your Auntie Barbara – why you din go dere?'

'Is that what you expected me to do?' I said.

'Well, you could have.' She looked at me. 'Besides, I knew you was okay.'

'How?'

'People... I used to ask people.'

'Like who?'

'Barbara,' she said. 'You used to visit her an'... an' other people.'

Tears filled my eyes. 'You love him more than you love me, Mum. I can't believe it. For his money?'

'I... No, Erica. It wasn't dat.'

I glanced at Millie and lowered my voice. 'I was your child. You, my mother. I was pregnant. Did you know if I had enough food to eat for your grandchild there' – I pointed at Millie – 'to be healthy?'

'I... I was vex, then I was too ashame' to come an' look for you.'

'Exactly,' I said.

'I am sorry,' she said, a glisten in her eyes.

'You put him before me. You've put him before me ever since we moved in with him. That man who promised you marriage, but never delivered, who cheats on you constantly. Who had eyes on your own *daughter*—'

'Stop,' she said. 'You don't understand, Erica. So, I should let him put de two of us out? An' where we was going to go? Me, you an' a baby?'

'I had Leo,' I said.

'You had Leo an' who I would have? Where I would go?'

I looked at her in disbelief. 'Where do other women like you go? Women who leave crappy relationships for... for whatever reason. They go and—'

'Go an' find another place to live *where*? Go an' beg de government for a little money to help make ends meet, live in... in—? I don't *want* dat for myself again.' She began to cry.

I stood up. Millie began fussing. 'Honestly, Mum,' I said.

Part of her dilemma I could see, but was living with a man like Mr Frank her next best option?

She sniffed. 'We caa put all of dat behind us?' She looked over at Millie. 'Look... look you waking de baby.'

'She's fine,' I said, under my breath.

'I'm sorry, Erica. Let's put dat behind us, *on*?'

She was doing the deflection I'd learnt to accept from her.

'Do you love him, Mum?'

'I... of... of course. He... he have a good heart.'

'Where? How did you arrive at that conclusion?'

'All dose presents he was giving you—'

'Didn't I leave them for you and him when I left? Mum, it's not all about gifts and nice things! Where's the *love*, Mum? His love for you?'

'It's dere,' she said. 'No matter what you or anybody say. Frank love me.'

'Okay.' I sighed.

There was no disputing that I'd missed her in my life. She worshipped Millie, and from that first visit from her when I was in hospital, not a day passed without contact from her. She was doing her best for us to reconnect, but couldn't say goodbye to Mr Frank and whatever he was giving her. Leo was working any extra hours he could get at the advice centre, and it was great having her company on the days she visited.

What Mum needed to do was to get the strength to stand on her own two feet. She'd been with Mr Frank for eleven years at the time and my understanding was that she didn't have to make any contributions to the household. He paid all the bills. What she earned at the sweet factory was all hers. But she could still take him to court and get something from him to help get a place of her own. But she didn't want to do that. She wanted to be with him.

I deliberately stopped discussing her relationship with Mr Frank with her. She didn't complain about him to me. She was *my* mother – I wasn't hers. Mum was of a different generation: as much as I loved Leo, I couldn't see myself staying with him at any cost because of the comfortable lifestyle being with him brought. The adjustment wasn't easy for me, but I manoeuvred around it.

Months later, he showed up at my door with his balding head, pot belly and crooked smile.

'Mr Frank?' I gasped. 'What are you doing here? Where's Mum?' I was expecting to see her standing alongside him. And was already thinking of the reprimand I was going to give her for bringing him to my home.

'Seems like you don't want me to see your baby, so I bring a little something for you.' He looked me up and down suggestively, then held an envelope out to me. 'You looking good so quick.'

'What the—?'

'I can help you out, you know. Anytime you need. We can help each other. Your mother won't know, if you don't tell her.' He smirked.

I'd given him a hard stare. 'You... you think I would—? And you've brought me *money*?' I said, stunned at his presumptuousness. 'You... how *dare* you think I'd... Don't you dare come back here again, you... you *dirty* old—' I slammed the door in his face.

I said nothing to Mum, nor Leo. But weeks after Mr Frank's visit, the envelope he'd tried to hand me reappeared amongst our mail. He'd dropped it through the letterbox, my name written on it. Angry and disgusted, I'd picked it up and started carving a slot in the day for me to dispose of it – get it out of my house and back to where it belonged.

Leo wasn't intrusive. If a letter or card arrived addressed to me, he wouldn't spend time wondering or asking what it was.

My biggest dilemma was whether to tell Mum.

CHAPTER THIRTY-ONE

Relief that Mum seemed to be fine after her ordeal brought high expectancy to the day. There was something to look forward to and be happy about. Optimism entered my life. Mum was safe.

My hope was that they'd discharge her after doing the brain scan, then we all – me, Mum and Auntie – could go home together.

But Auntie had arranged to go back home with Cousin Headley. 'Jus' in case dey keep her in,' she said.

Mum was downstairs having the scan when we got to her ward. So we sat by her bed waiting, me feeling disappointed not to have been there when they'd taken her down for it. That I'd arrived too late.

Twenty minutes later, they wheeled her back in and I was able to ask the nurse who came with the porter how Mum had been overnight.

She spoke to me away from Mum's bed. 'She slept okay, with the tablet Dr Medouze prescribed, but once she is up – well, you know how it is. It's home she wants to go and she wants to know where certain people are. Sister Joan' – that was the woman in the nun's habit – 'keeps her company when she can.'

I asked if she thought Mum would be able to come home today.

'Dr Medouze will have to take a look at the scan and discuss it with you. It's for him to decide,' she said.

'Would that be this morning or in the afternoon?'

'I'm not sure. I will check with Sister Whitley and let you know.'

She left and came back to say that Dr Medouze was still at Queen Mary's hospital. And that Mum could probably go home after lunch.

'I tell you don't let dose people make Ione stay longer dan necessary in here, eh. You hear?' Auntie warned after the nurse left.

Just then, Cousin Headley walked in with a dark-skinned woman, a little taller than me. 'Look who I bring to see you!' he said, jovially.

'Hello. Hello. Good morning. Good morning, Cousin Ione, Cousin Barbara. Hello.' She looked at me, unsure. 'Cousin Erica?' she asked, in her husky voice.

'Er... Yes. Hello,' I answered.

'I'm Hannah. Your cousin.' She looked at Cousin Headley.

'Oh. Okay. Nice to meet you,' I said.

Auntie and I made way for them to get closer to Mum's bed.

'Dey taking good care of you in here?' Hannah asked, settling herself into one of the chairs by the bed.

Mum scrutinised her visitor's face, looked at Cousin Headley and said: 'Your girlfrien'?'

Auntie Barbara and Cousin Headley laughed.

'Eh-eh. No. No,' Hannah said. Hannah didn't look any older than mid-forties. Cousin Headley was ten years younger than Mum, so old enough to be Hannah's father. What was Mum thinking?

'Your cousin Hannah dat's dere,' Cousin Headley said. 'Cousin Sonia daughter.'

'Ohhh,' Mum said.

Hannah smiled, displaying gappy teeth. 'All of us are cousins,' she said.

The others had gone and Mum was in the middle of lunch, when a nurse came in to say Dr Medouze was ready to see me.

He was looking more formal today, in a white shirt and dark trousers.

'How are you?' he asked, shaking my hand again.

'Anxious about the scan, if I'm honest,' I said.

'I thought we could discuss it,' he said. 'Let's take a look in here.'

We went into a cosy room with two chairs, and a computer on a small desk, where he sat facing the screen. I sat next to him, the muskiness of his aftershave under my nose.

'I'll just get them up,' he said, sliding the mouse around until a large image of a brain appeared on the screen.

'Your mother has clearly been having some TIAs – transient ischemic attacks,' he said.

'Mini strokes.' I'd read about them online.

'Yes.'

I stared at the screen, the oval-shaped image representing Mum's brain. Dr Medouze pointed the cursor at some small white dots on the image. 'These,' he said, 'indicate some of the TIAs she's been having. As you can see, she's had several. And if you look here you can see the shrinkage—'

'Mmm.'

'These TIAs can lead to major strokes.'

'I understand, Doctor,' I said, moving my eyes from the screen.

This scrutiny was forcing me to see Mum as an object – her

brain as a thing to be studied. It dismissed the real, active person I'd known and loved all of my life; whom I couldn't imagine being without. It was reinforcing the knowledge that Mum would never be the same again. That screen gave confirmation of the unmistakable truth that I'd never have the mum I'd known back. Here was confirmation that she'd be leaving me: gradually, bit by bit, or suddenly, with little or no warning.

'So, we'll put her on a mild blood thinner for now and see if that helps.'

I took a deep breath. Pragmatism and rationality told me I should get as much information on Mum's condition as possible. But I couldn't. I didn't want to hear any more on that subject.

'Doctor, do you think she'd be better off in England?' The burning thought at the back of my mind found voice. It was worth getting a second opinion.

'You mean, if she had stayed there?'

'No. For me to take her back there now. Soon.'

Dr Medouze leaned back in his seat. 'I...' His eyes fell on Mum's file, then moved to my face. 'I wouldn't recommend it.' He shook his head. 'It wouldn't be good for her.'

I took another breath and swallowed, past the lump in my throat. 'How soon can she come home?'

He glanced at his watch. 'Any time you like.'

'Thank you, Doctor.'

'It's not easy, I know.'

'No, it's not.'

He gave me a lingering look. 'Keep her safe,' he said. 'And take care of yourself.'

'I'll do my best.' We both stood up and left the room, him allowing me out first.

After getting Mum dressed and paying the bill, which came to $3,300 and some change, we set off for home, with Mum drowsy in the passenger seat. Later, Auntie insisted on staying the night with us.

'Is jus' to keep you-all company,' she said.

I wasn't sure if it was to keep an eye on me, or on Mum, or for her to feel closer to her sister, but it made the evening feel cosy. Like a little celebration that Mum was home. I found myself in a bit of a tiswas, trying to make sure everything was as it should be, especially for Mum.

Clearing the spare room where Mum had stored what she had left of Mr Frank's things, hadn't left my to-do list, so Auntie had to sleep with Mum, which she said she preferred.

As I helped Mum in the shower, the temptation to quiz her rose again. Did she still have no recollection of what had gone on with her over the last three days? How many buses had she got on? Had anyone taken advantage of her in any way? How was I ever going to know?

With the two safely in bed, I sent texts to Millie and Delia, even though they weren't likely to see them until the morning.

In bed, lying on my back, I closed my eyes, welcoming the sensation of my weight oozing into the mattress.

CHAPTER THIRTY-TWO

'Erica? Where you? Erica?'

'Uh? Uh?' I raised my head from the pillow. 'Auntie?'

She knocked then came into my room.

'What? What's that, Auntie?'

'She pee in de bed. Ione!' Auntie said.

Unable to believe it was already morning, I trudged along to Mum's room. 'Mum?'

'Ione?'

'Look me,' Mum answered from the bathroom. 'All... all my nightie wet.'

'You dat wet it,' Auntie said, from behind me.

'Me?' Mum replied.

'Of course, is you wet de bed, Ione. Is not me.'

'Come on, let's get this nightie off,' I said, going into the bathroom, forcing myself to tolerate the obnoxious smell.

Auntie went off to use my bathroom.

I left Mum to finish sorting herself out in the shower and stripped the bed, ready for cleaning.

'Morning.' Mum addressed Auntie, who'd returned to the bedroom all cleaned up.

'Morning?' Auntie glared at Mum, then turned to me. 'She forget she see me already.'

Mum trotted off to the kitchen with Auntie, who'd volunteered to make breakfast.

'*Mé koté* Frank? But where's Frank?' Mum was asking Auntie as I came into the kitchen.

'Ione, how many times people have to tell you...'

I caught Auntie's eye, gave a deliberate blink and gently shook my head. *Let it go.*

'Well, let me go at my home, dan,' Mum said, sitting upright, like a light had come on in her head.

Auntie and I both looked at her.

'But, Ione, you don't see you already at your home?' Auntie said, clearly irritated. She turned to me. 'Erica, thank you for de breakfast. I will see you all later.'

'Wait for me,' Mum said, looking round.

'Let Auntie go. She's in a hurry,' I said. 'I'll take you home in a minute.'

'Good, because I have to go an' cook for Frank,' Mum said.

Auntie had quickly made her way to the bedroom and returned with her overnight bag in hand. She let out a sigh. 'I'll see you-all, you hear?'

I offered to drive her over.

'Erica, is just five minutes down de—'

'Well, leave the bag. I'll drop it off to you later,' I said. I had to make things easier for her too, or I'd have two sets of carers to find.

'Well, all right.'

I took the bag from her, dropped it on a chair and went to see her off.

'Your workplace give you de extra time?' she asked at the gate.

'I haven't heard yet,' I said.

'Mmm.' She turned her eyes towards the sky and sighed. 'I will see you all later, den.'

I locked the gate behind her.

Mum had followed us as far as the veranda, where she sat. I left her there and went inside, leaving my bedroom door open to keep an eye on her.

Millie, then Delia rang, both wanting to say hello to her.

Mum went and sat at the kitchen table. Her script was the same for both of them: 'Hello, *ich mwen*. I'm all right. When you coming an' see me?' I could guess the questions they were asking her.

'Bet you're glad to get her home,' Delia said, when I took the phone back.

'Yes and no. Wait. That came out wrong,' I said, lowering my voice. 'It's good to have her home, but... honestly, Del, I can't see how I'm going to be able to leave any time soon.' I told her about my request for a couple more weeks' leave from work. 'Not sure if I'll get it, though.'

'Your boss is your mate, so it should be okay, shouldn't it?'

'Yeah, but whatever I ask for now has to be approved by the governors.'

'It's still better than resigning.'

'Listen, I've got to go,' I said. Someone was at the gate.

'Oh. Okay. We'll talk later, or tomorrow.'

'Morning,' I shouted, as soon as I hung up. 'I'm coming!'

It was Mrs Andrews.

'Good morning, good morning. I just pass to see your mudder on my way to pay some bills. I heard she was home,' she said.

'Good morning. Yes. She's inside,' I said.

'And I brought you a few mangoes.' She handed me a carrier bag, which I thanked her for, offered her a drink and a seat on the veranda, then went to get Mum.

'Mrs Andrews has come to see you,' I told her.

'Frank she come to see?' Mum replied.

'No, you.' I frowned. 'Go and say hello.'

I hurried off to get the water.

'Ione,' I heard Mrs Andrews saying, as I stepped past Mum in the doorway. 'How are you? You feeling better?'

'I'm okay,' Mum said. 'Frank is not here.'

'Oh, I know dat.' Mrs Andrews cleared her throat and looked at me, then diverted her gaze to Mum. 'I heard you were in the hospital.'

'Mmm.'

I handed Mrs Andrews the glass of water she'd asked for.

'I brought you some mangoes,' she told Mum, her eyes fixed on her as if assessing her every word and move. 'I'm glad you're safely back.' She flashed a look at me.

'Yes. We're glad she's safely back,' I said, a little uncomfortable with Mum's silence, which was coming across as unwelcoming.

'Well,' Mrs Andrews hesitated, shifting in her seat, 'I just wanted to say hello, Ione, and to wish you well.'

I thanked her on Mum's behalf. 'It's very nice of you to come. Isn't it, Mum?'

We both looked at Mum.

'How is Walter?' Mum responded.

'Walter?' Mrs Andrews said, frowning. 'Walter? My Walter? I wish he was here.' She paused. 'But you were at the funeral. Seven years ago.' She became still. Sadness fell into her eyes. 'Well... I have these bills to pay. Better go before this sun get too hot.'

'I'll walk you to the gate,' I said, standing up. 'I won't be a minute, Mum.'

'No. No. There's no need.'

'I need to lock it, anyway,' I said, quietly.

'I will see you again, Ione,' she said, looking at Mum, who replied as though they were old friends now.

'Her memory is very bad?' Mrs Andrews whispered to me on our way.

'Uh-huh.' I nodded and thanked her again for the visit.

'It can't be easy for you.'

I shrugged. 'No.'

CHAPTER THIRTY-THREE

I didn't get round to returning Mr Frank's envelope in time. Mum spotted it when she came to visit.

'Where you get dat from?' she asked, holding it up to me in the kitchen.

'What?' I turned around. 'Oh, Mum. I didn't want you to know about this.'

'Why – because you taking money from Frank behind my back?'

'Mum?' Her accusation took me by surprise.

'Dis is de same envelope Frank does use to pay his staff, an' I know his handwriting well.'

'It's not what you're thinking, Mum. I wouldn't be taking—'

'So what is dis?' she demanded.

I told her about him appearing at the front door and what had happened. 'I don't even know how the hell he got my address. Did you give it to him?'

'I...'

'All I want to say, Mum, is I plan to give his money back to him.'

'You mean to say, Frank find your address an' bring money

for you? How much is in dere?'

'I don't know and I don't care. I intend to give it back.'

'I taking it.'

'No,' I insisted. My suspicion was that she'd keep it and say nothing to avoid an argument with him. 'I have to give it back to him. He has to know I haven't kept it. I'm not playing games with him. I don't have to put up with him anymore and don't want him in my life, as far as I can help it.'

It took me a while to convince her to let me do it my way, and I wasn't sure if she believed or trusted I would give it back.

The fact that my mother had underlying suspicions that I might be encouraging her would-be husband to befriend me and give me handouts was more than unsettling.

As part of proving I wasn't hiding anything, I'd asked Mum when Mr Frank was likely to be home and, with Millie strapped to my front in the baby carrier, I got a bus to their house and knocked on the door.

She'd opened it to me, mouth gaping. Threw a furtive glanced over her shoulder, put a hand out and whispered: 'Give it to me. I will give it to him.'

'No.' And just like that woman had done on that Saturday morning all those years ago, I shouted out his name.

'It's all right,' Mum said, trying to quieten me.

I shouted his name even louder, until he appeared in the hallway.

'What—?'

'This belongs to you,' I said, holding up the envelope, with Mum standing between us. 'Here.' I threw it at him. 'I'm not my mother, or any of those other women you buy. I'll see you, Mum.'

I left her and him at their doorstep. It was their affair to sort out.

CHAPTER THIRTY-FOUR

Phillipa called and put an end to my wait for the governors' decision on my request for an extra two weeks' extended leave.

'I fought your corner,' she said. 'It's been approved.'

'Thank God for that,' I said. 'Thanks, Phil. I really appreciate it. Though I'm starting to think I should have asked for a month.'

'Oh. Things aren't getting worse, are they?'

'It's hard to say. It's just that I'm nowhere nearer to sorting things out for her.'

'Oh, dear.'

'Hopefully, I'll manage it in time. I'll see,' I said. 'It's just – if I'm honest, she seems to be getting worse. The doctor's just told me she's been having mini strokes.' I filled her in on the last few days' events.

'Oh, no,' she said.

'And now she's showing signs of incontinence.'

'Are there any services there that could help with any of that?'

'You're joking. And if there was, Mum would need to be

poor enough to qualify. Honestly, Phil, I'll never complain about the NHS again.'

'Have you thought about taking a sabbatical?'

'Sabbatical?' The idea scared me. I wasn't ready to say goodbye to my job, but it did mean I'd be able to keep it.

'It might be a good option since no one knows how long all of this will go on for with your mum...'

Phillipa's analysis put me on a roller-coaster where decisions about my life were being made for me. I was simply being dragged along.

'People can live for a long time with dementia.'

I wasn't wishing Mum dead, but Phillipa's last words rang like a warning in my ear, amplified fears of what lay ahead for me. I wasn't ready for retirement, and caring for the elderly wasn't my chosen profession. My job at Rushmeade fulfilled my life in a way nothing else could. I didn't have what it took to care for the elderly or manage dementia. That person wasn't me. I knew about efficiency, running a school, motivating staff, children – all those things that would enable me to make a superb headteacher, before retirement. *Oh, dread.*

'Think about it,' Phillipa said. 'I'm happy to argue your case again.'

Phillipa was kind, and a great line manager. I guess that's why we grew to be friends. But the longer I was away the heavier her workload would become. And a sabbatical would mean her having to get a locum. That locum might become another competitor for the headship next year. Then there was the possibility of not being able to take Mum back to England. Problems were escalating. I could see my opportunity for the post fading. There was a lot to think about, things to put in place and secure.

'Morning, *ich mwen.*'

'Morning, Mum.' *Wow.* She was standing behind me wearing a floral top over a red and black striped skirt, her head wrapped in the yellow head scarf she'd worn to bed. I didn't dare ask whether she'd showered. A visual inspection of her bathroom would clarify that.

It would be a quick breakfast this morning.

Outside was warm, but close, with the odd cloud passing over the sun, giving the impression that there may be some more rain later. I set Mum's cornflakes in front of her.

'Where's yours?' she said.

'I'm not hungry, yet.'

Mum's request to 'go home' after breakfast tied up nicely with my planned shopping trip. The hired car had been extremely useful in the past few days. I'd extended the rental period and it was sitting there with almost a full tank.

'Let's see what else you can wear,' I said, and coaxed her into changing into an outfit more in line with the style I'd known her to prefer. I left her to get dressed and called Auntie to ask if she needed anything from the shops. She said she didn't.

When I returned to Mum's bedroom, she was turning this way and that. 'My bag. Where's my bag?' she said.

I handed it to her. 'You not untying your head?' I asked.

'No. It's cole.'

We hadn't driven off yet when she started humming, 'I Can't Stop Loving You.'

I joined in, the words triggering a yearning for that special, intimate love I hadn't had for so long.

'What a nice song,' she said, when we stopped.

'Is, isn't it?'

'We used to really dance to dat.'

'We did.'

'Dey used to play dat at de dance.'

'Mmm.'

I parked and helped her out of the car. She was slower now, so we took our time.

'I've got a trolley,' I told her, as she picked a basket from the pile at the entrance to the store. 'Look.' I tapped the handle.

'Dat's for your shopping,' she said. 'I have my own things to buy.' She put her arm through the metal handle, holding it close, like it was hers for keeps, then, walked straight to the cereal aisle, stopping at a shelf with 'Special Offer' written in red under the cornflakes.

I'd mainly come for more incontinence pants. Her bedwetting hadn't been the one-off I'd hoped for. The toiletries section was to our left as we entered the store, but given Mum's tendency to wander and stray, I stayed close by.

'We don't need cornflakes, Mum,' I said. She walked further along, picked up a packet of porridge oats and dropped it in her basket. I picked up lentils, rice and a couple of other items from the shelf nearby. 'Come on. We need veg.' I pushed my trolley back to where she was standing. 'And toiletries.' She ignored me.

I would have been halfway through my list by now, if I'd come alone.

'I need butter,' she said.

The toiletries and veg sections were close enough to the exit door for me to see her if she tried to leave, so I left her in front of the fridges and rushed to the toiletries section, then swung over to the fruit and veg, constantly checking for the yellow scarf she'd insisted on wearing. When I quickly looped back to where I'd left her, she wasn't there, but couldn't have got far at the pace she walked. I scurried around, positioning myself at the tops of aisles so I could glance down them and keep moving. She had to be somewhere in there.

Spotting her, I released a breath I hadn't realise I was holding. She was speaking to a woman I vaguely recognised as our cousin. Hannah.

'There you are, Mum,' I said, wheeling my trolley closer to them. 'I've been looking for you.

'Cousin Erica,' Hannah said, taking her eyes off Mum to address me. 'I was jus' asking Cousin Ione if you was with her.'

'Hi, Hannah. I... I just went to quickly pick something up. She wants to do her own shopping,' I said, slightly embarrassed that I'd left Mum to her own devices. If Hannah was close to Cousin Headley she may have known a lot, if not all, about Mum's condition – and her antics.

'So how things going?' Hannah asked, walking alongside me, Mum ahead of us.

'Not too great,' I said. 'Mum's... well, getting incontinent now.' I pointed at the packets of pants in my trolley.

'I can walk with Cousin Ione, while you get the res' of your shopping, if you want?' she said. 'We can shop together.'

'Oh, it's okay, thanks, Hannah. I think we've finished now. I've got everything I came for. It wasn't much.'

'All right,' Hannah said, hesitating. 'Well, I'll see you again, eh?'

'Yes. Okay.'

She went closer to Mum. 'We'll see again, Cousin Ione.'

'Okay,' Mum said, waving to Hannah with the hand she was carrying the basket.

Hannah smiled and walked away, but as we drove past the first bus stop from the supermarket, I spotted her. I pulled over and called out to her.

She waved. I beckoned. 'Come. Where're you off to?' I said, when she reached us.

'Home,' she said.

'Where's that?'

'By Micoud side dere.'

'Oh, well, that's not far from us,' I said, relieved it wouldn't be too far out of our way to risk me getting lost. 'Come on. I'll give you a lift.'

She thanked me and got in. 'Cousin Ione, look, we meet again,' she said, tapping Mum's shoulder.

'Hello,' Mum said.

'You been living in Micoud long?' I asked, as we drove off. I couldn't believe she lived that close by and I hadn't met her before she showed up at the hospital.

'Not so long. I was here in Vieux Fort for a long while, but me an' my friend stop getting along, so...'

'You're close by then. Near us.'

'Yes. Cousin Headley tell me dat too.'

'So you must pop by. Come and say hello.'

'I know. I mus' get to know my fam'ly. Isn't it, Cousin Ione?' She leaned closer to Mum so she could hear her. 'I'm very grateful for the ride.'

Her place turned out to be a small wooden house tucked down a narrow track, off the main road running through Micoud village.

'Who is dat?' Mum wanted to know after we'd dropped Hannah off.

'Our cousin, Hannah,' I said.

'Hannah? What Hannah is dat?'

'She's our cousin Sonia's daughter.' I repeated what I'd heard Hannah say, though I hadn't a clue who this cousin Sonia was.

'Hold on, Mum,' I said, getting out of the car to open the gate so I could drive in.

'Bondyé.' She clung to my arm, jostled out of her seat and trudged past me, heading for the new kitchen door. I hadn't given her a key to it yet, so followed her to open it.

No. 'Mum, what's that at the back of your dress?'

'What?' she said.

I came closer and touched it. 'You're wet.'

'What...?'

'You... you're not wearing the pants I left for you to put on.'

'Pants?'

'I left them on the bed for you. What are you wearing?' I tapped her bottom again.

'What de hell you think you doing?' she shouted, slapping my hand away.

'Come on.' I took her arm, almost dragging her to the bathroom, afraid to let her go in case she sat down on something and soiled that too.

'What?'

'To wash. And...'

'I don't need you to come an' wash me,' she said, marching on ahead.

'You have to take the wet clothes off. Quick!' I shouted, close on her tail.

'I can...' She began to address me from the bathroom door.

'Come on. Take it off, Mum.' I tugged at her dress.

'Help!'

I moved closer in. 'What's wrong with you?'

'What de hell...? Take your focking hand...' She glared. 'Move from—'

She pushed me. Stumbling, I grabbed for something to help steady me, but I fell anyway, bringing her down with me.

'Ahhh!' Crippling pain rippled through my lower back. I couldn't move. 'Look what you've done,' I said, tears filling my eyes. 'I was trying to help...'

'You push me down?' she snarled, looking around, then grabbing the edge of the toilet bowl. 'Bastard.'

'If I'm a bastard, it's because you made me that,' I screamed, turning away, her words reminding me of my father's rejection. I couldn't bear to look at her and stayed where I was until the pain disseminated into discomfort and my back began to feel like it could belong to me again. Holding onto the sink, with great care and caution, I heaved myself off the floor.

We faced each other, hate spewing from our eyes.

'Sort your own pissy self out,' I said, hauling my aching body to my room. I locked the door and lay on the bed, wishing her – this life – all of it, gone.

Minutes went by before I heard: 'Hello?'

I didn't answer. Just looked at the door, tears trickling down my face.

'Erica?'

'Yes, Mum.' I was her child again, responding as I should. I got up, wiped my eyes and opened the door.

'You all right, *ich mwen*?' She was still wearing the soiled dress.

'No. No, I'm not,' I said.

'What's the matter?'

'Nothing. Nothing. It's all right.' There was no point in telling her. My back was bruised, sore from the fall, but I was willing to bet, despite any bruises on her body, that she'd forgotten the whole incident.

I moved past her.

'What happen to you?' she said.

'Nothing.'

'But you walking funny.'

'I'm... I'll be all right. Come on. You need to get changed.'

How was I going to leave her with someone and be sure this kind of thing wouldn't happen between them? They could lose it and react just as I had – or worse.

The conversation went on in my head all through helping her get cleaned up. Every new behaviour Mum displayed set me off balance. I could never be prepared. Never be near certain about what might come next.

· · ·

'You vex?' she asked later, watching me put the shopping away.

'I'm okay,' I lied, not allowing my eyes to meet hers.

She was the one with cognitive impairment. She was allowed to behave the way she did. I wasn't. I was supposed to exercise patience, respond to her with understanding and care. That's what all the advice said, and the rational part of me understood all of that.

But what about me?

What about my pains?

When will we be able to stop hurting each other?

CHAPTER THIRTY-FIVE

Millie was three when Leo left to go and work on a two-month project in Mozambique. He'd been hinting about it for ages, saying how he'd always wanted to visit Africa and this trip would be all paid for. I was halfway through teacher training then. Three weeks after he left, I discovered I was pregnant again. The coil had failed me.

He hesitated at first when I told him, over the phone, then said it was great. But his two-month project extended into three, then four, and then permanency.

'Everything will be all right,' Mum assured me. 'You never know, he could still come back.'

'What if something's happened to him and no one's told me?' I said, when my last few letters to him were returned with a note saying he was no longer working there. I resorted to digging through his papers to find other contacts: his mother, father – anyone whom he might have been in touch with.

I found his mum's address in Ireland. On one occasion, when I was pregnant, he'd taken me up there to meet her, but neither of them had been good at staying in touch with each other. Whenever I'd suggested he called to see how she was, he'd say, 'She can call me too, you know.'

I wrote and told her what had happened, sent pictures of Millie and asked if she'd had any contact from him.

She responded with a phone call. 'I'm so sorry about what he's done to you,' she'd said. 'Leaving you and the little one like that.'

She hadn't heard from him either. Didn't even know he'd gone to Africa. There was no contact for his father. They'd parted when Leo was eleven.

After that call to her, she promised she'd let me know if she heard anything from him and I said I would do the same for her.

Leo had truly abandoned us. Moved on. Left me and Millie behind. Obviously found someone else. There'd be plenty of beautiful and smart women out there to choose from.

Millie and I would become part of his past. And I had another baby on the way.

'How could he do this to me?' I asked Mum. 'And Millie. What am I going to do?'

'I will help you,' Mum said. 'You an' Millie an' de baby will be all right.'

Thankfully, I already had a cot, buggy – all the big things needed for a new baby. After I'd bled the savings dry, Mum helped me pay for Millie's nursery. When I got stuck, she picked her up from nursery for me, taking care of her at my place until I got in.

Making the psychological adjustment to being a single mum and being on benefits had me down for a while but, thanks to Mum, I never felt too hard up.

There were moments during the pregnancy when I'd fantasise about Leo coming home. But when labour came, it was Mum who was there, replacing him as my birthing partner, and the two of us marvelled at the bouncy eight-pounder I'd produced.

My Shane was a contented baby. There'd be a whimper when he was up and wanting his feed – I'd look across at his cot and see his little head bopping up and down.

That's why, months later, I couldn't understand what all the crying was about on that horrendous night, when the wind wouldn't stop wailing, and heavy rain thumped and thumped the windows like it was demanding to be let in. No amount of hugging, holding or rocking would console Shane. Not even humming the 'Hush Little Baby' tune that would normally lull him to sleep. As soon as I put him down, he'd be awake again, crying, pulling his little legs up towards his chest. It had to be wind, I convinced myself, a tummy ache – colic. Maybe he was coming down with a cold.

When I felt the heat coming from his body, I called Mum. 'Something might be wrong,' I said.

She'd come over, dripping wet, to stay with Millie, while I headed off in the ambulance, with Shane. His crying didn't stop. Still, I didn't expect it to be more than a cold. They'd give him some medication that would calm him, bring his temperature down and we'd be back home. That was my expectation.

But hours later, after being diagnosed with bacterial meningitis, my baby was dead.

Babies weren't tested for sickle cell in those days, so I'd never know whether he was carrying the trait. Years after that, we learnt that Millie and I were carriers. If Shane did have the trait, it would very likely have been a contributory factor to him dying from meningitis.

But if I'd taken him to the hospital earlier, they might have been able to save him.

CHAPTER THIRTY-SIX

The bad weather, a few days ago, had broken the trunks of two banana trees and a plantain, leaving them paralysed, heads on the ground. They'd need to be cut and got rid of, together with the rotting fruits and loose branches all over the garden. We'd been waiting for the gardener to come and tidy things up, so when a voice shouted from the gate, I thought it might be him.

'Oh, hi, Hannah!' I said. 'What a surprise.'

'I come an' see how you-all are,' she said. 'Cousin Ione dere?'

'Come in. Come,' I said, leading her in. 'I think she's in the front room. She might have moved, but let's see.'

Mum's engagement in conversations had declined since her stay in hospital. The vacant, confused expression was on her face more often. I'd wondered whether it was the new drug she was on, and was still monitoring it.

She was where I'd left her – walking around mumbling, between hums, touching and picking things up, as if to confirm what they were, then putting them back.

'We have a visitor,' I told her. 'Hannah's come to see you.'

'Hannah?' she said, like she'd never heard the name before.

'Good morning,' Hannah said, from the doorway. 'Is me, Cousin Ione. *Mwen sa ich Kouzen Sonia*. I'm Cousin Sonia's child.'

'You can go in, Hannah,' I said. She took slow and cautious steps into the room. I offered drinks.

'Water, thank you,' Hannah said.

Outside was where I was most comfortable, but I made an exception for Mum and Hannah's sake, and after getting Hannah's drink, sat in the sitting room with them.

Hannah was trying to get Mum to remember her visit to her in the hospital, using Cousin Headley as the link. When she saw how that was failing, she moved on to our meeting in the supermarket. Then Claire showed up.

She too wanted to see Mum. I brought her in. After ten minutes, Mum went back to humming again, and wandered out into the kitchen, oblivious to her visitors.

'Where you off to, Mum?'

'I don't know,' she said, and continued walking.

'I'll just see where she's going,' I said.

Claire and Hannah looked at me.

'Dat's okay,' Hannah said.

Mum took her time finding her room. I returned to the front room, apologised for Mum disappearing and suggested we sat outside. 'It's the Alzheimer's,' I said, quietly. 'She won't be able to wander out without anyone seeing her if we sit here.'

'Don't let me forget another reason why I came,' Claire said, reaching into her bag. 'Look.' She presented a ticket. 'I bought this for you.'

I took the small, square card from her. 'What is it?'

'*Jibyé Palé*, Talking Bird,' Claire said. 'They have a show nex' Saturday. I bought this ticket for you.'

'A show? You mean like music and—'

'A show. A... play.'

'Oh! That sounds nice.'

'You have to have a break from this house an' I know you love your mom like crazy, but you can't spend every day an' night taking care of her with no break, unless she sleeping.'

'Oh, yes. Dat's true,' Hannah said, smiling. 'It will make you laugh.'

'It's in Castries, so we will leave here around five-thirty,' Claire said. 'And I will drive.'

'It's very nice of you to think of me, but—'

'Come on. This is not your cousin?'

'Yes, by my mother,' Hannah replied.

'So? She can help?' Claire looked at me, head tilted.

'I'll think about it, but I'll reimburse you too, for this ticket.' Claire tutted. 'It's okay.'

'I'll see if Auntie won't mind—'

'I can stay with Cousin Ione for you, if you like, Cousin Erica,' Hannah said. 'What time next week Saturday?'

I looked at the little card. 'Says it starts at seven on here.'

The prospect of going out, to socialise, left me secretly excited. It would be a change from my current choice of spending evenings alone in my room, walking around the garden star-gazing, and sitting on the veranda tippling alcohol to numb thoughts of Mum's disease and everything else connected with it. It was an offer of a real time-out.

I ran it by Auntie to see what she thought.

'She's a nice girl. Headley seem to like her,' she said. 'An' you say you not going to come home too late.'

'And Claire said she'd take her home for me when we get back.'

'Take care with dat Claire though, eh,' Auntie said.

'Why?'

'People say she's a *zanmyèz*.'

'*Zanmyèz*?' I had to think quickly about the word. 'Lesbian – she's gay? Oh, yeah, I know. She told me. And it doesn't matter to me. She's one of the nicest people I've met here.'

'I jus' telling you, in case she like you in dat way.'

'She doesn't, Auntie. She knows I'm not gay. Honestly,' I added, exasperated by Auntie's suggestion.

'Jus' watch yourself. You mus' tell Hannah too.'

'Hannah's fine,' I said, firmly.

Closer to the day, the idea of having Hannah staying with Mum instead of Auntie started to make me a little anxious. The only person I knew who could tell me more about her was Cousin Headley. He assured me she was a good person. Trustworthy.

'But you know how difficult Mum can be,' I said. 'And Mum's only met her three times in the time I've been here.'

'An' when you not here, you think Hannah doesn't see her?'

I told him about the incident with the knife on the night I arrived.

'I know all dat. Cousin Barbara already tell me.'

What does Auntie not tell Cousin Headley?

After our conversation an idea came to me. I called Hannah and came clean about my ambivalence.

She suggested coming over to spend time with Mum. 'For her to get used to me.'

'And you to her,' I said. 'She's not always easy.'

'I know. I know,' she said.

'She can get violent – try to fight you. She can say nasty things as well.'

'Cousin Headley tell me already all how Cousin Ione is – how she does behave an' things like dat. I did look after my mother well before she die. I can manage her, Cousin Erica,' Hannah said.

Her words began to loosen a knot inside me.

'So which day you want me to come?'

I took a deep breath. 'When are you free?'

'Well, I don't have chil'ren, husban' or nothing like dat to put pressure on me. Is when you want me.'

We arranged a couple of days in the week, but she ended up doing three and managed Mum's quirkiness better than I did. Showed none of the irritability I did at times with Mum's behaviour and even managed to interest her in tackling one of the small jig-saw puzzles I'd bought a while back. Like with Cousin Headley, I could see pity on her face and in her eyes sometimes, when she looked at Mum or responded to her, but nothing Mum did or said reduced her to tears. She was more equipped for this job than me.

When I was on caring duty, hardly a day went by without tears. Caring for Mum was blighted by our past and my deep emotional connection with her.

'Why she would say dat?' I heard Hannah asking Mum while they picked limes from around the tree. Mum had accused someone in her imaginary world of saying something she wasn't pleased with.

'I don't know,' Mum replied.

'She should mind her business, eh?' Hannah said, clearly humouring Mum.

Observing them was a training course in itself. One I wouldn't pass with more than a grade C.

My sense of inadequacy aside, it was a relief to have found Hannah because she could do the things that needed to be done for Mum. Meaning I, and possibly Mum, could be spared a lot of emotional pain.

CHAPTER THIRTY-SEVEN

Claire kept me chatting all the way to the Morne, a hilly location overlooking the city. I told her about some of the plays I'd seen in England and how much I enjoyed live performances.

'You say you understand Kwéyòl good, eh?' she said.

I told her that I did.

'Everything, English lady?' she teased.

'Everything.'

We laughed.

'All right. All right. I believe you.'

It was still light when we got there. After parking the car, we began making our way to the entrance of what looked like a large gazebo, then Claire said: 'They don't let you eat inside, so you want something to eat before we go in?'

'Okay,' I said. We walked around the booths scattered close to the entrance to see what was on offer. Claire bought some nuts and whilst I waited for my float – a super light fried dumpling very popular in the Eastern Caribbean – Claire disappeared and returned with a plastic cup and a small bottle of fizzy drink.

'Wine okay for you?' she asked.

It looked like a rosé. 'Mmm.' I nodded and took the cup from her. 'Thanks.'

We joined the queue then two women came over and said hello to Claire. She introduced me and they said they'd see us inside. More people greeted her once we got in there.

'You're popular,' I said.

'I know a lot of people,' she said, laughing.

Seats were laid out similar to a regular theatre, getting higher up the further you got from the stage. We sat towards the front.

The performance was about to start when I heard a voice I recognised. I turned, and caught his eyes. 'Dr Medouze? Hi,' I said, giving a quick glance and a smile to the young woman sitting next to him.

He nodded. 'Nice to see you. How are you?'

'Okay,' I said, lowering my voice. Grateful the lights were fading because my smile came with a blush. I gave a light wave and turned to face the stage.

'Who's dat?' Claire whispered.

'Mum's doctor at the hospital,' I whispered back.

The setting was basic, with performers wearing mikes which I initially found off-putting. At odd moments I was distracted by Dr Medouze's voice and glanced back to look at him.

Intermission came. Claire said she needed the loo. 'I'll meet you over there.' She pointed towards the exit opposite the one she was about to take. Other people were spilling out through it. 'You can buy a drink or something. A float,' she said, when I asked if she wanted anything. 'And a small water.'

Fish and chips, St Lucian style, was available on this side. While waiting for the portion of chips I'd ordered, I scanned the area to see if I'd catch a glimpse of Dr Medouze and his friend.

'What you doing here?' Claire asked. She'd found me

leaning against a huge stone towards the edge of the hill, enjoying the breeze.

'Beautiful, isn't it, this?' I said, reluctant to take my eyes off the view of different coloured lights from the houses and passing cars, far off in distance below.

'I suppose so,' she said.

Does it take being a visitor to appreciate the beauty of this place?

Soon we were back in again and there was no sign of Dr Medouze or the woman he was with.

The play, which was about a young woman who was finding it difficult to choose between the two young men in her life, was as funny as Hannah had said it would be. The acting wasn't too bad either, and I'd laughed enough to put aside almost all worries about Mum, and whatever gloom there was waiting ahead.

CHAPTER THIRTY-EIGHT

It was Sunday. Mum was pacing. Talking to imaginary people Auntie would claim were spirits.

I called out to her. 'Lunch is ready.'

Hearing my voice, she changed direction. 'What you say?'

'Lunch. We're eating outside.'

The ceiling fan was spinning, but not doing enough to tackle the heat that would have sent me putting my head through an opened window if I'd been in England.

'All right,' she mumbled, peering at the food on the plate.

'Come on.'

She followed me out.

'Where's yours?' she asked, when I put the plate in front of her.

'I'm getting it, but don't wait for me. You can start.'

I came back with my plate and sat opposite her at the table.

'Mmm.'

A glance at her made me noticed small pebbles of perspiration on her forehead and cheeks.

'You see. You're hot too.' I took the piece of kitchen paper I'd brought for my mouth and dabbed her face.

'Thank you,' she said.

'You okay?' Her voice was low.

She was staring out, but not at me, her eyes smaller than usual. 'Mum? You okay?' I repeated. Her eyelids started to flicker. This wasn't a good sign. What was going on? I stood up. 'Mum?'

Her body jerked. She was about to have another one of those attacks. I rushed for the phone and called the Oriole's emergency service, then rushed back to her, flustered, scrambling through my mind for ideas – something I hadn't thought about that would force or jump-start her breathing back to normality. But all I could do was hold her. Pray that this episode wouldn't end in a disaster; that Mum wasn't going to take her last breath there, sitting at the table with me unable to help her.

To wait was all I could do, for the gasping to subside, but before that came a sudden surge as she emptied her stomach over herself and the floor again.

'Oh, Mum.' I pulled her chair away from the table and tipped the mess out of her dress. 'Mum?'

I stood supporting her head, looking down at her face, praying as hard as I could for the gasping to stop; for her to start breathing normally again. Half a minute later things began to slow down. Her head fell to the side and her eyes began to drift, like the last time. She was coming back.

CHAPTER THIRTY-NINE

We arrived at the Oriole and Mum was seen by a young doctor, to whom I explained what had happened. She said they needed to do tests again.

It took two nurses and me, holding Mum, continually telling her that taking urine directly from her, was necessary. I reassured her and myself, over her screams, that the ordeal would soon be over.

Half an hour later, she was falling asleep. I nabbed one of the nurses and asked what we were waiting for.

'Dr Medouze,' she said.

'And how long will that be?' I asked, and pointed out that Mum was tired and falling asleep.

She said he was on his way.

Forty-five minutes later, he hadn't arrived, but the female doctor came and said they thought it would be best to admit Mum. 'At least for one night, to monitor things.'

'Okay.' I nodded. 'But can someone tell me what just happened with my mother? Did she have a stroke?'

'Dr Medouze will look at her test results and discuss that with you,' she said.

I assumed she must be a junior doctor.

A banging sound made me lift my head off my arm, where I was leaning on Mum's bed. The nun, Sister Joan, was coming through the door with a tray. Until then, it had been quiet. Mum had nodded off and I'd almost followed suit.

The only other patient in the ward was two beds away with the curtain drawn, separating her from our side of the room. She was sleeping, sedated or something, because I hadn't heard a murmur from her. Though a nurse had been in to check on her.

I greeted Sister Joan.

'You come back to see us?' she said, coming towards Mum's bed. 'And how are you?'

'Okay, thank you,' I said. 'Mum?' I touched Mum's hand, sorry to have to wake her.

'Barbara?' she said, before even opening her eyes.

'We have something for you.' Sister Joan put the tray down and began adjusting Mum's bed into a more upright position. 'Why don't you let me help her eat,' she told me. 'I will sit with her. You can go and get something for yourself downstairs, or get a little fresh air.'

I looked at Mum and considered Sister Joan's suggestion.

'Come on. Let's eat something,' she said, helping Mum to sit up and adjust her pillows. She glanced at me again.

Nothing, not even water, had crossed my lips since breakfast. I hesitated.

'I won't be long, eh, Mum?' I said. 'Make sure you eat.' I thanked the nun and left, but went straight out of the building, inhaling deeply when I hit the outside air.

These dummy runs of how I was likely to lose Mum, witnessing her take what could be her last breath, were wearing. I needed comfort, reassurance. But there was no one to give it to me.

'Good afternoon.' Dr Medouze's now-familiar voice startled me.

Blinking back tears, I turned. 'Good afternoon, Doctor.'

He was standing close by, a grey stethoscope around his neck. 'Sorry, I didn't mean to frighten you,' he said.

'No. No, it's okay.'

'I'm running a little late. You're here for your mother?'

'Yeah.' I sighed. 'I brought her in earlier. I think she's had a stroke.'

'I'm sorry to hear that. Well, let's get inside and see what's happening with her.'

I walked beside him, the faint scent of his aftershave taking my thoughts away from Mum for a split second.

'What did you think of the show?' he said.

'Nice... it was nice,' I said. 'You?'

'If I'm honest, it was hard to get into it since I had to translate the patois to Beth – my cousin who was with me. She's visiting.'

'Oh,' I said. What was this relief in knowing that the woman was his cousin and not a friend?

'Then I had to leave for an emergency.'

'Oh. That's a shame.'

He held the door for me as we entered, and our conversation ended as we approached the nurses' station. I walked on to Mum's ward.

Minutes later, Dr Medouze came in, followed by a nurse. 'How are you feeling, Mrs Joseph?' he asked.

'Doctor?' Mum said.

'Yes, he's the doctor, Mum,' I said.

'Dr Medouze. Remember me?'

'Of course,' Mum said.

The nurse smiled.

'Now, let's see,' Dr Medouze said. 'I hear you've been

having some problems. Mmm?' He proceeded to examine her, spoke quietly to the nurse, then asked if he could have a word with me.

'Where you going?' Mum said, as I turned to leave.

'I'll be back in a minute. I'm just going to speak to the doctor,' I said.

'She won't be long,' Dr Medouze confirmed.

The nurse stayed with her.

'She's very protective,' he said, lowering his voice, as we went through the door.

Back in the same little room, we both sat down. There was no screen to look at this time.

Dr Medouze sighed. 'Sorry to see her back here so quickly.'

'Me too. Seems it's one thing after another with her Alzheimer's. Is that what brought this on? Can you tell from... from everything, if it was a stroke? The real thing?' I said.

He asked me to tell him what had happened before I brought her in.

'Mmm. Difficult to tell,' he said. Her motor movements seem okay. Though you may have noticed she's leaning to the left slightly.'

'I have. Should... should we do another scan? I mean, how can we be sure exactly what's going on? I was wondering if it was the tablets.'

He explained that, given the stage Mum's dementia was at, it wouldn't be cost-effective or beneficial to her already damaged brain to do another scan.

'Do you have help for her, at home?'

'Well... sometimes,' I said. 'My plan was to take her back to England with me, as you know, but since you and the other doctor – the psychiatrist – don't recommend I do that, I... I'll have to think of something else.' The care home came to mind. 'I... I wouldn't leave her if I didn't have to. But I have a job in

England, and there'd be things I'd need to sort out there. I just didn't expect all of this to happen when I came. And it's all happening so fast.' I didn't include my own sense of inadequacy in handling it all.

'Dementia can be like this, especially at the stage your mum is in.'

'What stage would you say she is in?' I asked the question I already knew the answer to.

'Late stage,' he confirmed, looking intently at me.

'Mmm.'

He leaned towards me. 'Are you okay about all of this?'

I looked away. 'I have to be, don't I?'

'We, doctors, can get so busy thinking about our patients, we forget how important the other people taking care of them are.'

'You... They do,' I said.

'I hope you have friends, family to help... you can talk to?'

'Yes.'

'Mmm. Your mother is lucky you're here.'

'Should we stop the medication she's on? Not the one to help her sleep,' I said.

'If you think they're helping her, I'd say continue.' He went on to explain the benefits of keeping Mum on the tablets Dr Peres had previously prescribed. 'At this stage of the disease, it's important to think about you too. Having to manage her behaviour.'

'So you don't think it had anything to do with the stroke?'

'I wouldn't say so.' He paused. 'It's swings and roundabouts. She has late-stage dementia, which brings its own issues, including behaviour that can be difficult to manage. The drugs can help to control that. Stopping it means you, or whoever is caring for her, having to manage the behaviour.'

I had to accept the inevitability – the damage dementia had done, and was continuing to do, to Mum's brain and the rest of her. The drug, even with its side effects, was the only way we could curb her unstable behaviour.

'But you do have to watch out for possible falls.'

'Yes,' I said.

'We will see how she is in the morning.'

'Okay. Thank you, Doctor.' I got up to leave. 'Doctor Medouze.' He looked up at me. I sat back down. 'How close would you say she is to... the end? I... I mean, can you tell?' I held my breath, fearful of his reply.

'Every stroke she has potentially brings her closer to decline, or may be fatal, but as for the end – the absolute end? She may stay the way she is for a while.'

His response said that Mum and I had some time, but he couldn't give me the definitive answer I wanted. Who could?

'Of course, you can see for yourself how quickly her condition has deteriorated recently,' he continued. 'But we can't predict. We have our limitations.' He gave a sympathetic smile.

'I... I know. It... it's just that I'd like to be prepared – well, as far as possible. But it doesn't sound like I can be.'

'There's only so much we can be prepared for with some conditions,' he said, giving me another one of his intent looks. This one I read as one of curiosity. What was he curious about? Did he think I was being uncaring or harsh to think about my mother's end, how soon or how it might be?

'Plus I need to plan, and make the right decisions for her care,' I said.

'I understand perfectly.'

How could he?

Mum was having her blood pressure taken when I got back to her. Then the nurse left us alone.

'When you taking me home?' she said. 'Why I'm here?' Her voice had taken that childlike tone again.

'You had a stro... you fainted,' I said.

'Faint? How you mean? When we going home?'

'Tomorrow,' I said. 'Hopefully.'

'So who's staying with me?'

'You've got the nurses and—'

'You not staying with me?'

'I'll stay for as long as I can,' I said.

'But Barbara tell me you going back to England an' is in a home you putting me,' she said.

'I... I'm not.'

'You staying?'

'Yes.'

'Because of me?'

'Of course, Mum,' I said.

'Because somebody need to take care of me,' she said. 'One daughter. Dat's all I have.'

Her words punctured me. What was I waiting for, to decide? Things were getting rapidly worse.

'I'll be here, Mum,' I said. 'For as long as I can. Everything will be all right.'

After losing Shane, I lived in a daze. Lost all meaning to my life. Everyone, everything, was nothing but a shadow. I took to my bed, the curtains permanently drawn. In that darkness, I saw only what I'd lost. The errors I'd made that had resulted in his death. My eyes opened or closed I saw him: his mass of black curly hair, gummy smile. I missed the scent of his dribble, the joy and beauty of him. Then that night: his crying, screaming, calls for help I couldn't give him. And when I did – too late. Only a miracle could have obliterated that nightmare, bring him home to me so we could become a family again.

'Remember you have another chile dat need you,' Mum told me. She'd been there coaxing me to eat. Trying to help me accept, again, what life had thrown at me. 'And me. I need you too,' she'd said.

She, Mum, was the strength I had, and needed around me. She saw to Millie, took care of us, never stopped telling me: 'Everything will be all right, *ich mwen*.'

CHAPTER FORTY

I was back in the house. Empty without Mum. Her new routine of going to bed early and sleeping till morning, had brought an end to the late-night pacing. But even when she was in bed and asleep, her presence was there in a calm and reassuring way. With that presence gone, I was left with the reasons why.

I hesitated before answering the phone. I wasn't in the mood for speaking to anyone, but it could have been Auntie checking on us or wanting something.

'Hello. Good evening,' I said.

'Good night, Cousin Erica.' It was Hannah. 'How are you? Cousin Ione all right?'

'Er, we're okay,' I said, not wanting to share any more than I needed.

'I'm sorry to be phoning late.'

'It's okay, Hannah.' It was only eight o'clock.

'I... I wanted to have a talk with you.'

'Oh. About what?'

'Well.' She hesitated. 'Cousin Headley tell me you might want somebody to stay with Cousin Ione for you to go back to Englan'.'

'Oh.' I was briefly lost for words. 'Well... I'm not sure about that right now.'

'Oh, I thought—'

'I... I might not be doing that any more,' I said, being deliberately vague. Hannah couldn't be the first to know about this big decision, which I myself was still trying to come to terms with.

'All right. Well, if you change your mind, let me know because I can help you with Cousin Ione, if you want. I don't have no work at de moment an'... well... is fam'ly... Let me know.'

I took a fleeting moment to consider it. 'That's good to know, Hannah. I'll think about it and let you know.'

CHAPTER FORTY-ONE

A restlessness tumbled into me. My decision to stay came with consequences. My life wouldn't belong to me in the way that it used to. Not now, nor in the near future. The new life I needed to carve out would need to be palatable, workable. For me and for Mum.

Help from Hannah, and maybe a second person, would make things more manageable. I'd promised Mum now. And, unless she'd forgotten, I couldn't change my mind, but an unsettling anxiety stayed with me through the night. Eyes wide open at one in the morning, with no one I could reach out to, I got out my notebook and added to the message I'd begun to Mum.

Before going off to the hospital, I called Millie.

'It's not forever,' she said. 'And Nannie needs you. Maybe she can't tell you, but she does. I could see how she'd be scared of you coming back and leaving her.'

'I know,' I said.

'And, oh, I was gonna phone to tell you – Adwin's clear. No trait. No sickle-cell.'

'He got the results?'

'Yes. We're fine.'

'That's the best news I've had for a while,' I said, a huge smile on my face. 'I'm so happy for you, Millie. For both of you. All of us.'

'Thanks for nagging us into doing it. What a relief.' She sighed.

'It is. I've still got lots to sort out in England, but—'

'I can help with anything you need me to do.'

'You might be sorry you said that,' I teased.

'I won't.'

I smiled as we disconnected. Then called Delia.

'For what it's worth, I think you've made the right decision,' she said. 'I mean it's your mum and you'd feel like crap if you left her and something bad happened and you weren't there to sort things out.'

'I know,' I said. 'But what about Millie?'

'Millie's grown, Erica. You've done a great job with her. She's independent, has tenacity and is doing well for herself. Watch out. There'll be a wedding and a baby soon.'

'I know.'

'You're doing the right thing, staying, but you can't be chained to your mum, girl.'

'Mmm. I suppose so.'

'Think of that wonderful lifestyle you'll have. Fresh food, sunshine, all that swimming, ooh. You'll be there for carnival, jazz, all of that fun stuff too. Your mum's forcing you into a good life!'

'We'll see,' I said, allowing myself to embrace the possibilities of cheer ahead.

'We will.' She laughed. 'But, seriously, give me a shout if you need me to do anything, yeah? Anything. I mean it. You hear?'

'Okay. I hear.'

Adjustments would have to be made, but telling Millie and Delia, and having them on board made my decision feel less daunting and right. I wanted to be there for Mum, but couldn't get away from my concern about leaving Millie in England on her own. She had Adwin, a couple of cousins, friends she was close to, but she'd be without me at hand.

After I'd contacted Leo's mum, all those years ago, she'd started sending birthday cards with the odd little gift for Millie, and invited us to Ireland to see her. I didn't make it, until Millie was around fourteen, and then we never went again because Millie didn't want to.

A couple of Leo's uncles, aunts and a few cousins had turned up to see her. But that had just made it worse for Millie. She'd said she didn't feel comfortable there.

'It was like they'd all come to look at me, Mum,' she said. 'Like they were curious or something.'

'But they're your family,' I'd told her. 'They were just being nice.'

'They're all white,' she'd said. 'And look at me.' Apart from the waves in her hair, no one would have guessed that her grandmother was Irish.

'They're still your family,' I said. 'Granny Catherine and all of the other Doyles are part of your heritage.'

'Doesn't feel like it,' she'd said.

It did feel odd, thinking Millie belonged in that white family, with their fair hair and thick Irish accents.

'Staying in touch with them might help you get in contact with your dad,' I'd told her.

'Let him try to find me,' she'd said.

Maybe her resentment of Leo influenced her decision to stay away. But what was mine? I'd considered inviting his mother down, but had told myself it was a long journey and I was unsure as to how it would work out.

If one of us, either me or Leo's mum, had worked harder at

staying in touch, it might have helped to bring Millie round, and she'd have had other family to call on, apart from mine, especially now that I wouldn't be that close by.

I left early for the hospital, so I might be with Mum when Dr Medouze was doing his rounds, but the traffic was bad and it took me longer than I'd expected to get there. The nurse confirmed that he'd already been in to see her, and it would be okay to take Mum home. She'd been showered and only needed to get dressed. I said I'd do that. Save her a job.

Mum was sitting on the side of her bed and lifted her head when I entered the ward.

'Morning, Mum,' I said, and asked how she was feeling.

'I... okay,' she said. 'I was looking for my slippers.'

'You going somewhere?'

I noticed the bed the other patient had occupied was empty. 'Where's the lady who was in that bed over there?'

She shrugged. 'I don't know.'

An hour later we were ready to leave.

I'd strapped Mum into the car and had just slammed her door shut when I heard his voice.

'Good morning.'

I turned, and a rise in body temperature I'd like to believe was due to the morning sun or the biological changes of menopause, struck me.

'I could tell that was you.' Dr Medouze smiled.

'From behind?'

'You're looking rested,' he said. 'How is everything?'

'Okay, for now, I think.'

'I'm hoping not to see your mum here again in a hurry.'

'You tired of seeing us?' I smiled.

'I didn't say you. It's always nice to see you,' he said.

'Oh. Oh, really?' My body temperature rose again.

'You should do that more often.'

'What?'

'Smile,' he said. 'Oh, but I'm embarrassing you? I'm sorry.' The glow on his face suggested I wasn't the only one blushing. 'Take care of your mum.' He stooped to get a look at her in the car, gave a little wave and stood up again. 'I'm here if you have any questions.'

I thanked him and got into my seat, where I sat for a few seconds watching him walk towards the entrance of the hospital.

'You like him?' Mum said, when we drove off.

'Like him? He's the doctor, Mum.'

'But I see how you looking at him. What he was telling you?'

'He was talking about you, mainly.'

'Dat's what you say.'

'Mum?'

'Uh-huh,' she responded.

It was moments, conversations like this, that I missed. When we could be not just mother and daughter, but women together. Understand each other and be okay. I treasured every bit of real-life communication and connection with her.

Waiting at the traffic lights, I noticed an old lady I could have mistaken for her. The mum that used to be. She was wearing a khaki sun hat, cotton trousers and a navy blouse. 'Hi, Mum,' I imagined me saying to her, this mum in the future we'd planned. I'd be smiling, feeling a warmth inside, layered with joyful possibilities. 'I've cooked lunch,' I'd say, or made bakes, a cake.

We'd go on that shopping trip we'd planned for the day, sit, have a cold drink, talk about life. Share a little gossip, maybe. We'd smile, find things to laugh about at a restaurant, bar or on the beach. Or we might simply enjoy being with each other at home. We'd capture the times when it was just me and her.

This mother I loved and who loved me. Yes, things could have worked out differently for us, if... if it hadn't gone the way it had.

I sighed and drove on through the changing lights. The woman I'd seen, way back in the distance now – how much of her was still there in the mum sitting on the seat next to me?

I touched her thigh. She looked at me. 'Huh?'

'Nothing.' I smiled. Then for conversation, added: 'Auntie might be wondering where we are.'

'Why?' Mum asked.

'It's past the time she normally calls.'

'Why you don't call her?'

'I will.'

As scary as it had been, to avoid the extra fuss, I hadn't told anyone yet about this episode with Mum.

I called Auntie when I got home and asked if she'd come over. She said she'd be down later. I wanted to tell her face to face.

'I've decided to stay,' I told her, when she arrived.

'You mean you not going back?' She stood as if frozen. Her eyes not leaving my face. 'You serious?'

I nodded.

'You not going back?' she repeated.

'Not now. Not yet,' I added.

'Ohhhh,' she sang, holding me close, swaying me from side to side. 'I'm so happy. So glad. What make you change your mind?'

'A lot of things,' I said.

'Oh, God.' She lifted her head to the sky. 'Dere is a God. Dere is a God.' She released me, showing that single dimple again.

CHAPTER FORTY-TWO

The number calling me wasn't registered in my phone, but I knew the voice as soon as he spoke.

'Hello. Good morning.'

'Dr Medouze? Good morning.'

'Yes. I hope you don't mind me calling.'

'No. Not at all. It's fine. Is... is there something... something wrong?' I asked, to dispel fears that he might be calling about something they'd missed or overlooked relating to Mum.

'No. Well, I hope not. How is your mother doing? Mrs Joseph?'

'She's here,' I said. 'We're managing.'

'Oh, good. I... I wanted to recommend a GP you could access for small emergencies, if you need to, for your mom. He has a special interest in the elderly and is on your side of the island. Your mother may already have a good one, of course – I don't know, but—'

'Oh. That's thoughtful of you,' I said, and quickly got paper and something to write with.

'Dr Mint does home visits and operates a twenty-four-hour service. I think that would be very useful for you.'

'Yes, it would.' It would also mean I wouldn't have to visit that doctor who'd prescribed paracetamol and aspirin for Mum for no apparent reason. 'Thank you so much for this, and all of your help.'

'Not a problem,' he said. 'I was afraid I might have missed you, that you might have already left for England.'

He'd remembered all of that?

'Oh. I've decided to stay,' I said.

'And not go back?'

'At least for now.'

'I'm sure your mother's happy with that decision. And you sound brighter.'

'It's for the best.'

'Your decision has changed my luck too.'

'Oh. How's that?'

'I was thinking,' he said. 'I wondered, if... if I could ask you to come out for a meal – a drink or something, with me? I could maybe show you some parts of the island you're maybe not familiar with? What do you think?'

'Ooo, gosh! That would be really nice, Dr Medouze.' I hadn't seen this coming, but it was adding more than cheer to my day.

'It's Keith, by the way,' he said, 'away from the hospital.'

'Okay. Keith,' I repeated. 'I'd really love that, Doctor—I mean, Keith.' I giggled. 'That would be really nice.'

'Can I call you, say, tomorrow? To confirm? A day and time.'

'Of course. But I'll need notice, so I can arrange a carer.'

'We'll talk soon then,' he said.

'Okay, bye. Oh, my God,' I said out loud, after putting the phone down. 'Doctor Medouze! Ooo!'

I was walking on air.

CHAPTER FORTY-THREE

Sorting through the rest of Mr Frank's belongings in the spare room wasn't something I was looking forward to, hence why I'd left it so long, but it had to be done. Especially as it meant getting rid of what was left of him in the house. Every time I'd suggested finishing off the job we'd started, after his funeral, Mum would get all worked up: 'I will do it,' she'd say. But it never happened. Did she dream that Mr Frank would come back, like I had with Leo all those years ago? If she'd kept them as mementos, none of it would be of any use to her now. And what was the point, anyway?

Clearing the room would free it for possible visitors, or if Hannah had to stay the night at any time. I mentioned it to Claire when she called to see how I was. She offered to come to the paupers' care home with me to drop the clothes off.

I didn't tell her about Mum's stint in hospital either. If I wasn't telling Auntie, I wouldn't be telling anyone – at least no one in St Lucia.

I made an early start. Hannah wasn't due in for a couple of hours, and I reckoned Mum would stay asleep, if I worked quietly. I wasn't going to go through anything. Just dump it all in rubbish bags and cart them away, so it wasn't going to take long. It would have been more satisfying to burn the damn things, but cruel when others could make good use of them.

Kitted out in a loose dress, intended for beach wear, head tied with one of Mum's old scarves, hands stuffed into rubber gloves, rubbish bags and cleaning tools at hand, I turned the handle on the door. Once inside, I pushed the window open. The view from there was similar to the one from my room: clear water merging with sinister greeny-brown as it met the mangrove, where new life survived feeding on the dead.

I'd only come to the funeral because of her. And it had taken me ages to decide, especially when the bastard had the nerve to die in the middle of spring term, which meant I had to attach some unpaid leave to the compassionate leave Phillipa had given me, because my 'father' had died.

'Nannie's taking this bad, isn't she?' Millie had said.

Mum's sore eyes and drooping face had said it all. It was the only concerning part of the occasion, since Millie had no attachment to him either.

Mum had already started wearing the customary mourning colours: the mark of respectability after losing someone close. But where was the respect he should have had for her during those thirty-nine years they were together?

From what I'd seen, the first three – when they were smoochy and she must have felt she was the centre of his life – were the best years she'd had with him. And maybe a portion of when they'd first come back to St Lucia to live. Three is a tiny piece of thirty-nine. His tiring of her came quickly, like a child with a new toy.

Leo had only given me a little more than that, but I'd been happy with him the whole time.

I had thought he was too.

'Why did you even come back here with him?' I'd asked Mum, while she and I cleared his things out of their once shared bedroom. His affairs were common knowledge by then.

She'd taken her time to answer. 'He did all dat business in England,' she said, 'but when we come here, I believed it would be different. He would change. Leave all of dat behind.'

'You should have left him,' I said. 'Ages ago.'

'Huh. Frank did jus' like too much woman, no matter what I did do to fill his belly an' satisfy him in de bedroom.'

My mind flashed back to that porn magazine I'd come across in their room when I was thirteen.

'One thing,' she added. 'He never stop me spending his money or ask what I do with it.'

'But did he love you, Mum? Do you really think he loved you?'

'He din leave me.'

'Because you let him do whatever he liked.'

'In Englan',' she said, 'I din have to see or hear about what he was doing.'

'But you knew.'

'He wasn't home a lot, but I... I could put it from my mind more. Is when we come here... here everybody in your business.' She sighed. 'Everybody talk.' She paused. 'You caa have everything in life, Erica.'

'What about love, Mum?'

'Frank did love me in his own kind of way.'

'What kind of way was that? Mum,' I said, when she didn't answer. 'I understand how hard it must have been for you before, when it was just the two of us, but I was happy then. I knew it would get better one day – when I finished uni and got a decent job. I'd take care of both of us.'

'Huh. An' how we was going to improve our life before dat time came? An' even if you was going to take care of us when you start working, dat would be for how long?'

'Anyway.' I sighed. 'He's gone now.'

'He used to go out, but always come back home. He would never leave me. He had promised me dat. Now' – her eyes circled the ceiling – 'is me alone have to live in dis big house.' Tears had filled her eyes.

'Oh, Mum.' I'd sat next to her and held her, wishing I could plug into her pain. 'You'll be fine, Mum,' I'd said.

Now, as I opened the first bag to fill it with his stuff, a rage pushed through me: anger that I had to be handling his clothes; that he'd sucked up the good years of Mum's life; been the cause of terrible friction between me and her; and that his money or whatever else it was about him had had Mum spellbound. Bonded to him, even with Alzheimer's.

I dragged four large bin bags of clothes to the kitchen door and went back in to mop the floors.

The lemon-scented bleach I'd used followed me out into the corridor as I went back out to let Hannah in.

CHAPTER FORTY-FOUR

I'd got changed and loaded the bags of clothes into the car, but where was Claire?

'Look me! Look me!' She called from the gate.

'I was about to call you,' I said.

'Your auntie inside?'

'No, Hannah.'

'Let me say hello.' She rushed past me, animated, then rushed back. 'Go get your things.' She lowered her voice. 'We going for a swim after.'

'What?'

'Go! Go! Come on. Somebody's there with your mum. We not going far.'

Claire had a way of injecting spontaneity and fun into my life. I hadn't had a swim in the whole month I'd been there.

Getting rid of the rest of Mr Frank's belongings was like disposing of the final pieces of him.

'Jus' drive like you're going home,' Claire instructed, after we got back into the car. I sighed. I'd never discussed my feelings towards Mr Frank with her. And though I was tempted to, doing it now would ruin this sense of release and promise I was determined to nurture. I drove, and grew a little nervous when she directed me past Sweet Lime Grove, where Mum was being taken care of by Hannah.

'Go straight. Take your time, eh,' she said.

I passed the empty plot I'd explored weeks ago, driving along a rocky road with attractive fenced-off bungalows along each side.

'It's nice down here,' I said. I wouldn't have known these houses existed if Claire hadn't brought me through there and was intrigued to take a closer look.

'Keep driving,' she said, until we came to a large building.

'A hotel?' I said.

'Uh-huh. Pull-up down there.' She pointed to where two other cars were parked. 'I'll give you room to change.' She got out, and stepped away, keeping her back to me. This was crazy, but fun.

I quickly slipped into my swimming gear, then ran to catch up with her. 'Ready!'

We walked a little further until, below a haphazard line of stony steps, I saw the sea. 'Oh, wow,' I said, following her down to a small beach where perfect blue water stretched out and away from two huge rocky formations on each side, like opened arms.

I threw my towel down, glanced at a couple lying on their fronts and rushed in, leaving Claire dipping her toe in the water, complaining it was cold.

'I'm staying in the baby pool,' she shouted out to me, from where the waves frothed as they hit the sand. I swam further out, then turned onto my back.

I was in a warm, salty bath with the sun over me. 'This is great,' I shouted out to her, turning onto my front again.

'You swim good,' she shouted.

I waved.

Water began falling on my face. A glance around confirmed a cloud had burst overhead. It was raining. I looked over at Claire.

'Passing shower,' she shouted.

I was wet anyway.

She was right – the rain soon passed. I looked up at the sky and saw a rainbow: blue and green joining yellow, into orange into a reddish pink, then into the blue sky again. There was more to being here than sorting out Mum's care and managing her dementia.

'In all the years I've been coming here,' I told Claire on our way back up to the car, 'I've never known this beach existed.'

'It's for residents only, really,' she said, 'but I bring friends here sometimes. A lot of people don't like to use it because of all the steps.

'They don't bother me,' I said. 'Gives me a pre-workout before I hit the sea. It's fantastic.' I spontaneously hugged her.

'If you was friends with me before, you would have known,' she said, laughing. 'But there's plenty more beach in St Lucia still, you know.'

'I know,' I said, 'but this one's my local.'

CHAPTER FORTY-FIVE

I said goodbye to a job I loved, the prospects of a headship and the plans I'd had for my retirement. Goodbye to a life I hadn't seen myself leaving, at least not for some time.

My new role was supervising Mum's care, making sure everything was in place to make what was left of her time with us as pleasant as possible.

She was slower. I suspected her medication might be partially responsible for that, though it could have simply been Alzheimer's, or a combination of the two. There were fewer words and active responses, though sometimes she could give a pleasant surprise by producing a perfectly formed sentence, like: 'When Erica come, she will fix it,' and it would tickle something in me. A joy. A hint of hope I'd have to remind myself to put away; to just accept and appreciate the positives. Take it for what it was: a fragment of lucidity.

She slept more, ate less and didn't wander around much anymore. The humming had slid into a constant, engine-like sound, which was only there when she was alert. Forget about a song.

Her eyes didn't tell the onlooker what she was seeing, but I could still look into them and claim those small, vacant, searching eyes as Mum's.

Sometimes I would lie next to her and look into them, and she'd smile.

'Who is your mother?' she'd say, and a barrage of emotions would fall into me.

'You,' I'd say. 'Ione. Ione Joseph.'

She'd frown, as if confused.

I was going to lose her. That day, the next – in days, months to come. Who knew when? But she needed me more than ever right now.

Mr Frank's money had brought her financial security, and was helping her to get the best possible care.

Employing Hannah took the day-to-day care for Mum out of my hands. It brought more normality to my life, gave me time for myself. The space enabled me to better appreciate the time with Mum. The emotional roller-coaster I'd been on with her had stopped corkscrewing. Fears of failing and letting myself and Mum down had subsided, and given me space to reflect, go to the beach, even paint my toenails, which I did in preparation for my first date with Dr Medouze – now Keith to me.

I'd put it off for long enough.

Over dinner, he had explained that he was divorced with two grown children who'd moved to America with their mother. We'd talked, joked, and I had done my best not to discuss Mum's condition with him.

Seeing him initially had brought up the times Mum had been in the hospital under his care, but the more we talked, the more those thoughts faded.

CHAPTER FORTY-SIX

I'd returned home from what had become my regular afternoon swim. Cousin Headley's vehicle was parked close to the gate. I figured he'd come for a visit, or brought Auntie over after taking her shopping, but there was a strange quietness around.

'Hannah?' I called out, though she'd be too far to hear me, if she was in the bedroom with Mum.

'Where is everyone?' I mumbled. Then I reached the veranda and they were sitting there, all eyes on me: Auntie, Cousin Headley and... Millie.

'Hello, Mum,' Millie said.

I stood frozen. 'Millie...! You—'

'I wanted to surprise you.' She rushed to me, almost tripping down the steps.

'Oh, my God,' I said. 'You're here!'

We held on to each other for a while, tears brimming in my eyes. 'Where's Adwin?' I said.

'He couldn't make it at such short notice,' she said. 'And I couldn't wait. He'll be here next week.'

'Oh, Millie, I can't believe it! And you' – I looked at Auntie and Cousin Headley – 'you were in on all of it.'

We laughed.

CHAPTER FORTY-SEVEN

The reliable sun in this part of the world was spreading brightness wherever it could. There was the heat that came with it too, however, and although it was only eleven o'clock, a minute in that heat was enough to bring on a sweat.

I escaped from it under the mango tree, though not intentionally, because I'd popped under there to see if I spotted any turning or ripe-and-ready-to-pick fruits overhead.

Millie was asleep. Jet-lagged, no doubt. I'd made breakfast, and left Hannah tending to Mum.

'What you doing?' Millie appeared wearing her shortie pyjamas and flip-flops.

'Oh, you're up?' I said.

'Yeah.' She came closer. 'You gonna pick some?'

'Thinking about it. Otherwise the birds and bats will have them.'

'Oh, what a life, eh?' she said. 'You not climbing the tree, are you?'

'Course not.' I chuckled. 'Pass me that long pole over there.' I pointed at the *kali* leaning up by the clothes line.

'Oh, Mum,' Millie said, the pole not yet in her hand. 'These are beautiful, aren't they?'

'What?'

'Orchids. These orchids. Gosh, wish I could preserve some of these.'

'They're out?' I rushed over. 'Oh, wow! I hadn't noticed,' I said. Most of the buds on the long purpley stem hadn't yet popped open, but some had, displaying a peachy-pink flower with yellow inside. They *were* beautiful.

I recalled the last time I'd checked on them with Mum. 'When dey send flowers, I'm happy,' she'd said.

'We'll bring Mum out later to see them. She'd love that. Come on, I'll make you some breakfast. There's fresh bread.'

'Creole loaves?'

'Mmm.'

'What about the mangoes?' Millie said. 'It can be my starter.'

We picked a few of the ripe ones I was able to reach, washed them under the outside tap and put them on the table.

'Good morning, Cousin Erica, Millie. You all right?' Hannah said, leading Mum out onto the veranda.

'Morning, Cousin Hannah. Morning, Nannie,' Millie said.

'Hey, Mum, you're just in time,' I said. 'Come. Come and have some mangoes with us.' I took Mum's hand and led her to the table.

'I will get her apron,' Hannah said.

By the time she'd returned, I'd already peeled the skin off one side of a mango for Mum, and she, Millie and myself were biting our way through the orangey flesh, juice dripping down our hands and arms, running onto the table.

'Mmm. Can't get these in England. Gorgeous, aren't they?' Millie said, smacking her lips between a bite.

'Uh-huh. Gorgeous,' Mum repeated. 'Pal Louis, for Erica.'

'For you, Mum.' Millie looked at me, her mouth covered in juice.

'For all of us,' I said.

'Wait. Wait!' Millie said, taking the last bite off her mango seed, then rushing out to the garden. 'Look, Nannie. It's your orchid.'

'Fl... flower,' Mum said. A huge smile took over her face, mango juice all around it.

EPILOGUE

Mum, I write this knowing that you'll never be able to read it. And if someone took time to read it to you, it would come across too jumbled. You'd struggle to make sense of it all. But I'm writing it anyway, for release.

I'll bet it never occurred to you, back then, when you were first diagnosed, that this sickness life had brought to you would end up swallowing a huge portion of my life too? I hadn't seen it then either. But I'm coming to terms with it.

It's too much to expect, I know, but I wish that back then, we'd understood what the disease meant in its totality and had handled it differently. Wish we'd taken time to have honest and open conversations, to help iron things out and tidy up the loose ends. Wish it was possible to have been given something like a road map, to make us aware of the cracks, bumps, collisions and near-misses we were going to encounter along the way. The only thing we'd been sure of was that this sickness would bring about changes in your brain. You'd be confused, your memories squeezed out. Then you'd be gone.

As bumpy and challenging this time with you has been, it's given me a chance to consider and reflect on many things, including the painful choices you felt you had to make for your own security.

You've taught me to accept the good, and to work with the rest. And I'm grateful for that.

We don't know how much more time we have. But know that I'll be here, continuing to manage whatever challenges present along the way. Because we have to push through or manoeuvre around obstacles, don't we, Mum? And keep going forward. I'm grateful that you've brought me here to this beautiful place, to make the most of what's left of your life with you.

It goes without saying that I'll miss you. Huh. I'm missing you already and still find it hard to see myself in a life without you, but as you've always told me: Everything will be all right. It will. And you'll always be alive, here inside of me. I love you, Mum.

A LETTER FROM STEFFANIE

Dear reader,

I want to say a huge thank you for choosing to read *My Mother's Gift*. If you did enjoy it, and want to keep up to date with all my latest releases, just sign up at the following link. Your email address will never be shared and you can unsubscribe at any time.

www.bookouture.com/steffanie-edward

I've spent years taking care of my mother who suffers from Alzheimer's. But in writing this novel, I wanted to explore the challenges for someone like Erica – who has unresolved painful issues with her mother – and then has to decide whether to give up a life she loves in another country, to come and take care of her. I also wanted to explore issues around the vulnerability and powerlessness that comes with old age.

I hope you loved *My Mother's Gift* and if you did, I would be very grateful if you could write a review. I'd love to hear what you think, and it makes such a difference helping new readers to discover one of my books for the first time.

I love hearing from my readers – you can get in touch on my Facebook page, through Twitter, Goodreads or my website.

Thanks,
Steffanie

KEEP IN TOUCH WITH STEFFANIE

www.saedward.com

 facebook.com/Steffanie-Edward-101943815246620
twitter.com/EdwardsaEdward

ACKNOWLEDGEMENTS

To Isobel Akenhead, for your hard work, patience and understanding during my bout of illness whilst writing *My Mother's Gift*, Belinda Jones, for your sharp copy-editing skills, Alexandra Holmes and the rest of the Bookouture team, working behind the scenes to make this story, and the presentation of it, such a beautiful one.

Writing this novel has been a strong emotional challenge. Thank you, Patsy Knight for helping me push through the boundaries.

Heartfelt thanks to my children, Marvyn and Shikila, my family and friends for your support and for convincing me that this story was worth telling.

A big thank you to Terrence Elliott for introducing me the Kwéyòl word 'zanmyèz,' and Jason Joseph, at Kwéyòl Sent Lisi, for guidance on the spellings of Kwéyòl words which haven't yet been included in the dictionary.

Once again, a huge thank you to my mother, Patricia Edward, who was the impetus for me to begin writing *My Mother's Gift*.

Printed in Great Britain
by Amazon